Jacob Hiltzheimer, Jacob Cox Parsons

Extracts From the Diary of Jacob Hiltzheimer

Philadelphia, 1765-1798

Jacob Hiltzheimer, Jacob Cox Parsons

Extracts From the Diary of Jacob Hiltzheimer
Philadelphia, 1765-1798

ISBN/EAN: 9783337120481

Printed in Europe, USA, Canada, Australia, Japan

Cover: Foto ©Raphael Reischuk / pixelio.de

More available books at **www.hansebooks.com**

EXTRACTS FROM THE DIARY

OF

JACOB HILTZHEIMER,

OF PHILADELPHIA.

1765-1798.

EDITED BY

HIS GREAT-GRANDSON, JACOB COX PARSONS.

PHILADELPHIA:
PRESS OF WM. F. FELL & CO.
1893.

PREFACE.

The extracts contained in this volume are from the diary of Jacob Hiltzheimer, who at the age of nineteen years left his native city, Mannheim, on the Rhine, for Rotterdam, where he embarked on the ship Edinburgh, James Russell, Master, and arrived at Philadelphia, September 5th, 1748, and three days later took the usual oath of allegiance. Soon after his arrival he was apprenticed to John Nagle, a silversmith, on Front street. At the expiration of his term of service, finding that the confinement of the store was not congenial to his active disposition, he decided to engage in farming and the raising of fine stock, and commenced by leasing land in the suburbs of the city. He took part in the campaign to resist the encroachments of the French on the river Ohio and the lakes to the westward, and for his services was entitled to a portion of " back lands," under the King's proclamation of October, 1762. During the war for independence, he sided with the colonies, attached himself to the First Battalion, City Militia, and was also connected with the Quartermaster's Department, in which he rendered valuable service to the army in the field. He became a prominent member of the Patriotic Association. As Street Commissioner, for three years he discharged the duties of the office in a manner worthy the emulation of public servants at the present day. He was elected in 1786, a Representative of the city in the Assembly, and served for eleven consecutive years, being Chairman of the Committee on Claims, and on other important committees. In all movements of a public and charitable character he took an active and prominent part : was Vice President of the German Society, an early member of the Society for Promoting Agriculture, the Society

for the Promotion of Domestic Manufactures, and the Fire Department.   In 1761, he married Hannah Walker, of a Quaker family, and
established his home on the east side of Seventh street, just below the
corner of Market street.   After passing through the epidemics of
1793 and 1797, he died of yellow fever, September 14th, 1798, and
his remains were interred in the cemetery of the German Reformed
Church (now a part of Franklin Square), of which he was a member
of the vestry for many years.   Jacob Hiltzheimer's daily record of
thirty years affords ample evidence that he enjoyed in a large measure
the confidence and esteem of his fellow citizens, and also sheds a
bright light on his domestic career.

   The extracts from the diaries are continuous from September of
1765 to September of 1798, with the exception of the years 1771, 1775
and 1776, the books containing which are lost.

                                        JACOB COX PARSONS.
   NEW YORK, *September, 1893.*

EXTRACTS

FROM THE

DIARY OF JACOB HILTZHEIMER.

1765.

September 11.—Captain Friend arrived; Andrew Hamilton went ashore at New Castle.

September 14.—Andrew Hamilton reached Philadelphia to-day—the first time since his arrival from England.

October 8.—Took a ride with Andrew Hamilton, to try his black colt.

October 26.—My mother-in-law died at seven o'clock this evening. [She was buried in Friends' Ground on 28th.]

October 31.—My newspaper was delivered in the morning, being the last before the Stamp Act goes into force.

November 19.—With wife and son Billy, went to Germantown to see Catharine Klages and Michael Heil married.

December 23.—Breakfasted at five o'clock at Mrs. Gray's, with Enoch Story, Samuel Morris, Dr. John Cox, Mr. Petit, John Cadwalader, and Levi Hollingsworth; then set out for Darby fox-hunting. The number of hunters was thirty, who, by eleven o'clock, killed three foxes. Dined at Joseph Rudolph's, and at evening returned home with Hollingsworth. The other hunters remained over night for another hunt in the morning.

2

December 27.—Set off this morning at five o'clock with Thomas
Mifflin, Sam. Miles, Jacob Hollingsworth, and young Rudolph, from
my house; proceeded to Darby to meet the other gentlemen
hunters; from there to Captain Coultas's house, and to the woods.
About thirty-five gentlemen attended with thirty dogs, but no fox
was secured.

December 30.—Dined at Garlick Hall, on invitation of Robert Erwin,
with Joseph Fox, Thomas Willing, William Parr, Joseph Wharton
and sons Thomas and Joseph, John Ross, Tench Francis, Samuel
Mifflin, James Benezet, Wm. Jones, Judah Foulk, John Biddle,
Jacob Lewis, Henry Elves, Humphrey Robeson, Daniel Rundle,
Samuel Hassell, Peter Reeves, John Palmer, Dr. C. Evans, and after
dinner we were joined by William Fisher, Captain Coultas, and
Jonathan Humphreys.

1766.

January 3.—Took Joseph Galloway and Thomas Mifflin in my sleigh
to the Middle Ferry [also called Humphreys'].

January 24.—Attended a cider frolic at Greenwich Hall with the following gentlemen : Robert Smith, Robert Erwin, William Jones,
Richard Footman, Mr. Adcock, Captain Mushett, Philip Kinsey,
James Johnston, William Lloyd, F. Trimble, Humphrey Robeson,
and Samuel Hassell.

January 25.—Samuel Miles sent me a quarter cask of wine.

February 7.—Accompanied Daniel Wister to the meet at Hannah
Williams's, where we met the gentlemen hunters. Peter Wikoff
wore the brush.

February 22.—Went up town to Nicholas Brosius' funeral.

March 2.—With my wife attended the burial of Mrs. Dean.

March 4.—Attended Court to give my reasons why I did not serve as
a juryman last term.

March 18.—Went over Schuylkill to meet D. Wister and his brother
William, and brother-in-law, Owen Jones, to shoot pigeons.

March 19.—Attended at Robert Smith's house-warming, with Joseph Fox, John Lawrence, Samuel Mifflin, Will Parr, Tench Francis, T. Francis, Judah Foulk, Henry Elves and son, William Bard, Joseph Wood, Dr. Phineas Bond, R. Keen, and Robert Erwin.

March 24.—Mr. Willing brought the news from Maryland that the Stamp Act had been repealed.

April 6.—The Court House bell was rung twice to-day for fires.

April 7.—An express arrived last night from Maryland confirming the report of the repeal of the Stamp Act, for which news the bells rang all day.

April 16.—Daniel Wister went with me to the Schuylkill to see the great freshet.

April 29.—All the public offices were opened to-day.

May 12.—William Jones's wife was buried to-day.

May 19.—This day received a copy of the repeal of the Stamp Act on a half sheet paper from the printer, and at night drank punch at Robert Erwin's with C. Gordon, James Pearson, and Mr. Hutchins.

May 20.—To-night the citizens in general illuminated their houses for the repeal of the Stamp Act.

May 21.—A great number of gentlemen had a dinner at the State House, during which several great guns were fired.

May 29.—Daniel Wister and myself went to the Green to see a £10 race between Joseph Hogg's and John Buckingham's horses.

June 4.—Being the King's birthday, dined on the banks of the Schuylkill in company of about 380 persons. Several healths were drunk, among them Dr. Franklin, which gave great satisfaction to the company. A long boat was taken there on four wagon wheels, and many great guns fired.

June 24.—Received the news that Daniel Wister had a son born and named John.

July 6.—My Lord Hope's carriage and horses arrived.

July 30.—My wife gave birth to a son at three o'clock this morning.

August 1.—In the evening went to Mrs. Gray's, and drank a bowl of punch with William Jones.

August 20.—Robert Erwin gave a beefsteak dinner at the Bettering House to J. Fox, Jacob Lewis, Joseph Redman, John Palmer, Robt. Smith, John Drinker, Wm. Jones, John Parish, Nicholas Hicks, Isaac Coates, Joseph Allen, and myself.

October 12.—This morning the Highlanders, Captain Stuart, came from Lancaster.

October 21.—Attended the funeral of Daniel Wister's son; he was five months old.

November 12.—Five horses started for the £60 purse. Trial, Merry Andrew, Sterling, Valiant, and a mare belonging to Colonel Armstrong. Trial won the purse.

November 13.—Four horses started in the race to-day—Smoker, Merry Andrew, Sampson, and a little roan, belonging to Joseph Richardson. Smoker won.

December 11.—Opened my cask containing ten saddles and twenty-four bridles, received from England.

December 16.—Spent the evening at Mrs. Gray's with William Jones, Robert Smith, and Robert Erwin.

1767.

January 1.—Very, very cold! Delaware frozen over. Three sleigh-loads of us went to Darby to Joseph Rudolph's,—Joseph Fox, Robert Smith, Robert Erwin and wife, William Jones and Mrs. Gray, his intended, and two daughters, Hannah Gardner, John Biddle, Leonard Stoneburner, my wife and self.

January 3.—Called in my sleigh for Mrs. Reynell, took her to see the Bettering House, and then left her at Edward Penington's.

January 6.—Went to Middle Ferry (Jonathan Humphreys') to see how high the water was at twelve o'clock last night. It moved the chair-house about 100 yards. Thomas Shoemaker and I measured at the hay barrack, below the house, where the water left a mark, and found it had been five feet four inches.

January 14.—Spent the evening at John Biddle's, with Robert Erwin, Robert Smith, and William Jones.

January 20.—Set off from Jonathan Humphreys' to a fox hunt with the following gentlemen: Zeb. Rudolph, Joseph Jones, Mr. Pallard, Cornelius Francis, Charles Willing, Sam. Morris, Anthony Morris, Richard Bache, and James Massey, huntsman. We afterward dined at Massey's house.

February 2.—To-night with my wife, Daniel Wister, and Timothy Matlack, attended the play called " Cato."

February 8.—Took a walk to near the brick kilns with Emanuel and Jacob Carpenter, Daniel Wister and Adam Kimmell. This afternoon William Jones and Mrs. Gray were married.

February 13.—My wife and I went to the play and saw acted Romeo and Juliet.

February 14.—At noon went to William Jones's to drink punch, met several of my friends, and got decently drunk. The groom could not be accused of the same fault.

June 15.—Drank punch at John Hughes's, who lately married Stephen Paschall's daughter.

July 1.—Last night heavy rain with thunder and lightning. The Moravian meeting house was struck.

September 4.—Timothy Matlack, J. Lukens, Palmer, and myself measured the new race track very exact, and find it lacks 144 yards of being two miles.

October 13.—Four horses started in the 100 guinea race: Selim, Granby, Old England, and Northumberland. Selim won.

October 23.—James Hamilton, Samuel Powell, and Francis Hopkinson returned from England.

October 26.—General Gage reviewed the troops on the Commons.

December 12.—The gentlemen hunters let a fox loose at Centre Woods, which afforded an agreeable ride after the hounds till dark. The fox ran up a tree on the Schuylkill side, and when Levi Hollingsworth climbed up after him, it jumped down and was killed.

December 17.—In the evening came James Wharton, Tench Tilghman, Samuel Hudson, Zebulon Rudolph, and Joseph Jones.

December 26.—From Rudolph's the following gentlemen, Samuel Miles, Levi Hollingsworth, Israel Morris, Joseph Jones, Samuel Nichols, Zebulon Rudolph, and Jeremiah Warder, went to Lower Tinicum fox hunting. There we were met by Charles, Richard, and James Willing, and after riding about the woods until two o'clock, without the sign of a fox, we returned to Joseph Rudolph's and dined.

December 31.—Daniel Wister was weighed to-day, 270 pounds; and I, 161 pounds.

1768.

February 1.—This afternoon Captain Coultas was buried from house of Charles Jenkins in Church ground, [corner Fifth and Arch Streets].

February 13.—Took a ride with James Webb, Jr., Sheriff of Lancaster County, to the Middle Ferry, and spent the evening at John Biddle's with Robert Smith, Robert Erwin, and Francis Trimble.

February 22.—Bought a horse of George Rosell, four years old, for our Governor Penn—gave £28 for him.

February 23.—Rode to Point No Point, met Edward Roberts, who showed me his new house, and though not quite finished is very fine.

February 27.—Attended a barbecue at Robert Smith's country house and from there went to William Jones's, Greenwich Hall, with the following gentlemen: Joe Fox, Samuel Morris, Samuel Miles,

Samuel Nichols, Robert Smith, John Smith, Robert Erwin, William Jones, Francis Trimble, Captain Mushett, Captain Jones, and Henry Elwes.

February 28.—Attended the burial of Charles Jenkins.

March 7.—Went with Mr. Erwin to Mr. [Richard] Hockley's, and from there up town to a little Dutch woman, who told him where to find four shirts that had been stolen from him.

March 12.—Drank punch with Levi Hollingsworth, who was married last Thursday to one of Stephen Paschall's daughters.

April 15.—Went to the Widow Coultas's vendue ; bought seven wild cherry tree chairs at 25 shillings and one arm chair at 60 shillings.

May 13.—Set out this morning at four o'clock, on Skewbald, and reached Lancaster at six in the evening, although he is now fifteen years old.

June 26.—This afternoon, with my two sons and Daniel Wister, went to Joseph Galloway's place to eat turtle.

July 10.—This afternoon went with John Backhouse and Thomas Shoemaker up to Joseph Galloway's place to dine with Daniel Wister, William Wister, Timothy Matlack, John Fox, Jacob Barge, and others.

August 10.—Spent part of the evening at John Biddle's with Dr. Smith, John Lukens, Thomas Livezey, John Paul, Robert Hooper, and Robert Erwin.

August 12.—Went up Wissahickon Road to set up mile stones. Dined at Leberon's with Hugh Roberts, Pearson Smith, Edward Milner, and John Lukens, Sr., and afterwards, a little beyond his house, we placed the XIII mile stone.

August 16.—This forenoon called at William Hamilton's place over Schuylkill.

August 29.—About nine o'clock this morning a soldier was shot for desertion in front of the Jews' burial-ground wall.

October 4.—This afternoon started for the £100 purse, the gray horse Northumberland, bay horse Granby, and bay mare Strumpet; the gray won two heats.

October 6.—Started for the Ladies' purse, Mr. Morris's colt Luggs; Mr. Coryell's bay mare Bungtown Maid; Mr. Peterson's horse Brinton; my mare Pallas; all three years old. Luggs won; made the first heat in 4 m. 17 s.; second heat, 4 m. 23 s.

October 8.—The City Plate of £50 was run for by Strumpet, Ladylegs, Nancy Dawson, and Granby; Strumpet won.

October 9.—Dined at Galloway's place with Israel Waters, Daniel Wister, Jacob Barge, Joseph Fox, Timothy Matlack, and Owen Jones.

November 5.—Dined at Greenwich Hall on beefsteaks, with Joseph Fox, W. Parr, Sam. Morris, Judah Foulk, Clem. Biddle, Robert Erwin, William Jones, Andrew Bankson, and Philip Kinsey.

December 5.—At night came here seven black horses belonging to the Duchess of Gordon.

December 12.—Went to Darby to burial of John Rudolph. Israel Morris, Samuel Nichols, Joseph Jones, and myself carried the corpse to the grave in the Friends' ground at Darby.

1769.

January 3.—To-night went to the play with Israel Waters to see " A Bold Stroke for a Wife."

January 13.—Dined at Greenwich Hall with Sheriff Joseph Redman, Sam. Morris, Robert Tuckness, Robert Erwin, Reynold Keen, John de Haas, and Andrew Bankson.

January 15.—I had to dinner with me Emanuel and Jacob Carpenter, Joseph Redman, Samuel Morris, Daniel Wister, and William Jones.

February 11.—My horse fell with me at the Barracks and hurt my arm.

March 5.—Robert Hopkins's house at Point No Point was burned to the ground yesterday.

April 6.—Dr. Kearsley, Colonel Jones, and W. B. Hockley drank tea with me.   •

April 10.—My three children were inoculated by Dr. Kearsley. '

April 13.—John Holland was branded in the hand at the State House for manslaughter.

April 15.—Dined on fish at Greenwich Hall with Joseph Fox, Samuel Mifflin, William Parr, Judah Foulk, Tench·Francis, Reynold Keen, Andrew Bankson, Henry Drinker, Joseph Wharton, Edward Penington, Captain Story, Dr. Evans, Robert Smith, Robert Erwin, William Jones, James Hartley, and Mr. Bard.

May 12.—In the morning took a ride with Joseph Redman in my chair. Drank punch with Henry Keppele, Jr., and wished him joy on birth of a son. Afterwards went to see the race between Mr. J——'s horse, Sportsman, and Dr. Kearsley's black colt, 3 years old, for a quarter cask of wine. Sportsman won.

July 7.—Went with wife and son Tommy to Galloway's place, and dined with John Wister and wife, Daniel Wister and wife, the Widow Chancellor, William Wister, and George Smith and his mother-in-law.

July 13.—Took John Reynell and wife out in his own wagon with my horse.

July 22.—Dined at Greenwich Hall with Joseph Galloway, Joseph Fox, John Ross, Abel James, Thomas Tilbury, Samuel Bryan, Tench Francis, Joseph Wharton, Robert Smith, and others.

August 24.—Yesterday put two men to work on the race track, and this afternoon drove Daniel Wister's pair of horses thrice around the track.

August 25.—My wife and self attended the funeral of Samuel Ash at Darby; he was buried in Friends' ground there.

August 29.—At four o'clock this morning we looked at the comet, near the Seven Stars.

September 2.—Timothy Matlack, my two sons, and self went up to

Joseph Galloway's place to see Whitehead Jones raise Daniel Wister's barn, and after dinner had a bull bait. ·

September 9.—Last night Penington's lumber store burned down, caused by lime slacking. Walked to Centre Woods, where I found above one hundred trees blown down.

September 13.—Whitehead Jones and myself laid a trunk at the race-ground, and Jonathan Humphreys sent his team for a day's hauling.

September 14.—Went to see the English cattle which arrived a few days ago.

September 28.—At noon started for the £100 purse the following horses: James DeLancey's bay horse, Lath; Mr. McGill's bay horse, Nonpareil; Governor Sharp's gray mare, Britannia; Richard Tidmarsh's gray mare, Northumberland. Lath won.

September 29.—Started for the £50 plate, Archibald Dick's gray colt, William Baxter's filly, James De Lancey's brown filly, Dr. Kearsley's black colt, and Mr. Leary's Old England. Three heats were run and the gray won.

October 17.—Spent the evening at the Widow Jenkins with John and George Ross, Jacob Carpenter, Henry Pauling, Squire Swope, Daniel Wister, Timothy Matlack, Peter Bachman, George Hitner, and Owen Jones, Jr.

November 8.—Went with Mr. Vorhees and John Hunt to the race ground, and had a race.

December 1.—Breakfasted at Galloway's place with Timothy Matlack, Daniel Wister, and Hoffman. In the afternoon, with wife, attended the burial of Mrs. Coultas—body taken from the Widow Jenkins's house to Church ground.

December 2.—Dined at Greenwich Hall with Thomas Lawrence, Joseph Fox, Joseph Redman, Colonel Francis, William Parr, Captain Morrell, Joseph Wharton, ˈDr. Evans, George Roberts, and other friends.

December 5.—Attended William Hamilton's vendue, and bought three pigs for 19s. 6d.

December 15.—With Robert Erwin went to Daniel Grant's, where we met John Lawrence, from Burlington, Joseph Wharton, Robert Smith, and William Jones; spent the evening there, and got home at midnight.

December 26.—Met the German Society at the Lutheran Schoolhouse.

December 27.—Joseph Fox, Captain Morrell, John Palmer, John Lukens, Robert Erwin, Edward Penington, Reynold Keen, and William Jones dined with me. Richard Bache came in after dinner was over.

1770.

January 1.—Accompanied Joseph Redman in his chair to Reynold Keen's place and dined with Clement Biddle and other friends.

January 7.—Sunday. Read a sermon delivered by Morgan Edwards on 1st inst., in the Baptist church in this city, wherein he modestly foretells his own death.

January 10.—Went to John Biddle's to see John Cameron, who is very ill.

January 19.—Doctor Kearsley took a bean out of the eye of my son Tommy, that has been in forty-five hours.

January 20.—This afternoon went to John Biddle's with my sleigh and took John Cameron, who is very ill and anxious to reach his home at Lancaster, as far as Stadelman's, 13 miles from the city.

January 21.—Remained all day at Stadelman's; Cameron very bad.

January 22.—Returned home with my sleigh, as the road is rough and very little snow. Promised Cameron to return with a carriage.

January 24.—Dr. Thomas Bond visited Cameron; he is growing worse.

January 25.—This morning at 6 o'clock John Cameron departed this life at Stadelman's.

January 26.—Sent my two men up to Stadelman's with a coffin for John Cameron and to bring his remains to the city.

January 27.—The corpse of John Cameron was brought to my house, and at four o'clock it was buried in the Presbyterian ground in the lower part of the city. Emanuel Carpenter and Daniel Wister were chief mourners.

March 3.—Took John Lukens and wife and William Scull in my sleigh to Camptown ; later went with Samuel Miles, his wife and sister, and my wife to Frankford.

March 6.—To-day James DeLancey, from New York, and Timothy Matlack, had a great cock fight at Richardson's, up Germantown Road.

March 10.—This evening the Amicable Fire Company met at the Widow Jenkins's. I paid 50 shillings toward the new engine made by Richard Mason, which is the eighth he has made. It is said that he made the first fire engine in this country.

March 12.—Spent part of the afternoon with Matthew Clarkson on Third Street.

March 15.—Edward Penington and Clement Biddle called on me with a subscription paper to encourage silk to be made here. I have subscribed 40 shillings. At night went to the church on Fourth Street [St. George's] to hear Mr. Pilmore preach a sermon for the benefit of prisoners, on Proverbs xxv, 21, 22.

April 2.—Took a sleigh ride, the "five mile round," with wife, sister, and son Tommy; stopped at Daniel Grant's and had a bowl of punch.

April 16.—Drank punch at William Jones's house with his new son-in-law, Anthony Morris.

April 21.—Took a ride with John Bullon to our race ground. Mrs. Duffield, Mrs. Clarkson, and Mrs. Hillegas spent the afternoon at my house.

May 2.—A race for £20 was run between Dr. Kearsley's gray mare and Alvaro Diornella's brown mare, bred by myself, a single two miles; the brown beat with ease.

May 3.—My wife and self attended the burial of John Wister's wife in Friends' ground.

May 5.—For a little diversion, this afternoon had a mile race between a bay horse and a bay mare of mine, and brown mare of Mr. Diornella; the bay horse won.

May 8.—Went up to Captain Macpherson's place [Mount Pleasant] and breakfasted with Alvaro Diornella, who has rented it for the summer.

May 17.—In the evening went to hear Mr. Whitefield preach at the New Building.

May 20.—Attended the funeral of a son of Henry Keppele, Jr.

May 23.—Took a ride with Edward Shippen to buy a pair of black horses.

May 24.—Attended Tench Francis's vendue, two miles from town, where I bought six acres of land at £33 per acre. At the same time was sold thirty-four lots, containing 331 acres, which amounted to £7544. [This little farm Mr. Hiltzheimer called Gravel Hill.]

June 13.—This evening went with Andrew Hamilton to Jonathan Humphreys' and had a bowl of good punch.

June 19.—Coming home with Owen Jones, Jr., from Galloway's place, met Richard Wister and Owen Jones, Sr., who made us return with them. At noon went to drink punch with Richard Roberts, on account of his being lately married to a young woman from Maryland.

July 9.—Went to Gravel Hill, and from thence to Tench Francis's. He and I took a walk to the Schuylkill.

July 11.—This morning left for New York Sir William Draper, who has been here about a week.

July 12.—Heavy thunder gust this afternoon. The lightning struck Sarah Emlen's two new houses on Market Street.

July 14.—Went to the State House this afternoon, where a meeting was called to consult about a further non-importation of goods from Great Britain, although the Yorkers have broke their agreement.

July 17.—Went to Gravel Hill with wife and children and there made a punch out of the new spring water, from the spring opened this morning.

July 23.—This afternoon my wife went to the funeral of old Mrs. Hillegas, in the Church Burying-ground.

July 28.—My wife and self spent the day at Fort St. David's with friends, and Mr. Alexander Alair was kind enough to cook for the company.

August 26.—With Thomas Wishard went to Bank meeting, on Front Street, to hear Rebecca Jones preach.

August 31.—Early this morning Timothy Matlack and myself went to the race track to see the brown colt Regulus run the two miles, which he did in four minutes and a quarter.

September 9.—I went up to the race ground to hear Mr. Pilmore, the Methodist preacher; he spoke from one of the stands.

September 15.—To-day read the first part of Goddard's article against Joseph Galloway and Thomas Wharton.

September 27.—This afternoon went to the town meeting at the State House, where it was agreed that further non-importation was necessary, a few articles only excepted. Joseph Fox, who was chairman, requested Charles Thomson to speak for him.

October 1.—Went to the State House to give in my vote for Judah Foulk for Sheriff; Joseph Fox, Michael Hillegas, Henry Pawling, Thomas Livezey, Thomas Mifflin, George Gray, Samuel Miles, and Edward Penington, for Assemblymen.

October 12.—At noon started for the £50 purse the following horses:

James DeLancey's b. f. Angelica,	1	4	1
Captain McDaniel's bl. f. Blackbird,	1	dist.	
Dr. Kearsley's bl. colt Steady,	3	2	3
Governor Sharp's c. f. Creeping Kate,	4	3	4
J. Hiltzheimer's b. colt Regulus,	5	1	2
James Boyd's g. colt Belt,	dist.		

October 20.—Dined at Greenwich Hall with the following gentlemen: Joseph Fox, Samuel Swift, John Chevalier, John Biddle, Thomas Wharton, Thomas Tilbury, Caleb Cash, John Mifflin, Dr. C. Evans, Henry Drinker, James Foster, Judah Foulk, and others. A number of the gentlemen went in a new stage wagon drawn by four horses.

October 25.—Set out for Long Island.

October 26.—Breakfasted and dined at Wilson Hunt's, at Maidenhead, from thence John Hunt and self proceeded to Woodbridge and lodged at Nathaniel Heard's.

October 27.—Proceeded to the New Blaze and Star Ferry, to Anthony Water's Ferry, to Powl's Hook Ferry, to East River Ferry, and came to Oliver Waters's, on Long Island, where we lodged.

October 28.—Dined at Waters's with Mr. Johnson, Mr. Gallomore, Mr. Read, Mr. Hilton, Nathaniel Heard, John Van Horn, David Reed, Mr. Hendrickson, and Elijah Lawrence. After dinner to Jamaica, where we lodged at a public house.

October 29.—Went to the race ground, Hempstead Plains, where started for the £50 purse the following horses:—

Dr. Kearsley's b. c. Steady, 4 years,	1	2
Mr. Hart's b. f. Blackbird, 3 years,	2	3
Walters & Hiltzheimer's b. c. Regulus, 4 years.	3	1

The rider of Regulus losing his cap, his second heat was given to Steady. Lodged at Valentine's.

October 30.—This morning a number of gentlemen had a fox hunt.

At noon five horses ran for another purse of £50. Lodged at William Furman's for the night.

October 31.—Crossed the ferry at the Narrows, reached Woodbridge, where we nighted.

November 1.—Returned to Wilson Hunt's. Will leave for home in the morning.

1772.

May 14.—Took a ride to my lot with Andrew Hamilton and Major Robert Bayard, to try a pair of horses.

May 17.—Went to church twice at the Academy, now being used by our congregation during the erection of our church on Race Street.

May 19.—Sold my pair of black horses, Gentle and Partner, to George Emlen, Jr., for £70.

May 22.—The Hon. Richard Penn, Governor of the Province, was married to Polly Masters last evening, and so was Samuel Meredith to one of Dr. Cadwalader's daughters.

July 12.—Mr. Cadwalader came after the bay colt Juniper. I sold him for £115.

August 4.—Took a ride with my wife to Schuylkill, to see two men and three women baptized, among them Hannah Gardner, formerly a Friend.

August 24.—Took a ride with George Mifflin to the race ground and drove around the track. After sundown there were fireworks at the State House.

September 4.—Early this morning James Buchanan, with his bay mare, Nancy Dawson, rode a match against time for 20 guineas. He was to ride fifteen miles around our race track in one hour, and he performed it in fifty-six minutes.

September 19.—With my wife and children went to see Jacob Bates perform in my lot, up Market Street, different feats of horsemanship on one, two, and three horses.

October 13.—Took a ride with Messrs. Huger and Izard, of South Carolina.

November 23.—This evening went to the Widow Spence's; there supped on venison with the following gentlemen: Robert William Jones, Richard Footman, Mr. Freeman, and Sutliff. Jacob Bates gave the supper on account of his leaving the city for Carolina.

December 11.—I received a letter from my brother-in-law, Conrad Eberle, in Germany, giving an account of my mother's death.

December 28.—Spent the fore part of the evening with Anthony Clarson at his lodgings; from there to John Biddle's with Joseph Galloway, Abel James, Judah Foulk, and William Parr. Being joined by Robert Erwin and William Jones, we went to Mary Jenkins's, and had supper about one o'clock.

1773.

January 10.—Called to see Samuel Miles, in Second Street, who is sick, and from there went to the burial of Joseph Pott's second wife (a Powell) from their house on Race Street. Samuel Emlen, who returned from England yesterday, preached.

January 17.—This afternoon attended the burial of John Biddle's wife; walked with Joseph Pemberton [son of Israel]; Samuel Emlen preached.

January 19.—Confined to my bed by an injury to my leg.

January 30.—Thomas Mifflin, Andrew Hamilton, Norton Pryor, and Mr. Stoneburner called to see me in my room.

February 4.—My wife and I intended to go to the burial of Clement Biddle's wife, but the weather being bad and I lame, we remained at home.

February 22.—Very cold! The Delaware froze fast last night. At 6 A. M. Daniel Wister's thermometer was 4 below 0, and 7 A. M. 2 below 0; Thomas Pryor's, the same hour, 0. It thus appears that it

3

is 2° colder in Market Street than it is in Water Street. Both ther-
mometers were exposed to the air.

February 27.—Andrew Hamilton spent the evening at my house.

March 1.—Dined at the new ferry, Penrose's, with ten gentlemen.

March 17.—Received a letter from John Allen in England, requesting
me to look out for two or three horses for John Penn, Esq.

March 27.—At 3 o'clock this morning a fire broke out in the store of
John Mease. The loss was considerable.

May 7.—Went to Falls of Schuylkill and dined with James and
-Charles Biddle, Jacob Bates, Philip Kinsey, Captain Heysham, John
Mease, R. Keen, Edward Milner, and others.

May 29.—Went to Robert Smith's place, now kept by Thomas Musher,
and dined with Joseph Fox, William Parr, Judah Foulk, Joseph
Redman, Charles Jarvis, Joseph Wharton, Richard Peters, Robert
Smith, Francis Trimble, Edward Milner, and others.

July 6.—Received a letter together with three mares from England, the
property of John Penn, Proprietor of Pennsylvania.

July 9.—Thermometer 92°. Went over the Schuylkill to the Liberty
Fish House; there dined with thirty gentlemen, at the invitation of
Robert Roberts. After dinner crossed the Schuylkill to General
Mifflin's house, to look at the wind-mill pumping water for his
garden.

July 27.—Visited Baker's on Vine Street to see the electrical fish,
where ten persons on taking hold of hands and holding the fish
received a shock.

August 26.—This afternoon John Allen, Esq., arrived from New York.
He recently returned from England, where he has been since May
4, 1771.

August 29.—John Penn with his lady arrived this afternoon; he is to
succeed his brother Richard as Governor of this Province.

August 30.—At 12 o'clock John Penn, Esq., was proclaimed Governor of Pennsylvania.

August 31.—This morning Governor John Penn came to my stables to look at his mares, sent from England, prior to his leaving. He was very courteous.

September 30.—Spent this evening at John Biddle's with Colonel Francis, Pearson Smith, Nathaniel Hyde, William Parr, William Jones, Judah Foulk, and Robert Erwin. Robert Erwin bought Garrick's house on Sixth Street for £520 at the Coffee House this evening.

October 11.—Entered my son William at the Academy, and paid the entrance fee, 20 shillings.

October 13.—In the evening went to the State House to hear the trial between the Proprietor and one Mr. Baron, concerning 244 feet of land on South Street. The attorneys for the Proprietor were Andrew and James Allen, and James Tilghman; for Mr. Baron, Edward Biddle, Joseph Read, and Joseph Galloway.

October 31.—William Jones, Thomas and Norton Pryor, and Charles Massey went with me to Mud Island to see the Fort, which was commenced about seventeen months ago. We all dined at Samuel Penrose's Schuylkill Ferry.

November 6.—Went down with Mr. Lawrence and Allen to Robert Erwin's place, called Primefield, to dine on beefsteaks with a number of gentlemen. I remember the names of the following: Judge Lawrence, James Allen, Joseph Fox, Turbot Francis, Tench Francis, John Kidd, Robert Morris, Anthony Morris, Richard Bache, Robert Smith, William Jones, George Roberts, John Lukens, Surveyor General, Samuel Hudson, Richard Peters, Captain St. Clair, Richard Footman, and Jacob Lewis.

November 16.—Entered my son Robert at the Academy yesterday.

December 25.—Samuel Howell informed me that the tea ship had arrived at Chester.

December 27.—There was a meeting at the State House, where it was agreed that the tea should be taken back to England.

1774.

January 22.—With Charles Massey and my two sons, went to the Schuylkill to see Massey skate. He is considered to be one of the best in the city.

January 26.—Attended the burial of William Ibison, from the house of Isaac Howell to Friends' ground.

January 29.—In the afternoon went down to the wharf to see the skaters on the Delaware; afterward to John Wister's, where I drank coffee with Richard Wister, Casper Wister, Daniel Wister and wife, Benjamin Morgan and wife, Samuel Miles and wife, and William Wister.

February 5.—Dined at Greenwich Hall with the following gentlemen: Joseph Galloway, John Lawrence, Samuel Mifflin, James Allen, William Parr, Major Harry Gordon, Major David Hay, Joseph Wharton, Charles Jarvis, William Jones, Richard Peters, Jr., John Shee, Joseph Fox, and others. On the way home the horses of John Lawrence and James Allen broke some parts of their harness, ran off, and left the sleigh. I went home on horseback, had my horses put into my sleigh, and drove down to Sam Casin's tavern and there found the gentlemen who had been cast away. We reached home before midnight.

February 7.—This morning George and David Seckel killed my big steer, named Roger, near six years old.

February 8.—This afternoon Roger was weighed at Seckel's slaughter house (1332 lbs.) in the presence of the following gentlemen: Timothy Matlack, Joseph Fox, Andrew Allen, James Allen, Samuel Mifflin, William Parr, Samuel Hudson, Josiah Hewes, Tench Tilghman, Samuel Massey, Reynold Keen, Andrew Hamilton, James

Wharton, Joseph Redman, Joseph Wharton, William Sheaff, and others.

February 10.—Took my wife in sleigh down to Mullin's, and had a beefsteak off my big steer Roger. Thomas Mifflin with a sleigh full of gentlemen joined us.

February 12.—Dined on "Roger" beefsteaks at Mullin's, on the banks of Schuylkill, with the following gentlemen: Major Hay, Major Hamilton, Thomas Lawrence, Thomas Lawrence, Jr., Andrew Hamilton, Richard Peters, Samuel Mifflin, John Kidd, James Allen, Tench Tilghman, W. B. Hockley, Joseph Fox, and others.

February 24.—Accompanied Andrew Hamilton to the Middle Ferry to see the ice move, which it did several times and then stopped.

February 25.—Went out to Joseph Ogden's at Middle Ferry and found the river clear of ice and people crossing, which has not been the case for near a week.

March 1.—Joseph Fox, Michael Hillegas, Samuel Rhoads, Richard Peters, Jr., and self went down to Province Island to attend the vendue of Samuel Penrose. Dined at the Ferry-house, now kept by Joseph Rudolph.

March 8.—Spent part of the afternoon at John Wister's, and drank coffee with Richard, Daniel, and William Wister.

March 10.—This afternoon my wife and I went to the burial of Judah son of John Lukens. A. Howell preached and I walked with John Little. From thence went to visit Charles Massey, who has been ill for over three weeks, and to Thomas Pryor's, where we spent the evening.

March 31.—With my sons Billy and Bobby set out on horseback for Wilson Hunt's, in New Jersey.

April 3.—Went to Maidenhead meeting-house and heard the Rev. Mr. Spencer preach the funeral sermon of Captain John Anderson, who died a few weeks since, and at the same time was buried his son Samuel. The text was Job xiv, 14.

April 5.—Arrived home to-day from my visit to Wilson Hunt and friends in New Jersey.

April 6.—In the forenoon attended court and was bound in the sum of £50 to appear at next court in the case of Galloway and Griffen. Drove down to Ogden's Ferry and had a shad dinner with Tench and James Tilghman, Andrew Hamilton, J. Hewes, William B. Hockley, and a young physician.

April 18.—Summoned to the Court House by Jacob Duché and Gibson Esqrs., to make one of a jury to decide whether John Perkins is to move out of the house of William Gray or not. We soon agreed that he should move.

April 24.—With Thomas Pryor, attended the funeral of George Kemble at the Church burying-ground.

April 27.—Thermometer at 2 P. M., 84½°.

May 3.—The effigies of Alexander Widderburn, Esq., and of Thomas Hutchinson, Governor of Massachusetts Bay, after being exposed for several hours in a cart, were hung on a gallows erected near the Coffee House, set on fire by electric fire, and consumed to ashes, about 6 o'clock in the evening.

May 4.—This morning the houses are all covered with snow.

May 5.—Cold enough to make ice, which near my front door measured from one-quarter to one-half an inch thick.

May 13.—In the evening went to the Academy to hear Rev. Mr. Pearsey (who is called the second Whitefield) preach on the text, Romans xiv, 17.

May 14.—Attended the burial of Samuel Howell's daughter; walked with James Wharton; from thence to Bank Meeting to hear Walker, an Englishman, preach.

June 5.—Attended for the first time our new church on Race Street, and took possession of a seat in pew No. 52.

June 12.—Returning from a ride with Thomas Pryor to the meadows, stopped at Mushett's and had some punch with Robert Smith, Robert Erwin, William Jones, Captain Jones, Captain Long, and Carpenter Wharton.

June 18.—This afternoon went to the State House and heard the following gentlemen speak on the Boston Port Bill: Charles Thomson, Joseph Reed, John Ross, James Allen, Thomas Mifflin, George Roberts, Rev. Dr. Smith, and John Dickinson.

July 13.—Gave the Rev. Mr. Pearsey a ride to the Falls of Schuylkill and from thence to Germantown Road and home.

July 25.—Went to the burial of Robert Glenn, from J. M. Nesbitt's, to ground in Pine Street.

August 2.—While observing my haymakers in Tilghman's lot, Tench Francis invited me to his house, where I met Thomas Willing, Esq., and we drank punch.

August 11.—To-day Mr. Middleton, one of the delegates from South Carolina, sent to my stables four long-tail English horses.

August 20.—This evening Thomas Cushing, Samuel Adams, John Adams, and Robert Treat Paine, delegates from Boston, came to town.

September 1.—Forenoon went to church to hear Rev. Mr. Weinberg preach a sermon suitable to the meeting of the great Congress in this city on Monday next.

September 5.—This forenoon the Congress met in Carpenters' Hall, forty odd delegates present, who chose Peyton Randolph, of Virginia, Chairman, and Charles Thomson (who is not a delegate) to be their Secretary.

September 6.—News was received from Boston of six men being killed by the soldiers of General Gage.

September 10.—A part of the new gaol, opposite the State House, was raised to-day, and to commemorate the event Joseph Fox and Edward Duffield, managers, gave the workmen a supper. Subsequently they asked a few of their friends to dine with them in the northeast corner room of the building—viz., William Fisher, Mayor ; Thomas Lawrence, Sr., Peter Reeves, Robert Smith, Robert Erwin, James Pearson, Reynold Keen, Judah Foulk, John Lukens, William Jones, William Gray, and myself.

September 15.—This forenoon went to the burial of Richard Hockley, Esq., in Baptist ground. I walked with William Hoffman, who is in bad health.

September 16.—Met the Amicable Fire Company at the Liberty Fish House, where I dined with about twenty members. The dinner was given by Robert Roberts. A dinner was also given by a number of gentlemen, in the State House, to the Delegates now sitting in Carpenters' Hall.

October 15.—About one o'clock Thomas Pryor and I started on horseback to dine over Schuylkill, but we had not gone fifty yards before I was suddenly seized by a great pain in my right hip and forced to return. Doctors Cadwalader, Bond and Kearsley, were immediately summoned to my bedside, but could give me but little relief.

October 17.—My pain still continued excessive, but with the help of a clever little Irish woman named Darrah, I got some relief by a clyster.

October 20.—The Rev. William Pearsey, chaplain to the Right Honorable the Countess of Huntingdon, called to see me.

October 21.—This afternoon Joseph Potts called, and feeling well enough I took a ride in his phaeton.

October 26.—Rev. Mr. Pearsey preached his farewell sermon in the Arch street Presbyterian Meeting-house.

1777.

February 12.—In the afternoon went with Robert Tuckness to the burial of Robert Smith, carpenter, at Friends' ground, Arch Street.

February 20.—Leased Province Island for three years at £700 per annum.

March 9.—Dined at Province Island with Colonel George Taylor, Colonel Brodhead, Colonel William Henry, Robert Erwin, Samuel Penrose, Jesse Bonsall, Matthew Jones, William Jones, Caleb Ash, Charles Jervis, and Captain John Webb. Webb has leased the tavern, ferry, and about eight acres of land for one year, at £90.

March 14.—Went out to the Schuylkill to see what progress has been made with the Continental stables, and there met Major Jonathan Mifflin.

March 18.—To-day staked out the light-horse stable at Schuylkill.

April 16.—With General Mifflin inspected the light-horse stables.

April 17.—Breakfasted at Mr. John Mifflin's with General Thomas Mifflin, Major Jonathan Mifflin, and Major Ottendorf. Spent part of the evening with Mr. John Hancock, president of Congress, in Chestnut Street.

April 22.—Captain Hart to-day is moving the Continental horses and wagons from Tench Francis's lot to mine.

May 3.—Received an order from the Council of Safety to prevent the cutting of wood at Centre Woods.

May 7.—Removed sixty-one Continental horses from Hog Island to Province Island.

May 22.—Went to Kensington with Generals Schuyler and Mifflin to examine the boats attached to wagons, and from thence to Province Island with General Mifflin. In the evening took a walk with Generals Schuyler and Mifflin, Mr. Middleton, and several Delegates to Congress to examine the bridge over Schuylkill and the stables.

June 2.—Went down to Province Island, where I sold 80 Continental horses.

June 6.—Above 30 wagons returned with loads from Sinnepuxent.

June 17.—Out by the Schuylkill met Generals Gates and Mifflin, with Mrs. Dickinson, and took them to see the Continental stables.

June 27.—Walked out to the Schuylkill stables to see the troop ·of light-horse that arrived last night.

June 30.—Found the Schuylkill stables filled with light-horse; visited also Governor Penn's woods to see the camp of the North Carolina troops.

July 13.—Called to see General Gates on Front Street, and from thence to church.

July 27.—Called to see General Mifflin, who left our army last evening, who informed me that the British are coming into our capes, where seventy sail have already appeared.

July 28.—This afternoon I paid Jacob Graff, Jr., for the house and lot at the southwest corner of Seventh and Market Streets £1775, and received the deed for the same.

July 30.—Accompanied Captain Van Heer to Province Island and then to the camp at the five-mile stone on Chester Road.

July 31.—At ten o'clock to-night His Excellency General Washington came to town with about 200 light-horse.

August 3.—Joseph Thornburg, Wagon Master General, spent part of the afternoon at my house.

August 7.—Visited the encampment near and about Germantown, and John Vanderen's mill.

August 24.—Sunday. A shower of rain in the morning. Our army, commanded by His Excellency General Washington, marched through this city, crossed the bridge over Schuylkill, proceeded four miles, and then turned back.

August 31.—Called on William Moulder to inquire what forage he had in store.

September 7.—In the forenoon went to Mr. Hancock's to see his lady off to Boston.

September 11.—His Excellency General Washington had an engagement with General Howe at Brandywine. [Mr. Hiltzheimer records that the loss of the British in killed and wounded was 1976, which was ascertained from an Orderly Book found on an officer killed at Germantown.—ED.]

September 14.—Went with my sons to Province Island to bring off the Continental horses, as the island is to be put under water by Colonel Joseph Penrose, under orders of General Washington.

September 16.—About eleven o'clock, General Coudray, with nine French officers, set out for camp over Schuylkill. The General being mounted in the boat, his horse became restive and jumped overboard with him, and the General was drowned. I was present when his body was recovered, toward evening.

September 19.—At one o'clock this morning news came to town that General Howe's army was crossing the Schuylkill at Swedes' Ford, which set many people moving. Congress and other public bodies left before daylight. I sent off George Nelson with the money, books, and papers belonging to the public to Abraham Hunt's, in New Jersey, and one load of my private goods to Peter Trexler's, in Northampton County.

September 20.—The reported crossing of the enemy proves to be untrue.

September 23.—The city much alarmed and people moving out.

September 24.—Left Philadelphia with my whole family; dined at Bristol, and from thence to Abraham Hunt's, at Trenton, where we were kindly received.

September 26.—This day the English entered Philadelphia.

October 5.—Sent off David Kinney with two wagons, with my goods, for Reading.

October 6.—Set out from Trenton with my family for Reading, crossed the Delaware at Coryell's, and was directed to one Armatage, Bucks

County, but he refused to give us lodgings, as did one Balderston, at the next farm, but at the third farm we were more fortunate.

October 7.—Reached George Taylor's at Galloway's Iron Works (Durham), where we had everything we could desire.

October 8.—Dined at Bethlehem, and then proceeded to Squire Peter Trexler's, who received us with great good will.

October 9.—Sent on Nelson and Kinney with the wagons, but remained another day owing to the rain.

October 10.—Arrived at Reading, where we were received by General Mifflin in his usual warm manner.

October 11.—Breakfasted with Colonel Mark Burd. Took a ride with the General to his farm, three miles from Reading, which he calls Angelica. In the evening removed my family thither, where was provided for us a good house, with the service of John Schmucker, the tenant.

October 12.—General Mifflin, Colonel Mifflin, Colonel Matthew Irwin, and Anthony Butler rode out to visit me.

October 13.—Rode into Reading and dined at Samuel Morris's with Hall, the printer.

October 17.—At 10 o'clock to-night John White arrived with the good news that General Gates had captured Burgoyne and his whole army.

October 23.—We heard great firing this forenoon.

October 25.—Called to see General Mifflin, who read me a letter, which gave an account of the destruction of two British men-of-war in the Delaware and the defeat of the Hessians at Red Bank.

November 8.—General Mifflin, his lady, Miss Rebecca Mifflin, the two Misses Morris, Hannah Sherman, and Colonel George Gibson called to see us.

November 11.—General Mifflin, Major Benjamin Eyre, and myself took a walk over part of the General's land. He owns 628 acres, for which he paid £9050.

November 13.—I dispatched Barney Hart with six teams for South Carolina.

November 16.—Lady Gates, en route for Albany, arrived at Reading, and then called at my house.

November 21.—Cloudy, raw, and some little rain. This morning after seven o'clock we felt the shock of an earthquake.

November 25.—General Mifflin and Colonel Lutterloh called to see me, and accompanied them to Reading, where I dined at the General's with General Conway and other officers of the army.

December 3.—General Mifflin had a stable raised by a few Continental carpenters, and had the following gentlemen to dine with him: Samuel Mifflin, Jonathan Mifflin, James Biddle, John Biddle, Joseph Wood, William Richards, Joseph Redman, Jr., Jonathan Potts, Levi Hollingsworth, Richard Humphreys, Mr. Hall, the printer, Samuel Morris, Jr., Mr. Crauch, Anthony Butler, Dr. Kennedy, James Searle, Benjamin Eyre, Mark Burd, and Matthew Irwin.

December 5.—General Mifflin, Colonel Jonathan Mifflin, Colonel Humpton and Colonel Baylow called to see me. In the afternoon I went to Reading to attend the burial of Mrs. Keen, and, with Jonathan Mifflin, Benjamin Eyre, and Richard Humphreys, carried her body to the grave.

December 7.—Dined with me Captains Nichols and Fanwick, both naval prisoners of war.

December 13.—Went to town with Captain Charles Souder, and dined with Mrs. Mifflin and her two sisters; the General away from home. After dinner was over, Mr. George Mifflin came in, who left Philadelphia last Wednesday. He told us that a pound of meat is worth 3s. 9d.; sugar, 3s. 6d.; tea, 35s.; quarter of a hundred of flour, 17s. 6d., all hard money; wood, £4, without hauling.

December 17.—Met John Biddle, Esq., in Reading, to arrange for hay for the poor Continental horses here.

1778.

January 14.—Returned with General Mifflin and Dr. Potts to Reading in my sleigh, where we dined with the General and Dr. Thomas Bond. After dinner two New England soldiers on a furlough called at the house—each of them had twelve fingers and twelve toes, and they informed us other members of their family have the same number.

January 16.—Joseph Gray told us that he had been in Philadelphia for one night, recently, to procure clothing, and that he went in and out unmolested.

February 11.—Generals Oliver Wolcott and Samuel Huntington, Delegates to Congress, breakfasted with me.

February 19.—Captain Daniel Joy remained with us over night, and is now gone on to Colonel John Patton's. •

February 23.—Four wagons reached here loaded with General Mifflin's baggage on their way to Yorktown.

February 27.—Richard Ross, one of Mr. Hancock's express riders, took breakfast with us.

March 6.—Colonel Bull, who nighted with us, set off to join his family in Virginia.

March 7.—Distributed 24 Continental horses among the farmers in the neighborhood to keep until called for.

1779.

February 22.—In the evening met the Republican Society at Duffy's Tavern, 32 members present.

February 23.—With Mr. Butler and Cranch, called on the Treasury

Board and made application for more money to pay accounts contracted in the late Quartermaster General's Department.

February 25.—This evening my horse, which has been used by Lady
Washington since 2d inst., was returned from camp.

March 9.—Spent the evening with Mr. John Lukens, where I met
General John Armstrong, Mathias Slough, his son, George, Colonel
Ephraim Blaine, Mr. Trent, and A. Dunham.

April 14.—This evening Francis Lightfoot Lee, a Delegate to Congress, and Abraham Hunt took tea with me.

April 15.—Spent the evening with Colonels Atlee and Jacob Morgan
at Mr. Barge's.

April 20.—Moved the horses of the Delegates to Congress from Mrs.
Kimble's to the Continental stables.

April 27.—Mrs. Barge, Mrs Jones, my wife, and George Nelson visited
State Island, from thence to Red Bank, Billingsport, and Fort
Mifflin.

May 4.—I went out to examine the fence around the Continental lot,
and from there across the Commons to the camp of Indians, who
arrived to-day.

May 8.—Accompanied Mr. Webster, quartermaster of artillery, to
Sheriff Claypoole, and gave bond jointly for a horse taken from
Abraham Kintzing by Colonel Will for the use of the United
States.

May 12.—Started John Grave's brigade of teams, loaded with
ammunition, for the Susquehanna, and went with them some distance over Schuylkill.

June 10.—Tench Francis, James White, and Norton Pryor called to
see me.

June 12.—In the afternoon went out to the Commons to see Colonel
W. White's light-horse reviewed by General Wayne.

July 15.—George Ross, Esq., was buried to-day.

July 16.—Went to the War Office and received instructions from the Board to examine horses and wagons bought for the public use.

July 22.—I have six men making hay in Jones's meadow for the Continental service.

July 29.—John Grau set off with his brigade of twenty wagons for West Point; thirteen of them are loaded with cannons.

August 6.—My son Robert set out for camp with a chestnut gelding for Major General Greene, quartermaster general.

August 7.—Forenoon went out toward Schuylkill on horseback, fell off, and was much hurt in my back. Colonel John Cox and General Armstrong called to see me.

August 23.—Fireworks were displayed at the corner of Market and Sixth Streets.

August 25.—Grau returned with his brigade of teams from West Point. I am sick with fever and ague.

August 28.—My son Robert and I rode out to Germantown and on the way met 160 prisoners, captured by Major Lee in a small fort at Powles Hook. Dined at Mr. Stoneburner's, who took me to a man near by, who put something on my arm to cure the fever and ague.

September 5.—James Smith and I accompanied to the Schuylkill Baron de B——, who is on his way to South Carolina to visit his brother, Count Pulaski.

September 18.—I sent by Mr. Scull two bills of exchange on France for $90 to purchase dry-goods.

September 20.—Went down to Greenwich Hall and dined on beefsteaks with the following gentlemen: Robert Morris, James Mease, Thomas Willing, John Nixon, Richard Bache, John Little, Tench Francis, Robert Erwin, William Jones, and William Gray. Mr. Joseph Redman was buried to-day.

September 21.—In the afternoon went to the burial of George Bechtel and walked with Richard Hunt. The second French Minister arrived to-day.

October 4.—Took my wife and daughter Hannah riding, and coming home we met a part of the militia running from the Commons toward the city, pursued by the President and militia light-horse.

October 5.—Two of the soldiers killed in the riot yesterday were buried to-day.

October 9.—Took two Hessian blacksmiths out of the new gaol to work in the Continental smith shop.

October 20.—Sent off a brigade of thirteen wagons loaded with boots for camp.

November 6.—Took a ride with Mr. Langdon, member of Congress, to my lot to look at my two sorrel colts.

November 8.—Mr. Gerry, member of Congress, requested me to drive his pair of horses in a wagon for half an hour.

November 11.—Mr. Barge and I attended the burial of the Hon. Joseph Hewes, member of Congress from North Carolina, whose body was taken from Mrs. House's, southwest corner Market and Fifth Streets, to Christ Church yard. The Rev. William White took his text from 1 Corinthians xv, 55.

November 15.—To-night sent for Dr. Kuhn to see my daughter Betsy.

November 17.—This morning the small-pox appeared on my daughter.

November 30.—To-day the small-pox made its appearance on my daughter Hannah.

December 8.—Colonel Wadsworth and Abraham Hunt spent the evening with me.

December 21.—Very cold; navigation in the Delaware closed by ice. Lady Washington arrived from Virginia with seven horses. [She set out for camp December 27th.]

4

1780.

January 2.—Very cold, with snow. Early this morning a fire broke out in Mr. Penn's house, on Market Street, occupied by Mr. Holker, the French Consul, which was consumed to the first floor.

January 18.—Attended the funeral of John Naglee, from the house of his son-in-law in Key's Alley, to Church yard in Arch Street. I served a four years' apprenticeship with Mr. Naglee, who was a silversmith, and lived with him from September of 1748 until he moved to the country in the spring of 1755.

January 22.—In the forenoon went to the ox roast on the Delaware; in the afternoon crossed the ice to Joseph Cooper's in my sleigh and pair of horses, Mrs. Barge and my wife with me.

January 28.—James Hunt nighted here with his brigade of sleighs to load provisions.

January 31.—My wife and daughter Kitty's schoolmistress, Mrs. Roman, was buried to-day.

February 24—Went to the Treasury Board and applied for money to enable me to purchase forage for the horses belonging to the members of Congress, agreable to resolve of Congress.

February 26.—McCutcheon and Carson took away my big cow, seven years' old (weighed dressed 1763 lbs), for which they paid me sixty-five guineas.

February 29.—Received an order from the Treasury Board on Mr. Hillegas for $20,000 to purchase forage, agreeable to resolve of Congress, 16th instant.

March 2.—This morning a flat boat, loaded with wood, reached Market Street Wharf—the first craft of any kind to come up or go down the river since December 21st of last year.

March 5.—Rode horseback toward Germantown, and dined with Doctors Shippen, Bond, and Craigie, and Thomas Smith and Joseph Shippen.

March 10.—In the evening my son William and I went to see Templeman perform on the wire.

May 14.—Gouverneur Morris, member of Congress, broke his leg by jumping out of his phaeton, as the horses were running away.

May 23.—All the militia went to the field, where they were reviewed by President Joseph Read and the French Ambassador.

July 14.—Am quite sick, and had to send for Dr. Glentworth yesterday; had Dr. Jones in consultation to-day, but they agree that I am in a fair way to recover.

August 1.—Went to the Middle Ferry and examined 80 horses purchased by Mr. Slough for the French army.

August 15.—To-day was qualified before George Bryan, Esq., according to resolve of Congress, to enable me to act in the Quartermaster's Department. Colonel Pickering has recently been appointed to that office.

August 19.—At midnight a fire broke out in the Continental smith's shop on Chestnut Street, which was destroyed, and also part of the carpenter shop near it.

September 3.—Our militia returned from Trenton.

September 7.—Intended to go to the burial of old William Allen, Esq., but was too late.

September 17.—Called to see Colonel Pickering, quartermaster general, at his house on Front Street, as he is about to set out for camp.

September 19.—In the forenoon George Mifflin and I went to the burial of Mrs. Reed, late the wife of Hon. Joseph Reed, President of this State.

September 29—Abraham Hunt came from Trenton and brought the news that General Arnold had gone over to the enemy.

October 11.—Called on Daniel Wister at the Quartermaster General's store and selected some clothing for the wagoners in the Continental service.

October 15.—Summers and Karch set out for camp with baggage for his Excellency General Washington.

November 5.—General Mifflin, Colonel Bird, Patton, and Miles breakfasted with me.

December 1.—Lady Washington arrived last evening and proceeded to camp to-day.

December 31.—Took a ride with Richard Peters, Esq., to his farm over Schuylkill.

1781.

January 1.—To-day Timothy Matlack and Whitehead Humphreys met on Market, between Fifth and Sixth Streets, and, after some words, proceeded to blows.

January 16.—Mr. Barge and I attended the burial of Mrs. Keen, the second wife of Reynold Keen. She was buried in St. Peter's Church yard. I also attended the burial of his first wife at Reading, December 5, 1777.

January 27.—Attended a meeting of the German Society, at the Lutheran schoolhouse on Cherry Street, concerning the charter recently obtained from the Assembly.

February 3.—Called at Mr. Barge's to see Colonel Michael Swope, who has been a prisoner since the summer of 1776.

February 8.—Major Edward Giles brought the news here from the southward of General Morgan's victory over the British.

February 26.—Colonel Miles called me up at one o'clock this morning to send an express to head of Elk.

February 28.—Visited the Ordnance Yard to inspect the cannon loading in wagons for the head of Elk. There are over one hundred and fifty horses in the brigade.

March 3.—Colonel Timothy Pickering and Richard Peters spent the evening with me.

April 13.—Attended a court-martial at the Barracks; two wagoners before us.

April 19.—James Willing called to see me, who is out on his parole from New York.

May 17.—The corpse of Colonel Samuel Mifflin was brought from Reading and buried here to-day.

June 2.—Went to the Assembly and heard Robert Morris speak concerning our currency and recommend to the House to take off the Tender Act.

June 27.—Early this morning some cannon were discharged on the river, and a ball from one struck my stable door, through which it passed, struck against the wall, and bounded across the street into Christopher Brierley's yard, who picked it up and gave it to me.

June 30.—Lady Washington arrived here from camp.

July 4.—Fireworks at the State House.

August 30.—His Excellency General Washington arrived about one o'clock. He has not been here since 2d February, 1779.

September 2.—Accompanied Colonel Dearborn, deputy quartermaster, over Schuylkill, to select a site for an encampment.

September 4.—Arrived 2500 French troops, and as many yesterday, among them 300 cavalry, who are encamped on the Commons on the east side of the Schuylkill.

September 5.—General Washington left for the southward. Jonathan Penrose has charge of the wagons that transport the cannon to head of Elk.

September 9.—Colonel James Thompson left for the Head of Elk with a number of horses purchased for the French army.

October 22.—Early in the morning an express brought the news that on 17th Lord Cornwallis had surrendered to his Excellency General Washington.

October 24.—The city was handsomely illuminated in consequence of Lord Cornwallis's surrender, but am sorry to have to add that so many doors and windows have been destroyed in houses of Friends.

October 25.—To-night there is fireworks in the State House yard.

November 3.—This afternoon the British colors, twenty-four in number, taken from Lord Cornwallis, were brought to this city by Colonel Humphreys, aide to his Excellency. At the Schuylkill they were met and escorted into the city by our City Light Horse, commanded by Captain Sam Morris, and delivered to Hon. Thomas McKean, President of Congress, at the State House. At night the house of the French Minister was illuminated to a great degree.

November 5.—Went to the State House and joined following gentlemen as a jury : J. Hazlewood, Colonel Knox, T. Briton Falkner, David Reese, J. Few, T. Middleton, Grant Porter, Charles Syng, and Peter Thompson. We tried a case between Dr. F. Phile and the Commonwealth of Pennsylvania, and Jeremiah Warder and J. Parker, concerning goods brought into the State from St. Thomas and proven to be British manufacture. Judge McKean gave us his charge about midnight, after six lawyers for several hours had addressed us. We proceeded to Baker's, opposite the State House, and there remained until seven o'clock before we agreed upon a verdict, which was that we would give the facts and leave the decision to the court.

November 6.—At eleven o'clock we met again and carried in our verdict, which was delivered to the court by our foreman, John Hazlewood. Messrs. Ingersoll, Bradford, and Coxe, represented Phile and the Commonwealth, and Wilson, Lewis, and Sergeant, Warder and Parker.

November 7.—Accompanied Tench Francis and William Gray to see the ox teams (fourteen wagons, fifty-six oxen) Francis brought the money from Boston with.

November 13.—One of the three spies arrested last Wednesday night in this city was to-day executed on the Commons. Edison, one of the three, confessed that their design was to rob the office of the Secretary of Congress of such papers as might be of use to the enemy. Edison was formerly a clerk in the office.

· *November 17.*—Tench Francis sold his oxen and wagons at vendue.

November 26.—His Excellency General Washington and his lady arrived from the southward.

December 3.—Met General Mifflin on Chestnut Street, when we called on Dr. Kuhn, who recently arrived with his family from Edenton, North Carolina.

December 6.—Inspected two brigades of teams from Bucks County for the use of the French army.

December 19.—My son Robert, who attended the hunt at Frankford, told me that General Washington was present.

December 26.—Met the German Society at the Lutheran schoolhouse, and was elected one of the overseers.

1782.

· *January 2.*—In the afternoon went to the schoolhouse and met the German Society to finish the business of December 26th last. General Baron Steuben was this day elected a member of the society.

January 10.—Went to the Assembly Room in the State House, where the Court met, and there joined the following gentlemen jurors: Peter Thompson, foreman; Jacob Barge, Jacob Graff, Robert Roberts, Mr. Askin, William Hall, Robert Cox, Mr. Canady, Thomas Nixon, David Rees, and William Webb. The case before us was a wagon-load of goods, proven to be British, brought from

New Jersey, stopped and seized at Frankford by Colonel McVough. Our verdict was in favor of the Commonwealth.

January 11.—Again attended at the State House, and met the following jurors : Peter Thompson, foreman; Jacob Morgan, Jacob Barge, Jacob Graff, George Hazlewood, Benjamin Compty, Lewis Grant, Mr. Porter, Mr. Falkner, Thomas Middleton, and Joseph Ogden, Jr. We decided four cases—British goods brought from St. Thomas, and seized by Dr. Fred. Phile, on behalf of the Commonwealth. The claimants were George and Caleb Emlen, Peter Carmack, Mordecai Lewis, John Clifford & Co. Our verdict was against the claimants. In the afternoon the same jurors, with the exception of Peter Thompson, in whose place came John Little, decided against the claim of Paul Simor for goods seized on a vessel.

January 23.—Timothy Matlack breakfasted with me, and explained the way the business in the recently established bank is conducted, and the issue of their notes.

January 30.—The Delaware is frozen over and many people crossing. James Cannon was buried in the Church burying-ground.

January 31.—While walking along Front Street met George Mifflin, who took me to Joseph Morris's to see his brother the General, who had come in from the Falls, but we learned that he had gone on the river to skate, in which exercise, by all accounts, he is very expert.

February 2.—Sold to General Baron Steuben a black horse, bald face, seven years old, for £45.

February 3.—Took a sleigh ride with my wife, daughter Hannah, and son Thomas to Joseph Warner's, six miles up the Schuylkill, and his wife returned with us to the city.

February 12.—Loaned Robert Erwin a wagon and two horses to assist in bringing ice from the Schuylkill to the ice-house of Robert Morris in the rear of his house on Market Street.

February 20.—George Nelson took John Brown out of prison for me, to serve for six months as a hostler, for which he is to receive $30.

February 28.—Spent an hour at Peter Summers's with General Potter, Thomas Smith, Esq., Joseph Gardner, John Lukens, and John Little.

March 3.—I went on horseback to General Mifflin's, at the Falls, and dined with Mrs. Mifflin, Captain N. Falkner and wife, and Susanna Morris.

March 10.—Doctor Kuhn called to see me again to-day—the first time since his return from abroad.

March 12.—General Knox and Gouverneur Morris set out for Elizabethtown.

March 22.—The Commander-in-Chief set out for the eastward. He has been in town since November 26th last.

March 27.—Governor Dickinson's house, occupied by the French Minister, was struck by lightning this afternoon and a man horribly burned.

March 29.—Colonel Pickering, quartermaster general, and Abraham Hunt, of Trenton, breakfasted with me.

April 7.—My son Thomas and I went as far as Gray's bridge to look after the horses I purchased for the French army.

April 9.—I took out of prison four men to take care of the public horses.

April 12.—Moved all the Continental wagons and other public property out of the lot of Mr. Logan, at the corner of Sixth and Chestnut Streets.

April 25.—Fast Day, recommended by Congress and ordered by President William Moore.

May 6.—My son Robert was bitten by a mad dog in his arm.

May 13.—There was fireworks on the State House yard this evening.

May 16.—John Bayard sold some wagons and harness in the Continental yard.

May 19.—Mr. Hunt's Peter came after the stallion St. Patrick, which he bought of General John Cadwalader. Sent after the two Hessian prisoners who ran off last night.

June 14.—My wife, Mr. and Mrs. Barge, and I went to the burial of George Nelson's wife in St. Paul's yard.

June 24.—My carriage and four horses returned to-day with the Messrs. Rutledge and Clymer, members of Congress.

June 30.—Went to church and there met General Lincoln, Secretary of War, who I did not know understood German. Perhaps he attended out of curiosity.

July 14.—His Excellency General Washington, from the northward, and the Commander of the French army, from the southward, arrived to-day.

July 15.—Some fine fireworks were exhibited to-night, and several hundred lamps lit in the square opposite the French Minister's house, in honor of the birth of the Dauphin. My family, with Colonel Ephraim Blaine, J. Chaloner, J. Smith, George Nelson, John Wilson, and others viewed the fireworks from the roof of one of my stables.

July 22.—Colonel J. Wadsworth breakfasted with us, after which we went to see Colonel Pickering, quartermaster general, and from thence to General Mifflin's to dinner.

July 24.—His Excellency General Washington left the city.

July 25.—Returning from a ride with my wife, saw the burial of Major Galvan in the Potters' Field. The Major shot himself last night through the head.

July 30.—Went to Front Street to see General Lincoln, Secretary of War, and Colonel Hodgdon set out for Carlisle.

August 6.—To-day Henry Keppele, Jr., was brought in a carriage from Peter Summer's to his father's house, on Frankford Road. [He was buried August 8.]

August 13.—Returned from Colonel Miles's at Spring Mill, and in the afternoon with Mr. Lukens laid out the streets through my Aunt Foster's lot.

August 28.—Paid Thomas Bond, Jr., £175 on account of the lot purchased on Seventh Street for £275. At noon went to the Coffee House and bought a stable on the banks of the Schuylkill, sold by order of Colonel Miles, D. Q. M., for £102.

August 29.—With my wife and son Thomas set out for Angelica, one of General Mifflin's farms.

September 2.—Dined at General Mifflin's with General St. Clair, Samuel Potts, John Patton, Alexander Graydon, Collinson Read, Drs. Bond and Wilson, and several others.

September 3.—Took a walk with General Mifflin, Dr. Bond and Wilson, the two Misses Morris, and my son.

September 4.—After dinner we left the General's farm, passed through Reading, and went on to Pottsgrove, and lodged at the Sign of the Bell.

September 5.—Set out early this morning and drove eleven miles to Read's to breakfast, but the meal was such an ordinary one and the girl that waited on us so untidy my wife could not eat anything. Dined at Steers's, and arrived at home by sunset. The colt, which the General gave my son, caused many detentions on the way.

September 6.—While we were absent from home, the whole of the French army passed through the city on their march to Trenton.

September 29.—After church called on Joseph Morris to inquire after General Mifflin, and was told that he was better than for several days past.

October 4.—General Lee, late of our army, and just from his farm in Virginia, was to-day buried in Christ Church yard.

October 8.—Went to the election in Germantown with Colonel Samuel Miles. Dined at Armatage's tavern with Colonels Miles,

Melcher, Warner, Cowperthwaite, and Dean, Mr. Jacob Rush, Joseph Jones and others.

October 29.—Spent the evening with Dr. Jones, who will set out with his family for Georgia, after an absence of near four years.

November 1.—Accompanied Dr. Jones, member of Congress from Georgia, and his family five miles up the Lancaster Road. Mr. Everly and family are with them.

November 4.—Met the members of the Amicable Fire Company at Thomas Palmer's on Market Street. Fourteen members present.

November 7.—To-day at noon John Dickinson was proclaimed President of this State from the Court House steps.

December 5.—Took General Lincoln in my chair to the meadows, and there met William Jones, after which we went to the Sign of the Buck and had a pint of wine.

December 17.—Called on General Lincoln at his lodgings, who is about to set out to visit his family near Boston.

December 20.—Met the officers of the German Society at the Widow Hess's in relation to the lot on Seventh Street.

December 23.—This morning the last of the French Legion left for Delaware.

December 26.—Met the German Society at the schoolhouse, and the officers went to the Widow Hess's to supper. Colonel Lewis Farmer was elected president, and Lewis Weiss, vice-president.

December 30.—With Mr. Barge went to the State House to serve on the Grand Jury, the members of which are: Zebulon Potts, foreman ; Ruben Haines, John Shee, Jacob Bright, Samuel Wheeler, Caleb Emlen, William Bingham, Samuel Caldwell, Robert Hare, Captain Davis, William Turnbull, Colonel R. Knox, Captain Ord, David McCullough, Derick Peterson, John Pringle, John Harrison, Jacob Barge, and myself.

December 31.—The Grand Jury met. The bill against E. Oswald, the printer, could not be decided, owing to the absence of witnesses. We brought in a true bill against one Stackhouse and four negroes, who robbed William Ball's house, on the Delaware, above the city, in November last.

1783.

January 1.—The Grand Jury considered the bill against Oswald, the printer, for libel. The following witnesses were examined: William Bradford, Esq., Francis Nichols, Dr. Gardner, William Harris, James Wilson, John Reynolds, Edward Bird, Michael Hillegas, William Lewis, William Blair, J. Ingersoll, and Moses Levy. After a long debate the bill was ignoramused, 16 to 3.

January 2.—The Grand Jury met at 10 o'clock. Three bills were presented against Hammer, Richardson, Tyson, Roberts, and several others, residing in Philadelphia County, for aiding and assisting four British prisoners in making their escape from Lancaster to New York. Captain Noah Lee and one Burke were examined, whereupon true bills were found and carried to the Court.

January 3.—Another bill was presented against Oswald, for printing a libel in the *Gazetteer* of October 1, 1782, which was ignoramused, 17 to 2. The jury found a true bill against G. B., J. B., and N. G., the three Commissioners, for giving their order to the Collectors to demand of the people a larger sum of money than the law directs on the Class Tax for enlisting men for the Continental army in 1781, on the evidence of E. Duffield, Michael Hillegas, and Tench Francis. In the evening presented our bills to the Chief Justice McKean, and Justice Bryan. We were reprimanded for not admitting the evidence sent by the Court in support of the charges against Oswald. The Chief Justice handed us back the bill for reconsideration.

January 4.—The jury met, and debated the bill returned to us yesterday, and agreed to make no change in it, and to return it to Court. Adjourned to Monday.

January 6.—Mr. Bradford, the Attorney General, returned the bill to the jury which we handed in against the three Commissioners, together with one which he had drawn up himself. But the jury disliked the form, and found one more to their minds and intent. At the same time, the jury agreed to a memorial, to be handed to the Court, in consequence of the reprimand given by the Chief Justice to us on Friday, which was signed by sixteen of the jurors.

January 7.—The jury met, proceeded to the Court with the bill against the Commissioners and our memorial, which our foreman requested be read in Court. This was not done, but the Chief Justice told us that the Court had no further business for us. We then returned to the tavern in Elbow Lane and paid our reckoning, $7 each.

January 14.—Took Mrs. Mary Clarkson, her youngest son, my wife, and daughter Kitty, in my sleigh the five-mile round.

January 22.—Went to the Coffee House, and bought one-fourth part of the Congress stables, next to Eighth Street, for £49.

February 3.—Met at the German Reformed school-house the Vestry of that church, to which body I was elected last month.

February 13.—The speech of the British King arrived in town, in which he acknowledges the independence of the American States. Took a ride to Gravel Hill, and met General Mifflin and Baron de Fox in the General's phaeton.

February 15.—To-day was hanged Stackhouse and two negroes, who robbed William Ball's house. The other two negroes concerned in the robbery were reprieved.

March 13.—To-day we received the news by Captain Barney that the treaty between England and America is only provisional until terms are agreed on between England and France.

March 24.—Yesterday the sloop Triumph, commanded by the Chevalier Duquesne, arrived in thirty-six days from Cadiz, bringing the news of the confirmation of a general peace.

March 27.—Scott and Watkins began to pull down my part of the Continental stables.

April 3.—Returning with my wife from a ride, stopped in Arch Street to see the flying horses (wooden).

April 9.—Went with James Pearson to Gravel Hill to take an account of the damage done to my house and fences by the British during their occupation of the city. Also met the vestry of our church, and made out the account of damages done by the British to the church. Captain Rinnet arrived with dispatches from Sir Guy Carleton, informing Congress that the preliminary articles between England and France had been exchanged February 3d, and between England and Spain February 9th, and from that date two months hostilities between England and America will end.

April 10.—The account of damages done by the British to my property, £191 15s. 8d. was delivered to Gunning Bedford, Esq., at the Court House.

April 14.—Met at Thomas Palmer's, Nathan Sellers and William Turner, to settle by order of Court a dispute between Adam Poth and Borden and Croft. We found that there is justly due by Adam Poth £31 10s. 10d.

April 16.—Went down to the Court House, where the City Magistrates appeared and caused William Will, Sheriff, to proclaim to the people at large that all hostilities by land and on sea are at an end between America and Great Britain.

April 18.—At the request of John Holker, Esq., my son Thomas and I left for Wilmington to examine the French troop horses.

April 19.—Examined 249 French troop horses and then returned home.

April 27.—Mr. Barge and I, in my chair, set out for Lancaster. Lodged at Joe Webb's, on the Horseshoe Road near Dowingtown.

April 28.—Dined at New Holland, and from thence went on to Lancaster.

April 29.—Took a walk with Captain Webster and Captain Joy to look at the former's garden. In the afternoon went to Jacob Meyer's and then to Adam Weber's to see two horses belonging to British officers run a two-mile heat.

April 30.—Went to the Court House to see the dragoon horses advertised for sale, but the dragoons would not deliver them on account of the pay due to them yet.

May 2.—Arrived home from Lancaster at sundown, and found my daughter Hannah ill with the measles.

May 29.—Called on the Hon. Mr. Holker and settled with him for keeping and selling several horses he purchased of the Duke who commanded the French Legion.

June 1.—My son Robert, while at Chester, saw William Bingham and Robert Hare, with their wives and children, go on board of Captain Truxton's vessel for England.

June 23.—Took my daughter Hannah to Mrs. Roman's school, as she will not go to that of her sisters.

June 25.—When I returned from my ride with my wife and two daughters I found the light-horse gentlemen in my yard and about my house, to be ready to protect Governor Dickinson from being insulted by the riotous soldiers from Lancaster, who demanded their pay of Congress. This demand affronted Congress so much that they agreed to sit at Princeton, New Jersey.

July 4.—In the afternoon a triumphal car, prepared by Mr. Mason, attended by a number of boys and girls dressed in white, was paraded through the streets of the city, this being the memorable day independence was declared.

July 10.—Thomas Palmer, Joseph Rakestraw, Michael Shubert, and myself moved the Amicable Fire Engine from the house on the south side of Market, a short distance below Sixth Street, to Sixth Street above Market, on the ground of Miss Deborah Morris.

July 12.—My men brought from the meadows a man who was injured by a bull on the road, and was informed by William Jones that the doctors say he cannot live.

July 18.—Took a ride with my wife up the Germantown Road to see the camp of 1500 soldiers who came from General Washington's army two weeks ago.

July 21.—At the request of Colonel Pickering, quartermaster general, accompanied him to the camp at Mrs. McMaster's place, two miles from the city, to examine the hay there, estimated at ten tons.

July 27.—Attended the burial of Philip Moser. [The Widow Moser appeared in church with her new husband November 9, 1783.]

July 31.—Met at the Indian Queen the following gentlemen : General James Irvine, Major Armstrong, Colonel F. Johnson, Colonel Jacob Morgan, Dr. John Morgan, and Mr. Burd, a committee of officers who served in the Colonial wars, for which service we are entitled to some back-lands under the King's proclamation of October, 1763.

August 2.—Drank tea at Matthew Clarkson's with his wife; have invited Major Gibbs and Captain Williams to dine with me to-morrow.

August 10.—Mr. Dunlap moved into my house yesterday, at £120 per year. When I returned from church, was told that the chimney had been on fire.

August 14.—At the Indian Queen met General Ewing, Vice-President of this State, General James Irvine, Colonel F. Johnson, Major Armstrong, and Dr. John Morgan, on our back-land claims.

August 15.—In the afternoon, went with George Mifflin to Bush Hill, to the burial of the very wealthy James Hamilton, Esq., aged 72 years. Among the seven or more clergymen present was the Rev. William White, who performed the ceremony. Samuel Emlen, a Quaker, spoke fifteen minutes.

August 16.—Dined at Mrs. Matthews's, on turtle, with William Jones,

5

Robert Erwin, R. Keen. A. Tybout, Joseph Rakestraw, John Biddle,
Dr. Glentworth, Peter Z. Lloyd, and James White. In the evening,
drove my wife and daughters to camp and drank tea with Captain
Joseph Williams.

August 22.—Called to see Andrew Hamilton, who is confined to his
bed with gout. He requested me to aid in procuring four or five
horses for his brother, who has had a great fortune left him by their
uncle, not less than £150,000 cy. ; to Andrew and his children, not
above £40,000.

September 8.—Called to see General Mifflin, on Vine Street, but he
was too ill to receive friends, and from there went to see Miles &
Morgan's new sugar house, the fifth floor of which is now ready.

September 11.—Mr. Abraham Hunt drank tea with us, after which we
walked to the Indian King to see Joseph Smith, who is interested
in the stage line to New York, by which passengers are taken as
far as Newark in one day, and to New York for breakfast next day.

September 27.—Went to Miles & Morgan's sugar house, Vine Street
near Third, being erected by William Hicks, bricklayer, and Colladay, the carpenter. A supper was served in Colladay's carpenter
shop to Colonels Miles and Morgan, Eyre, Farmer, and Will,
Major Boyd, Messrs. Michael Hillegas, Jacob Rush, Jacob Negley,
Peter Wager, Schaeffer, Christopher Ludwick, and others.

September 29.—At midnight Captain Topham sent for me, being very
ill, and desired that I would try to persuade his children to embrace
the Reformed religion and attend the church to which their mother
belonged, it being her wish on her death bed.

October 6.—The Committee on Back-Land Claim met at the house of
Colonel Miles, when Doctor Morgan was appointed to go to Virginia to attend the Assembly, for which service he is to receive
£ 125.

October 17.—The Dutch Ambassador, Mr. Van Berkel, came to my
house to see two of his horses tried.

October 28.—Took a ride with Honorable Ralph Izard to Blakeley Island to look at Adam Gerger's horses and cows, a number of which were purchased.

November 4.—Loaned Mrs. Mifflin a horse for her servant to ride to the General's farm near Reading, and inform him of his being appointed President of Congress.

November 5.—Frederick Kuhl and I were qualified by Isaac Howell, Esq., to act as Street Commissioners.

November 7.—Called to see Abraham Hart at Mrs. Paul's Indian King, and from there to the Court House, where I met the Street Commissioners for the first time.

November 8.—The Street Commissioners met at my house, then proceeded to Fifth Street, and to the dock in Third Street.

November 12.—Honorable Mr. Izard's horses and cattle were put on board a vessel for Charleston, S. C. General Washington's baggage teams set out for that excellent commander's residence in Virginia.

November 19.—Met the officers of the German Society on Race Street. At the meeting the address prepared by Lewis Weiss to be handed to Hon. Van Berkel, Ambassador from Holland, was considered.

November 22.—Dined with Hon. Thomas Mifflin at his house on Vine Street, with the following gentlemen: Hon. James Reed, Colonel Lutz, Mr. Reiss, Lincoln, Colonel Clement Biddle, Mrs. Mifflin, and her two sisters.

November 29.—About twenty minutes after ten o'clock this evening I felt the shock of an earthquake as I was walking through my room up stairs, which lasted half a minute.

December 8.—Abraham Kintzing and I went to Germantown, to the burial of Leonard Stoneburner's wife. His Excellency General Washington arrived from the northward.

December 15.—The illustrious General Washington, after commanding

the armies of the United States above eight years, and has given
the Americans possession of New York again, set out this day for
his seat in Virginia. He was escorted a little way beyond the city
by their Excellencies De la Luzerne, French Ambassador, on his
right, and John Dickinson, President of this State, on his left, and
the City Troop in the rear, the Hon. Robert Morris and his lady
in a carriage in advance. I think it is not likely that I shall have
the honor of seeing that great and good man again, and, therefore,
do sincerely congratulate him on the noble resolution he has made,
not to accept public office hereafter, but to pass the remainder of
his days in private. This is undoubtedly the surest way to preserve
the honors he so justly acquired during the late war.

December 20.—Attended the examination of the scholars of Mr.
Brown's school, corner Third and Vine Streets, both in English and
French.

December 26.—Met the German Society at the Lutheran schoolhouse, and, after transacting our business, proceeded to Captain
Esterly's to supper.

1784.

January 18.—Went to Chestnut Street and brought home my fire-
buckets. Was informed by William Moulder of the death of
Joseph Fox, from a fall off his horse this morning.

January 20.—Went to the burial of Joseph Fox. Arthur Howell, a
Quaker, spoke at the grave. Went to Matthew Clarkson's on
Arch Street to warm my feet.

January 22.—The Street Commissioners engaged in having the rubbish cleared off Market Street, between Fifth and Sixth, so that the
people may have a free passage to view the triumphal arch erected
on Market Street. It is about forty feet high, with paintings on
the east side by Mr. Peale. At dark, just as the lamps were being
lighted, the painting caught fire by accident and was consumed,

together with the fireworks, which were on top. A rocket stick killed a woman. This sudden accident created the greatest confusion among the people in the street and the horses and carriages, so that many persons were injured and wearing apparel lost. The arch cost £600. Thus all the labor of weeks, for the celebration of peace being made, came to naught, and for the night turned into sorrow.

February 13.—Took my wife and George Mifflin in my sleigh to General Mifflin's place at the Falls, where we viewed the heaps of ice piled up on the shore by the high water.

February 14.—Paid $9 for a cord of hickory wood, which is more than I have ever given since going to housekeeping. It is said the price has reached $16 this winter.

February 16.—Went in my sleigh with wife, son, and daughter over the Delaware on the ice to Joseph Cooper's, but finding him from home, we returned. I observed a large number of wood sleighs crossing.

February 18.—Met the Street Commissioners at the Coffee House, and from thence we walked along Market and Second Streets, and gave notice to all persons who expose goods for sale on the street, contrary to law, to remove them.

February 20.—Took my wife a sleigh ride. In the evening met at the Court House my brother Street Commissioners, Francis Gurney, John Purdon, Samuel McLane, Frederick Kuhl, and Peter Kraft.

March 1.—In the House of Assembly the committee, who have been examining the charges of fraud in Colonel Sam Miles's accounts, made by Comptroller General Nicholson, made their report, which acquits Miles.

March 6.—Went to Ogden's Ferry and rode over and back on the ice, and from there went to the Delaware, where I saw numbers of wagon and sleigh loads of wood coming over to Vine Street and above.

March 13.—A vessel reached the dock to-day, the first from either up or down the river since December 24th last.

March 15.—Drove out to Ogden's Ferry to see the damage made by the ice breaking up. It swept away all the wooden buildings, and the water was five feet two inches high on the first floor of the house.

March 16.—The Street Commissioners selected sites to dump the dirt from the streets. Called to see Mr. Ogden at the ferry, who told me that two of his horses had been drowned, but one of his colts had got into the house and up the stairs to the second floor, and was saved. Several of his boats were carried off by the ice, which compelled him to discharge his gun to attract the people on shore to rescue his family, which was accomplished about daylight. In January of 1767, when Jonathan Humphreys was ferry keeper, the water rose to nine inches on the first floor, and he never imagined it could reach five feet and more this time At one time he feared the house would be carried into the river. We measured one cake of ice wedged among the trees and found it to be thirteen and one-half feet thick.

March 18.—On horseback I viewed every paved street in the city, and met the Commissioners in the evening.

March 20.—Sent my man with three horses up to the Honorable Robert Morris' country seat, Springettsbury, to bring back the fire engine belonging to the Amicable Fire Company, which was taken there yesterday, when the house was on fire.

March 24.—Took George Mifflin with me to his brother's at the Falls, and stopped at the Fish House [St. David's], where we saw the ice piled up twenty feet. If it had not been for several white oak trees, the house would have been carried away. Mr. Mifflin and I measured the water mark on the first floor, and found it to be seven feet six inches.

April 10.—Went up town to William Fisher's wharf to examine some paving stone for the public use. Attended the sale of the street dirt at the dumps, after which the Commissioners went to the Indian Queen and had some wine and punch.

April 13.—I took my wife a ride along the Schuylkill to the Falls, to show her the destruction caused by the ice. Many large masses are to be seen still in the neighborhood of the Fish House. We called at General Mifflin's place.

April 20.—Attended the burial of Thomas Pryor's housekeeper, an old maid named Susannah, who has lived in the family for many years. Samuel Emlen spoke at the grave half an hour.

April 22.—With my fellow Commissioners passed through certain streets of the city to notice whether they are obstructed by goods contrary to law.

April 26.—The Street Commissioners met at my house and agreed that men be set to work to take up the pavement across Market Street and Seventh. Then we went down to Isaac Snowden's and there met Gunning Bedford, carpenter, and Lowry, the mason, and consulted with them concerning the arch to be built over the dock.

May 1.—Went to Lawrence Seckel's place, which William Rush rents, and dined on beefsteak and shad with Gunning Bedford, Isaac Snowden, William Sheaff, David Seckel, Wertz, Wager, Habacker, David Schaeffer, John Baker, Philip Odenheimer, Philip Hall, Thomas Penrose, Francis Johnson, George Campbell, Daniel Clymer, John Morris, and others. His Excellency General Washington arrived here from Virginia. [Washington left the city May 18.]

May 4.—Plunket Fleeson and three of his neighbors waited on the Commissioners at the State House to complain of the street dirt being hauled to Fourth Street before the schoolhouse.

May 6.—The Commissioners met at Seventh and Market Streets and had James Pearson regulate the water course across Market Street, and in the afternoon Peter Kraft and myself staked out Seventh Street across the Strangers' Burial-ground.

May 10.—To-night the fireworks were exhibited by Mr. Peale on Market Street in place of those destroyed in January last.

June 5.—We have had men at work on Market Street every day this week. Went to the foot-bridge over the dock to see the trunk laid.

June 15.—Returning from church I saw the Free Quakers leave their meeting-house at corner Fifth and Arch Streets. This day a week ago they held their first meeting in the said meeting-house.

June 18.—Met Samuel Wheeler at the bridge, where he has a number of men at work filling in Hollander's Creek, and from there went to the Sign of the Buck and had a bowl of punch.

July 6.—The Commissioners began to view the streets which citizens wished repaired. Began at the fifty-foot street on the south side Market, between Sixth and Seventh Street, and proceeded out Market to Ogden's Ferry ; from thence in to South Street, down to Penn ; thence up the Dock to Second Street, and there parted until evening.

July 14.—Afternoon went to the Dock, and, two Commissioners with me, entered the new arch under Second Street bridge and walked up to Walnut Street bridge, and found the smell disagreeable.

July 15.—Inspected Quarry and Bread Streets, and went in the afternoon to the Dock to see what progress was made.

July 17.—Toward evening the American aerostatic balloon ascended from the new Work House yard. It was made of silk. The man who was in it cut the rope as the balloon struck the wall, and dropped out, which caused the fire to fall out of the stove; and the balloon was consumed when half a mile up in the air.

July 22.—With my wife and son Thomas, set out for Jersey, and arrived at my friend Abraham Hunt's in Trenton.

July 23.—Mr. Hunt and I breakfasted with General P. Dickinson. We found him busy looking after the stone house he is having built at the end of his wooden building, about a mile out of Trenton.

July 30.—Left Trenton about eleven o'clock, dined at Bristol, and reached home by sunset.

August 5.—Before breakfast I went with three of the Magistrates and four Street Commissioners down to Penn Street, to see whether we should pave it, but a majority being of the opinion that the street between Penn and the river, called New Street, ought to be paved first, it was so agreed.

August 6.—Went down to New Street with the Commissioners and Mr. Moulder, a regulator, to see what the descent of the street from South to Lombard alley is: seven feet and eleven inches. Looked after pavers on the fifty-foot street south side of Market, above Sixth Street.

August 10.—Andrew Geyer, Peter Kraft, and myself gave the name of Turner to the fifty-foot street south side Market Street.

August 13.—Looked after the work in Carpenter Street.

August 14.—At one o'clock went to the Falls and dined with General Mifflin, when we arranged to go to New York next Friday to settle our Continental accounts.

August 15.—Returning from church, I observed people crowded about the Free Quakers' meeting-house, and was told that they were waiting to see the wonderful Jemima Wilkinson, who had preached. I remained until she came out to get in her chair. She had on a white hat, but no cap, and a white linen garment that covered her to her feet.

August 17.—Mr. Geyer and I set the teams to work in New Water Street. Jonathan Penrose took us home with him, and gave us a drink of punch. We were told that he was recently elected a Magistrate of Southwark.

August 20.—Visited Colonels Pickering and Miles, and coming home went to the new Quaker meeting-house, on Arch Street, and heard Jemima Wilkinson preach. She looks more like a man than a woman.

August 21.—Set out for New York with Abraham Hunt and my son Robert. Dined at Bristol, where General Mifflin overtook us. The Hon. Henry Laurens, who had just arrived from Europe, called me to his room to inquire how he could secure horses for his carriage. My son turned back to Philadelphia, and we went on to Trenton, the General to Williamson's tavern and I to Mr. Hunt's.

August 22.—The General, a little girl, E. Johnson, and his negro, Terego, breakfasted at Princeton, dined at Major Egbert's, in Bruns-wick, and had supper at Mr. Sayre's tavern, in Perth Amboy.

August 23.—Crossed from Amboy to Staten Island, passed through Richmond to Bergen Ferry, and dined at the ferry house. Joshua Musserne, Esq., came and dined with us. It being exceedingly warm after dinner, Mr. Musserne's people put our horses and chairs across to Bergen. The General went by water and I by land, and he reached New York before me. We lodged and kept our horses at Ellsworth's, No. 19 Maiden Lane.

August 24.—General Mifflin and I called on William Denning, and asked him when he could take up my public accounts, which is the business which brought me to New York. On being informed that he could do so at once, in the afternoon I took the accounts to his clerk, Mr. Simmons, and, at the same time, a letter wherein General Mifflin, quartermaster general, appointed me to purchase horses and wagons for the Continental service, allowing me a commission of two per cent.

August 25.—Called to see General Robert Howe, Mr. Jacob Morris, and John Morin Scott, Esq., but did not see the latter, and am to call again. Met with Messrs. Matlack and Chandler, went to their store, and wrote a letter to my wife.

August 26.—This afternoon took a ride up the East River and returned down the North River; met John Levy, Jr., stopped at Cummings's, and had a drink of wine and water.

August 27.—Took a ride before breakfast to look at the chain-pump. After breakfast T. Bache went with me to Brockholts Livingston, Esq., about my claim of £176 19s. against General Robert Howe. I called on John Morin Scott, but only saw his son Lewis. Went to the coffee-house kept by Cornelius Bradford and met several old acquaintances, among them Colonel Isaac Melcher. In the afternoon I was arrested by a Deputy Sheriff with a writ for £100, for a horse Dr. Charles McKnight says he lost out of the Continental stable in Philadelphia while in my charge. Mr. Ellsworth kindly became my bail. [Dr. McKnight lost his case 24th June, 1787.]

August 28.—General Mifflin accompanied me to Mr. Livingston's, to whom I gave two guineas to defend the suit Dr. McKnight has brought against me. Crossed the North River to Powl's Hook and dined with Colonel Lutterloh and Isaac Melcher, Alderman Lott, Henry Sheaff, Mr. Denny, from Virginia, and two other gentlemen. The General returned to Philadelphia.

August 29.—Forenoon attended the German Reformed Church, Rev. Daniel Gross, and afternoon the Lutheran Church, Rev. Mr. Kuntz, formerly of Philadelphia. After church Mr. Von Puhl and I took a walk about the city, and on my return to my lodgings found my son Robert there.

August 30.—Sent my son to General Lewis Morris's, nine miles from the city, but he failed to find him at home. Mr. Ellsworth and I called on John Levy, Jr., and were well received, and were given a light lunch with wine and punch.

August 31.—Left New York to-day, my son to follow me on Thursday. Breakfasted at Newark. At Elizabethtown met Colonel James Thompson, and we dined at Woodbridge. Nighted at Major Egbert's in Brunswick.

September 1.—Set out at four o'clock and had breakfast at Kingstown. At Trenton I dined with Mr. Hunt, made a short stop at Bristol, and arrived at my home at eight o'clock and found my family well.

September 3.—Before breakfast met Magistrates Plunkett Fleeson, J. Howell, and Paschall, and my brother Commissioners, at Samuel Pleasants's, to view the common sewer that leads through his garden. We all agreed that it was not sufficient to receive all the water from Market and Fourth Streets at the time of a smart shower of rain, it being only two feet eight inches in diameter. Inspected the work on Carpenter and South Streets.

September 6.—Met the Commissioners in the Indian Queen Tavern yard this evening and sent two laborers down into the common sewer to walk up to Market Street and measure it. They reported it to be four feet six inches and in some places only four feet in the clear.

September 14.—Michael Wartman began to plow in Penn Street to prepare it for paving.   ·

September 16.—Four Commissioners met at the corner of Fourth and Market Streets, with Plunket Fleeson, John Gill, Isaac Howell, and Benjamin Paschall, Magistrates; two Regulators, James Pearson and William Moulder. Several street matters were decided, the main one concerning the common sewer at Fourth and Market Streets. Much has been said about carrying the water above ground, from Market Street along Fourth to Walnut Street, but being told by the regulators present that Fourth Street at Chestnut must be lowered nine feet seven inches from what it is at present to allow the water a fall of five-eighths of an inch in every ten feet, it was apparent to all that it was impracticable for surface drainage. It was agreed that the old sewer be cleaned out this fall and to erect a new one next spring, to effectually prevent any overflow.

September 18.—Workmen are putting down a wooden gutter on Seventh Street between Chestnut and Walnut Streets.

September 21.—My son Thomas and I stopped at Rush's, where we had beefsteak and punch with William Govett, Samuel Hudson, J. Williamson, Abraham Kintzing, J. Baker, Philip Odenheimer, and Philip Hall. The workmen are digging a gutter on Carpenter Street.

September 25.—The Hon. Henry Laurens took away the pair of horses I sold him. With three Commissioners went to Ogden's ferry and examined the street next to the Schuylkill, which John Dunlap has opened through his lot, and wants his neighbors to do the same.

September 27.—Took a ride with the Hon. Cyrus Griffin in his carriage, to try a pair of black horses he purchased of the Hon. Von Berkel, the Ambassador from Holland. To-day the House of Assembly broke up without adjournment, by reason of a bill being introduced for enfranchising non-jurors, and which was only carried by the Speaker's vote. About twenty withdrew.

September 30.—Colonel Jeremiah Wadsworth set out for Hartford with his son; they just arrived from France.

October 4.—The Street Commissioners notified people along Front Street to remove rubbish from before their property and to repair the footway.

October 14.—Received of Isaac Snowden, Treasurer, £38 for my last year's services as Street Commissioner.

October 19.—At noon went to the Widow Matthews's tavern with Colonel William Coates, Captain Simons, and another gentleman, and had some punch.

October 22.—Andrew Geyer and I took a walk to view the bad places in the streets north of Market Street.

October 25.—Met several gentlemen at Mr. Funk's tavern, in relation to the petition to the Assembly to have the market extended on Market Street to Fourth.

October 27.—Workmen and teams were engaged yesterday in removing the dirt from Market Street.   Richard Willing and Scott, members of the Assembly, dine with me to-day.

October 29.—Gutters are being laid, one in Walnut and Seventh Streets, the other in Eighth and Arch Streets.   James Pearson, Regulator, with a board of the Street Commissioners, regulated Eighth Street from Market to George Street, and found a descent of five-eighths of an inch in every ten feet from Arch to George Street, which was considered sufficient to carry the water across Market Street.

October 31.—I packed up my books and papers while General Greene was quartermaster general, and sent them to William Denning, Esq., in New York.

November 10.—Called on the wheelwright who is making a closed box for the Street Commissioners to carry off the refuse about the market.

November 12.—Mr. Joseph Ogden, at the ferry, invited me to his house to drink punch, on account of the marriage of his daughter to Thomas Palmer yesterday.

November 15.—Superintended the laying of the trunk at Tenth and Market Streets.

November 20.—The Commissioners went to Vine and Ninth Streets, and agreed that the streets are to be repaired next spring to make them passable and to prevent the brickmakers from digging into them.

November 24.—At noon went to the burial of Andrew Hamilton, whose body was taken early this morning from the city to Bush Hill, and from the house carried to the grave alongside of his uncle.   The Rev. William White performed the service.

November 26.—Hard rain last night and to-day.   Went on horseback to view the several cross streets from Vine to South and west of Fifth, to see which way to draw off the water where it stands in ponds.

November 29.—Mr. Barge, Andrew Carson, and I went to Brown's tavern on Arch Street and there met eight members of the Assembly in relation to extending the market in Market Street up to Fourth Street.

December 15.—Surveyor Thomas Hutchins, just from the backwoods, where he has been running the line between Virginia and Pennsylvania, drank tea with us.

1785.

January 5.—Attended the burial of Dr. John Morgan's wife at St. Peter's Church. Walked with George Mifflin; snowing at the time. The Rector's text was I Corinth. 15th chapter, from the 20th verse to end of chapter.

January 12.—William Richards and John Purdon came to my house and we examined the Commissioner's books to ascertain the cost of cleaning the streets and hauling off the dirt for one year, and found it to be £1118 15s. 5d., from which sum is to be deducted street dirt sold, £140. We have also used for paving the streets 1871 loads of gravel.

January 17.—Took my wife half a mile over Schuylkill to see a chain made of iron eight feet long tested for strength. It withstood five and a half tons, but broke on adding another ton. The experiment was made in order to know what number of chains will be necessary of that size for a bridge over the Schuylkill.

January 19.—Made an examination of all line houses standing on the streets. General Mifflin and his lady called at my house with a letter from R. B. Lloyd, of Maryland, and at the same time told me he had purchased Mr. Graff's house, on Market Street, for £2600.

January 22.—My wife accompanied the two Misses Morris to see General Mifflin's house on Market Street. Messrs. Boyd, Richards, and I examined the law regarding broad wheels.

March 1.—The Street Commissioners contracted with the following persons to keep the streets clean during the ensuing year :—

Alexander Miller, Lower District,	£330
William Young, Middle District,	190
Michael Wartman, Upper District,	270

March 6.—Attended the burial of Hon. Joseph Reed, from his house on Chestnut Street to the ground on Arch Street above Fifth. He was chosen member of Congress just as he arrived from England, about four weeks ago.

March 7.—I went up Second Street, with the intention of attending the burial of John Morris, Esq., but came too late.

March 16.—Took a walk down to Third Street, to look at the workmen pull down the old gaol and workhouse. To-morrow the old material will be sold.

March 26.—I have been sick since the 18th inst., and have Dr. Kuhn in attendance. General Mifflin and Richard Lloyd came to see me.

April 16.—Messrs. Geyer, Kraft, and I went out Vine Street, and met David Rittenhouse, Tench Francis, Matthew Clarkson, Nathan Sellers, S. Garrigues, Joseph Rakestraw, Hugh Roberts, and my son Robert, surveying and leveling the ground for a canal from the Delaware to the Schuylkill. They found the highest point to be near Broad and Vine Streets, 39½ feet above low-water mark in the Schuylkill. We dined at Mr. Garrigues's country house, near Poplar Lane and Fourth Street. After dinner Colonel Jacob Morgan arrived, and we went with him to level up Master's or Negley's Run, as far as the division line between the Mifflin and Taylor estates.

April 23.—Went to the State House yard to look at the rows of trees Samuel Vaughan, Esq., donated, and is directing the planting of. Met Mr. Dean, who asked me to go up with him in one of the rooms in the State House to see the printing of money, and saw Bailey and his press at work.

April 29.—Met seven Magistrates, six Regulators, and five Street Commissioners at Nathan Boys's, on Front Street, to determine the watercourses in the southern section of the city. It was decided that the water be turned down South Street into the Delaware, from the west of Fourth Street, and that a sewer is necessary for the purpose. We cannot do anything before obtaining a law from the Legislature.

May 2.—Went to the St. Tammany Anniversary, at David Beveridge's place over the Schuylkill, late Reese Meredith's. A large number of gentlemen collected, with tickets in their hats which cost 8s. 4d., but afforded us ample food and drink. The first thing done was, the gentlemen formed a ring, and chose James Read, Esq., their Chief; Timothy Matlack, his Secretary; and the following gentlemen the Chief's Council: George Bryan, Plunket Fleeson, William Moore, Frederick Phile, Esqrs.; General Daniel Hiester; Colonels Coates, Dean, Will, Boyd, Wade, Eyre, Proctor, and Jonathan Bayard Smith. In the evening I met our fire company and paid my fines.

May 7.—Dined at General Mifflin's, with General Brodhead, Richard B. Lloyd and his wife from Maryland.

May 9.—Mr. Richard B. Lloyd and his family left to-day for their seat at Bunnett's Point, Maryland. I observed in this day's paper that Abraham Hunt, of Trenton, was married to Miss Dagworthy at Elizabethtown on the 4th inst. He has been a widower since March 6, 1784. Took a ride with my wife over Schuylkill by the upper bridge, and returned by George Gray's, which is much the best bridge.

May 24.—The Street Commissioners were met at the Court House by the Board of Wardens and the Managers of the House of Employment, to consult as to whether the Collectors of Taxes to the several Boards shall receive or not the paper-money just issued.

June 4.—Messrs. Boys, Geyer, and I went to Market and Fourth Streets, and gave directions at what height to set the centres for the arch. It is to have a floor of three-inch plank, with a hollow of four inches in the middle; the cross-pieces to extend across the founda-

6

tion, and a large stone to be laid over them, so that they can be taken out, without injuring the foundation or wall, in case the floor should want repairing.

June 11.—I went on horseback, and three of my associates in a light wagon, to Captain Van Heers, at the Falls of Schuylkill, and there had some catfish soup. I walked over to see General Mifflin, who told me that he had been laid up for two weeks, and that this was the first day of his going out.

June 19.—This afternoon my wife got very sick, and Dr. Kuhn ordered her to be bled in the foot.

July 11.—The Commission tried Mr. Vaughan's water-cart. We are laying a trunk on Vine Street, opposite Mr. Penn's place.

July 15.—Agreed with Tench Francis for all the gravel the Street Commissioners may need at 6d. per load.

July 27.—The Street Commissioners went to the State House concerning the presentment of the Grand Jury, as published in the *Daily Advertiser* of July 18th, when Mr. Ingersoll, their attorney, informed the Court that they felt themselves aggrieved by the said presentment, and charged with neglect that did not belong to them, for, early in the season, they appointed scavengers to clean the streets for twelve months, in accordance with law. Mr. Chief Justice McKean replied that the gentlemen must have been unacquainted with the laws of the State, or they would not have presented the Street Commissioners, as it appears very plain that they are not the delinquents.

[*July 28.*—Went to Trenton and neighborhood, and returned home August 5th.]

August 8.—Took my three daughters to Harrowgate to show them the mineral water, and baths. We met several friends, and, after a lunch, returned home.

August 22.—Our men began to plow in Market Street between Seventh and Eighth.

August 23.—Very hard rain last night, so much so that the water over-flowed the arch at Market and Fourth Streets and ran into Mr. Cooper's cellar. This is the first overflow since the new arch has been added.

September 1.—At 4 o'clock this morning, took my daughter Kitty and Betsey De Camp to F. Lee's stage-wagon on Market Street, where it starts for New York. The girls are to stay in Trenton until Dr. De Camp comes for them from Hopewell.

September 13.—Two of my colleagues went with me to our gravel-pits, where we have four teams hauling gravel to Market Street. From there we drove over Schuylkill to look at young Mr. Penn's place.

September 14.—The Hon. Benjamin Franklin arrived at Market Street wharf and walked up to his house.

September 16.—We are hauling gravel to Market and Eleventh Streets and spreading it. Went down to see the workmen employed making steps from Front to Water Streets, at two points. In the afternoon took my wife and daughter Hannah a ride over Schuyl-kill, to show them Mr. Penn's place adjoining Isaac Warner's.

September 21.—The Commissioners met on Market Street to examine the pavers' work; some part of it is badly done, and we decided it must be gone over, and they must do better work; otherwise, they will be discharged.

September 18.—Returning from my visit to Trenton, I called at Mr. Edward Duffield's. He was absent from home, but Mrs. Duffield entertained me kindly with dinner and wine.

October 4.—Remarkably hard rain all night. In the morning went on horseback to view the water-courses on Vine, Race, Arch, Market, Eighth and Ninth, and Pine and Dock Streets. Went to the State House, and was drawn on a jury: Matthew Clarkson, foreman; Messrs. Whitesides, Henry, Hysham, Harbison, Dean, Harrison, Cornman, Stocker, Bispham, Morgan, and myself.

October 14.—In the evening rode to my lot and near there met General

Mifflin, his wife, and her sister. Loaned the General my horse to ride home, his pair of horses having too much of a load to go to the Falls.

October 29.—The Hon. Benjamin Franklin was proclaimed President and Charles Biddle Vice-President of this State. The Commissioners viewed Eighth Street from Market to Spruce Street near the Hospital, and so down to the river, taking in part of Pine Street.

November 11.—Went to the Assembly, where C. Pettit, James Wilson, and William Henry, of Lancaster, were re-elected Delegates to Congress, and Arthur St. Clair and John Bayard in the place of Dr. Jackson and J. Gardner.

November 12.—Richards and I inspected the streets of the Middle District, of which William Young is scavenger, and found Front Street and part of Second Street in bad order.

November 14.—This morning the Commissioners met at my house and determined that the three scavengers clean all the streets that are dirty throughout the city in one week.

November 16.—Met Samuel Vaughan on Walnut Street concerning the planting of a row of trees on said street from Fifth to Sixth Streets.

December 19.—We laid the bridge over the run on Race Street and made our teams go over it with their loads. After Messrs. Boys and Richards joined me, we went down the Schuylkill to George Savell's tavern and had a bowl of good punch.

December 23.—My son Thomas came home to spend Christmas with us. In the afternoon took a ride to William Standley's place at Point no Point, and stopped at Thomas Hopkinson's to see his colts.

1786.

January 1.—Had to dine with me Colonels Farmer, Will, and Melcher, and John Vaughan.

January 2.—Met the Vestry in the German Reformed schoolhouse, and at night the Society for Promoting Agriculture at Carpenters' Hall.

January 11.—Colonel J. Wadsworth breakfasted with me, after which we went on horseback to see General Mifflin at the Falls, but he had gone to his farm near Reading. The Vestry of the German Reformed Church distributed £32 17 s. 6 d. among the poor of the congregation.

January 13.—Went to the burial of John Ogden, whose body was taken from the house of his brother-in-law Thomas Palmer, on Market Street, and buried in Friends' ground. Young Savery spoke at the grave.

January 14.—Dined at Thompson's Indian Queen with my colleagues of the Street Commission, Nathaniel Boys, Andrew Geyer, Peter Kraft, William Richards, and John Purdon.

January 16.—Summoned to the State House for jury duty. The Judges, in their red robes, were Chief Justice McKean, Jacob Rush, and George Bryan. The names of the jurymen were: Abraham Markoe, Richard Bache, John Steinmetz, John Moylan, ——Donaldson, John Pringle, William Turnbull, Andrew Doz, George Emlen, Robert McKnight, Alexander Todd, and myself. We determined two causes.

January 19.—Last night the Delaware froze fast. Went with my colleagues, the Street Commissioners, to Isaac Snowden, Esq., our treasurer, to settle, our last year's accounts with him. The following gentlemen dined with him: Jerediah Snowden, Gunning Bedford, Samuel McLane, Nathaniel Boys, Andrew Geyer, William Richards, Peter Kraft, John Purdon, and George Hovey.

January 25.—In the afternoon came Messrs. Boys and Geyer, as per agreement, to examine our carters' accounts, to get at the number of loads of gravel the public had from Mr. Francis's gravel pit in Fourth Street last summer, being 808 loads. Mr. Kraft came to see us, told us that our colleague, William Richard's wife had brought him two sons at a birth this day.

January 28.—Several vessels came up to the city to-day. Navigation has only been stopped about ten days.

January 31.—Forenoon went with General Mifflin to Mr. Rittenhouse's, from thence to his house on Race Street, where came Messrs. Stoneburner and Kintzing concerning some public accounts. In the afternoon, Stoneburner and Kintzing, William Rush, George Nelson, and John Grau came to my house with regard to some accounts Stoneburner and Kintzing have against the public for horse and team hire.

February 1.—In the afternoon William Richards, Captain Boys, and I met on Chestnut Street, at the bank door, and went to Mr. Thompson's and drank a bottle of port wine. At night Mr. Hunt came here; at the same time a fire broke out in a carpenter's shop in Cherry Street between Fifth and Sixth Streets, which was consumed.

February 3.—In the forenoon went to see my fellow-countryman, Colonel Lewis Farmer, in Arch Street, near Fifth; drank punch and wine with a very large number of gentlemen, on account of his being married last night. Went to the Upper Ferry with four of the Street Commissioners to settle about some stone.

February 7.—In the evening met at Carpenters' Hall the Society of Agriculture, eighteen members present. We agreed that a gold medal be given to Colonel George Morgan, of New Jersey, for having the best farmyard of any the Society has information of. Colonel Morgan can say that he received the first medal given by the Society.

February 10.—This afternoon Peter Kraft and I took a ride to my lot, from thence we went across to Mr. Robert Morris's land on the

Schuylkill and to Vine and Race Streets, to view the work we have done as Commissioners last fall. Andrew Geyer met us and we went to Mr. Pole's place and drank a bowl of punch.

February 11.—In the afternoon met at Captain N. Beyer's, agreeable to appointment with the Street Commissioners, to consult concerning the cleaning of the streets for the ensuing year.

February 13.—To night went down to Abraham Kintzing's to see my wife home; she spent the afternoon there.

February 16.—In the evening went to Mr. Thompson's, at the Indian Queen. There met my brethren, the City Magistrates, agreeable to appointment, for the purpose of arranging the mode of cleaning the streets for the ensuing year. Present: Edward Shippen, Plunket Fleeson, Joseph Wharton, William Rush, and Isaac Howell, Esqrs.; Andrew Geyer, Nathan Boys, William Richards, John Purdon, Peter Kraft, and myself, Street Commissioners.

February 18.—In the afternoon the Street Commissioners met at my house. We examined Sixth Street, near the Workhouse, and from thence went to Captain Boys's, where we drew up an advertisement and offered a reward of £5 to any person that will inform of the persons who deposited quantities of filth out of cesspools on Seventh, Eighth, and Ninth Streets.

February 21.—Forenoon went to Mr. Francis Hopkinson's, on Race Street, concerning a letter from Joseph Borden, of Bordentown, to me; from there went to see Colonel Samuel Miles. At night met the Commissioners at the Court House.

February 22.—This evening Mr. Andrew Geyer came to my house, when we examined the Street Commissioner books for some years back concerning money advanced by the Hon. John Penn and others, in 1770, for the Street Commissioners to pave Fourth Street between Walnut and Spruce Streets. We found that all the lenders have been repaid between the years 1774 and 1777, as may be seen in a book at the Court House.

February 23.—A. Geyer and I went to Benjamin Chew, Esq.'s, and showed him the book wherein it is entered that the Hon. John Penn had been paid the £100 he advanced the Commissioners for paving Fourth Street. The reason we went to Mr. Chew was, that he claimed the said money and was told that Mr. Penn had not received it. We left Mr. Chew quite satisfied that he was misinformed, and that he was sorry he had called on the Commissioners for it.

February 24.—At night went to the Court House. Dined with General Thomas Mifflin, at his house on Race Street.

February 27.—In the afternoon went to Gravel Hill, afterward to Sixth Street, near the Workhouse, where I met Peter Kraft, overseeing Morton making three bridges by order of our Board.

February 28.—In the forenoon attended the Assembly ; at night met the Street Commissioners at the Court House.

March 2.—Forenoon went to the Assembly. In the afternoon went to the burial of old Mrs. Kintzing. She was taken from her son-in-law's house, William Prichard's, on Front Street below the drawbridge, and buried in the churchyard in Arch Street. Her son, Abraham Kintzing, went to the burial, but did not walk as a mourner, nor did he go into Prichard's house, where his mother died, because he and his sister have been, and are now, at variance with each other.

March 4.—Forenoon went to the Assembly room and spoke to several members concerning the market house to be extended.

March 6.—Went to John Drinker's and offered him Joseph Dobbins's lot. This evening went over to Mr. J. Dunlap's, where was Isaac Gray, Esq., member of our Assembly. Our conversation was about extending the market in High Street from Third Street.

March 7.—Breakfasted with General Mifflin, Speaker of the House of Assembly. Mr. George Nelson and I went to Mr. Benjamin Stillé's office concerning Nicholas Knight's Continental account. In the afternoon Mr. Peter Kraft and I took a ride to look at the bridge in Race Street, near Schuylkill. In the evening went with L. Stoneburner to Carpenters' Hall, and there met the Society of Agriculture.

March 12.—Went to church in the forenoon. After church, Colonel George Woods, Member of the Assembly, and I went to General Mifflin's, at the Falls, there dined with the following gentlemen : Mr. Evans, Mr. Harrison, Mr. Prizor, Mr. Meminger, Colonel Howard, Colonel Menges, Captain Barry, and Captain Gibson.

March 13.—Had to dine with me the following gentlemen, all members of Assembly : General Mifflin, Colonel George Woods, from Bedford ; Mr. Evans, from Chester ; and Colonel Will, for the City.

March 18.—Afternoon went to the Northern Liberties and gave my vote for two Overseers of the road, Mr. Brown, of Kensington, and John Hart, at the Three Mile Run. Afterward met the Street Commissioners at Captain N. Boys's, to consult as to which of the streets are to be paved this season.

March 19.—In the afternoon my wife and the Widow Matthews went to see Mrs. James White in Front above Vine Street ; myself and daughter Molly took a ride in my chair by Gravel Hill.

March 20.—Engaged all day concerning the cleaning of the streets for the ensuing season.

March 21.—In the afternoon we, the Street Commissioners, with four of the Magistrates, viewed the several streets that want paving. Afterward went to the Indian Queen, there fixed the price for Wartman and Miller to clean the streets for one year, £550 each, and to attend with their cart at every house once a week. Present at Thompson's Indian Queen the following : Plunket Fleeson, Isaac Howell, John Gill, William Rush, and Joseph Wharton, Esq. ; Peter Kraft, Andrew Geyer, Nathan Boys, William Richards, John Purdon, and myself, Street Commissioners.

March 22.—In the afternoon the Street Commissioners met at Captain
N. Boys's, and from there we went to Mr. Isaac Snowden's and
spent the evening.

March 23.—In the forenoon the Assembly passed a law for extending
the market houses on High Street. I planted two Lime trees on
Seventh Street at the house John Dunlap lives in, for which I paid
15 s.

March 24.—Went to Gravel Hill, and then to William Standley's place.
In the evening met at my house Messrs. Boys, Geyer, Kraft, Purdon,
and Richards, Street Commissioners, and after tea we went to Carpenters' Hall, where met a committee of the Society of Agriculture
at their request concerning the making of a piece of road in Market
Street, near the Public Square.

March 25.—Forenoon I went to William Jones's meadow; coming
back, went to Cristy's at Morris's place, to look at his large heifer.
In the afternoon took a ride to Schuylkill and round by Gravel
Hill with Colonel Samuel Miles. Afterward met the Street Commissioners at Captain Boys's, where A. Miller and M. Wartman
signed the contract as scavengers of the streets for one year, for
which they are to receive £550 each.

March 29.—Breakfasted at DeWitt's tavern, Trenton, where we lodged,
and Colonel Miles and I left for Colonel George Morgan's, at
Princetown, on purpose to see his farm and farmyard. He received
us kindly, and showed us every improvement about his place, and
after we had dined with him we returned to Trenton, drank tea at
Mr. A. Hunt's, and supped at DeWitt's.

March 30.—Colonel Miles and I went to see Messrs. Bird & Wilson's
works, near Trenton Falls, thence to McElroy's, where we met Mr.
A. Hunt, his son Pearson, and my son Robert. We all dined here,
then stopped a little while at the Ten Mile Tavern, and arrived at
Philadelphia by sunset.

March 31.—In the afternoon attended at the State House, where was
collected a very large number of people to hear the members de-

bate concerning the charter of the bank. The Hon. Robert Morris spoke the whole afternoon. Took two members home with me to tea, Wheeler and Bull; afterward went to the Court House.

April 1.—Forenoon attended again at the State House. The following members spoke in favor of the bank : Fitzsimmons, Robert Morris, and George Clymer, Esqrs.; against it: Smiler, Whitchild, and Findlay, Esqrs. The question was then put ; 28 in favor of the bank, and 41 members against it.

April 4.—At six o'clock this evening met the Society of Agriculture at Carpenters' Hall ; I left the Society, and met the Street Commissioners at the Court House.

April 5.—Forenoon attended at the House of Assembly. The House lowered their salaries from 15s. per day to 12s. 6d. ; and the Speaker's (General Mifflin), from 22s. 6d. to 20s. a day, and the members of Council to 12s. 6d. per day, and the Secretary to the Executive Council from £750 to £600 per annum, for himself and clerk.

April 7.—Forenoon went to Mr. Matthew Clarkson's, and shewed him my deeds for the house and lot at the southwest corner of Market and Seventh Streets. In the afternoon went with my brethren, the Street Commissioners, to view Lombard Street, in order to find out the owners of the lots who extended their fences into the street. Afterward went to a raising frolic at Robert Erwin's. The company dined in the new house this day raised on Market Street, near Seventh Street. It is only one month this day since Erwin begun digging the cellar. At night, met the Commissioners again at the Court House.

April 8.—In the afternoon met the Magistrates with my brethren of the Street Commission ; then went and viewed the sewer, back of the Workhouse ; from thence went to Cedar Street, and from thence to J. McCutcheon's tavern. There we resolved that the Common sewer, above mentioned, be built this summer, from the wall of the Workhouse, down to Fifth Street, and about 100 feet east of said street, to a house-wall ; and likewise agreed that Sixth Street, from

Market Street southward to Carpenter Street, be paved, and Dock Street, between Third and Walnut Streets, be paved; provided the arch under said street is sufficient and in good repair to receive all the water conveyed to said arch. Concerning the water-course, or courses, on Cedar Street, it was left undetermined. The gentlemen present were: Edward Shippen, Joseph Wharton, John Gill, Isaac Howell, and William Rush, Magistrates; Nathan Boys, Andrew Geyer, Peter Kraft, John Purdon, William Richards, and myself, Commissioners.

April 9.—In the morning went to church; then went with Mr. Tench Francis to General Mifflin's, and dined with him at his place at the Falls, in company with John Gill, Esq., Cadwalader Morris, Colonel Mentges, Doctor Ross, Tench Francis, Mrs. Mifflin, and her two sisters.

April 11.—Forenoon gave my two youngest daughters a ride in my chair to Aunt Foster's lot, where my people were repairing the fences.

April 12.—Went with John Purdon and marked out the ground for a ditch in Spruce Street near Schuylkill, to drain off the water. In the afternoon gave my wife a ride in chair.

April 13.—Peter Gordon, Esq., from Jersey, spent the evening with me yesterday. To-day I went to Spruce Street and set Henry Grotts to making the ditch Mr. Purdon and I staked out yesterday.

April 14.—Forenoon went to Spruce Street again, where two men are at work making a ditch. Afternoon went with my wife to Laskey's slaughter house, to see the beef of the five-year-old steer I sold him for £30. Afterward we went to Point-no-Point, to William Standley's place, and in the evening went again to look at the ditchers.

April 15.—In the morning went and looked at the ditchers. My daughter went to Gravel Hill in Mr. Samuel Vaughan's wagon, and in the afternoon I attended at Isaac Howell's, Esq., concerning Mary Biddle's quarrel in the neighborhood and her abuse of me. Henry

Hart was bound for her good behavior for three months in the sum of £20.

April 16, Easter Sunday.—Went to church twice.   Peter Gordon, Esq., and Mr. Patterson, from Maryland, spent the evening at my house.

April 18.—In the afternoon met at the corner of Race and Fifth Streets the Magistrates and Regulators, William Pollard in Front Street, ——— Craig in Second Street, and William Rush, Esq.   Pollard and Craig are newly-elected.   We viewed Cedar Street again.

April 19.—In the forenoon William Richards and I went to see the ditchers at work in Spruce Street.   Took the public plow to the blacksmith to have it put in order for plowing in Lombard Street to-morrow.   In the afternoon gave my wife a ride in chair up Ridge Road, through Turner's Lane, and down Germantown Road.

April 21.—In the afternoon went to Mr. Samuel Vaughan's, in Chestnut Street, and gave him an account of the weight and size of my large cow that was sold to Mr. McCutcheon for 65 guineas.   Her four quarters weighed 1347 ℔s.   Likewise gave him an account of two large oxen, the first slaughtered March, 1774, the four quarters weighed 1332 lbs., the other in March, 1776, quarters weighed 1240 ℔s., an account of which Mr. Vaughan told me he would send to England.

April 22.—In the afternoon took a ride to Spruce Street to see whether the ditch we are making draws off the water, and found that it must be made deeper in some places before it will answer the purpose.

April 24.—Forenoon went to the Court House, being summoned on a Grand Jury.   A jury was made up before I arrived and a fine put down to me, but telling the Judge, Edward Shippen, that I attended at the State House, expecting that it was there I was wanted, and when I found my mistake came directly here, but too late, however, the Court readily excused me, for which I returned thanks.

April 27.—Forenoon took a ride to the workmen on Spruce Street,

Cedar Street, and Lombard Street, and afternoon went with my wife in chair and examined the ditch in Spruce Street again.

April 28.—In the afternoon went with my wife to the meadow; coming back, went to the ditch in Spruce Street and from thence to the bridge on Race Street, where we met Captain Geyer. At night met the Street Commissioners at the Court House.

April 29.—Forenoon went to the ditchers, from thence to South and Lombard Streets. In the afternoon went with my wife to Gravel Hill, from thence to Race Street bridge, and Spruce Street again.

May 1.—Forenoon went with Peter Kraft to Cedar Street, and set two men to making a ditch; from there went to Spruce Street, near Schuylkill, to look at that street, and then to Race Street, to Edward Pole's place, on the banks of the Schuylkill, where the Sons of St. Tammany are to dine to-day. Afternoon went with General Mifflin in my chair, son Robert on horseback, dined at the Falls. At four o'clock the General and I went to Venderin's Hill, and there met a number of men concerning the altering the road up or around said hill.

May 2.—Forenoon met the Street Commissioners at William Richards's, and from there we went to view Sixth and Race Streets and Cresson's Alley; then three of the Board went to Cedar Street; Andrew Geyer and myself went to our workmen at the gravel pit in Fourth Street. In the evening met the Society of Agriculture at Carpenters' Hall, and afterward the Street Commissioners at the Court House.

May 3.—Forenoon attended the ploughing of Sixth Street, and part of the afternoon the laborers loading the carts. In the evening gave my wife a ride to Gravel Hill.

May 4.—Before breakfast and in the afternoon attended the laborers in Sixth Street. At ten o'clock, forenoon, went with my wife and daughter Kitty to the grand concert in the 'German Reformed Church, in Race Street; paid five shillings a ticket. In the evening

Dr. DeCamp and his daughter Betsey, and likewise Mr. A. Hunt, came to my house from Trenton.

May 5.—Attended the workmen in Sixth Street in the fore- and afternoon ; at night met the Street Commissioners at the Court House.

May 10.—Forenoon went with Mr. Andrew Geyer, in my chair, to the following places, where we had people at work : gravel pit, Race Street, Vine Street, Eighth Street, Spruce Street ditch, and in South or Cedar Street. In the afternoon we made use, for the first time, of our new plow in Sixth Street, which John Purdon had made agreeable to his draft, but we soon found that it did not do so well without a cart as with it. Therefore Captain Geyer and myself agreed to follow my mode lately put in practice, to hitch the plow with a chain to the axletree of the cart, which is the best and easiest way to plow the hard-trodden streets.

May 11.—Attended the workmen in Sixth and Arch Streets fore- and afternoon. This afternoon my son Robert went for the first time to meet the Light-Horse, commanded by Captain S. Miles, in his uniform.

May 13.—Attended the workmen plowing a ditch in Eighth Street and in Vine Street.

May 14.—Before breakfast took a ride with my wife, in chair, up Germantown Road and down Ridge Road. Went to church fore- and afternoon.

May 15.—Before breakfast put my big sorrel, leader of my train, and my gray chair-horse in General St. Clair's light wagon, and gave my four daughters and Betsey DeCamp a ride up Point Road, across below Frankford, and down Germantown Road. Attended the workmen plowing in Eighth and Vine Streets, fore- and afternoon.

May 18.—Attended the plowing in Sixth Street, between Market and Arch Streets, likewise in Eighth Street.

May 19.—Attended the workmen in Sixth Street, and plowing a ditch in Sixth, between Walnut and Chestnut Streets. In the afternoon went with Captain Geyer, and attended to filling up the side of the bridge at Ninth and Race Streets, which G. Morton made yesterday, and likewise to covering the trunk in Eighth Street. At night met at the Court House.

May 20.—Forenoon attended the workmen in Sixth Street and Arch Street. Afternoon went in chair with my wife to Abel James's place, to look at —— Thompson's large cow.

May 22.—Our servant maid, Rosina, was impertinent to her mistress.

May 23.—Forenoon attended the public workmen on Sixth Street. At noon Mr. Paris gave Mr. Geyer, Mr. Kraft, and me a bottle of Rheinish wine. In the afternoon met the Vestry at the schoolhouse to examine the tickets that have been handed in the last two Sundays for and against renting the pews in the church to families. There appeared votes for family pews, 19; and against it, 62. The latter part of the afternoon I attended to the spreading of the dirt on Arch Street.

May 24.—My men brought the cow from Abel James's place which I bought from Thompson for £18.

May 29.—This morning my two sons went to the meadow and brought off my cattle, as all the meadows along both rivers are overflowed, occasioned by the southeast storms and high tide. This morning, as is said by the people along the wharves, the tide has been seven inches higher than it has been at any time since the stores have been erected along shore. In the afternoon I took a ride to the meadows, and found that they were covered with water, more than I ever saw them.

May 31.—Forenoon went with Judge Pendleton as far as George Gray's Ferry, to see how his horses behave, which he bought of Mr. Vaughan for £120, to go to the Warm Springs in Virginia. In the afternoon met, agreeable to appointment, Captain Boys, Peter Kraft, and Andrew Geyer on Lombard Street, to view the new piece of pavement.

June 1.—Went in chair with my wife, and showed her the water that is over the meadows. It came quite up to the corner in the road, where it makes a turn to George Young's, and we saw in several places where it reached the upper rail of the fences. It is said that the meadows were never so much covered with water since they were banked in.

June 2.—Attended the laborers on Chestnut, between Ninth and Tenth Streets, in the forenoon, and in the afternoon went with four Commissioners to view the ditch on Spruce Street and the gravel-pit on Market Street.

June 3.—The Street Commissioners, agreeable to appointment, met at my house concerning the engaging of masons and material for the common sewer from the Workhouse to Fifth Street, and likewise concerning the expense of the books, wherein every lot of this city is to be entered, and to be kept by the Regulators.

June 4.—Forenoon went to church. This afternoon General Dehaas was buried.

June 5.—Attended the plowing and laborers on Sixth Street, and, afternoon, went with my wife to the meadows, and found that the water had disappeared.

June 7.—Forenoon set some of our laborers filling up the ruts on Race and Vine Streets; in the afternoon went to Mr. Logan's stone quarry by myself. Coming back, met Captains Boys and Geyer in Wartman's light wagon, going to the same place, and turned back with them.

June 8.—In the evening I, with three of the Street Commissioners, met Messrs. Bedford, Nevill, and Parson, Regulators, at the Widow McKinly's, to consult with them and to ascertain of Mr. Nevill and Collins their charges, and what they are doing to the books, wherein every square of the whole city is laid down, and the size of every owner's lot put down that has been regulated since the year 1782. The charge of the two gentlemen mentioned will be £33.15s.

7

June 11.—Went to see Mr. Rittenhouse's door on Arch Street, where an attempt was made last night to get in the house by some villains. They nearly got out one of the panels of the door, but did not get in.

June 15.—Mr. Nathaniel Hunt, from the Jerseys, dined at my house. In the afternoon went with my wife to Gravel Hill, where my men began to haul hay into the barn.

June 17.—In the forenoon, according to appointment, met the rest of the Commissioners at the common sewer at the Workhouse, and agreed to set hands to work on Monday next.

June 18.—In the afternoon went to church. My son Robert and daughter Kitty returned from the country.

June 20.—In the morning went to see our laborers at work at the sewer near the Workhouse. My people fetched from William Standley's to my stable one load of hay. In the afternoon went with my wife to Gravel Hill. From thence to Mr. Standley's. Drank tea there with his daughter and son-in-law, Godfrey Twells. At night went to the Court House.

June 21.—Forenoon went with the Commissioners to Eighth Street, to the Workhouse sewer, to Shewel's Alley, and to. Coleman's Alley.

June 22.—In the forenoon went to the burial of Isaac Shoemaker, and walked with Jacob Cooper. Went with my four daughters to Mr. Standley's to get cherries. In the evening my son Thomas, just from Trenton, came to Gravel Hill to see us.

June 23.—Forenoon went to Doctor Thomas Bond's place to look at his hay; at the same time he paid £24, which was the full balance of his account due to me. My people fetched part of a load of hay from William Jones's barn to my stable. In the afternoon finished putting in the hay at Mr. Tilghman's lot, and brought that on my one acre lot home. My wife and I went to William Jones's meadow to look at our cattle. At night went to Court House.

June 24.—Took a ride up to the Falls to see General Mifflin, but found he had gone up to his farm near Reading. In the afternoon went with my wife to the five-acre meadow.

June 25.—Went twice to church, and in the evening took a ride with my wife over Mr. Gray's ferry and came back by Ogden's ferry, or rather Bridge's.

June 28.—Timothy Matlack, who has just arrived from Georgia, breakfasted with me. Forenoon attended with the Commissioners at the common sewer near the Gaol, and at Mr. Pine's well in Eighth Street, and afternoon the laborers and teams in Sixth Street, south of Market Street.

June 29.—Attended the workmen in the afternoon in Sixth Street, and went to the common sewer with Messrs. Geyer and Kraft adjoining the Gaol wall.

June 30.—Attended the plowing in Sixth Street adjoining Chestnut Street, which was done by Alexander Miller's teams. At night was at the Court House.

July 1.—In the afternoon went with my wife to Tinicum to look at some hay of John Garret's. Bought two stacks of him, about six tons, at £5 per ton, to be taken away in six weeks. Coming back met with Adam Geyer and William Sheaff. The former took us to his house on Blakely's Island and gave us a glass of very good wine.

July 2.—Before breakfast gave my two youngest daughters a ride up Germantown Road, across Turner's Lane, and by my Gravel Hill lot home. Went to church forenoon and afternoon.

July 3.—Forenoon attended the plowing in Sixth Street. Dined with my brethren, the Street Commissioners, Boys, Geyer, Richards, Kraft, and Purdon, at the tavern opposite the State House. After dinner I met the Vestry at the schoolhouse, and from thence went to Germantown to Matthew Clarkson's to bring home my wife and daughter Hannah, who were taken there this morning by my son Robert.

July 4.—Forenoon went to the church in Race Street to hear Major William Jackson's oration delivered to the Pennsylvania Society of the Cincinnati. Afternoon went to Governor Samuel Morris's fishing house on Isaac Warner's place, and there dined on fish and beefsteaks with the following gentlemen: Samuel Morris, Gouverneur Morris, Tench Francis, John Lawrence, Richard Bache, John Wharton, Robert Roberts, William Gray, Robert Irwin, Jr., Andrew Tybout, Joseph Rakestraw, George Clymer, Joseph Ogden, Jr., Peter Brown, Samuel Wheeler, Benjamin Scull, J. Howes, and others. Brought John Lawrence home with me in my chair.

July 5.—Forenoon attended in Sixth Street, Eighth Street, and the common sewer near the Gaol. In the afternoon went with my men to William Standley's place and fetched a load of brushwood to make a shade for my cows in Mr. Tilghman's lot.

July 7.—Forenoon attended the plowing of Sixth Street to Chestnut Street, and afternoon went with my wife to Gravel Hill and got two of my men to clean out the spring. At night went to the Court House.

July 8.—Had my servant maid, Rosina Schaeffer, taken to Lewis Weiss's, Esq., on account of her insolent behavior to my wife and myself. Mr. Weiss ordered her to the Workhouse.

July 9.—Went with my wife to Leonard Stoneburner's at Germantown, and after dinner we took a walk to his wheat field (eight acre piece), which he intends to reap to-morrow and expects to get twenty-seven bushels per acre.

July 10.—Forenoon attended at the work at the common sewer adjoining the Gaol. Afternoon went to the five-acre meadow with my daughters Mary and Betsey, where my people were making hay.

July 11.—Had my wheat cut in Mr. Tilghman's lot. My wife and son William came to Gravel Hill; then she and I went to Mr. Standley's place at Point.

July 12.—In the afternoon met at Captain Boys's the Street Commissioners, and about six or eight of the Southwark gentlemen, concerning the water courses about Cedar or South Street. Mr. Hurst asked all of us to his house and gave us some wine and punch.

July 19.—Went with the Commissioners to Captain Boys's; from thence we took a view of Dock Street, between Third and Walnut Streets, to prepare the same for paving. Afterward Mr. Kraft and I went to Witman's and Bellew's to inquire concerning the gravel taken out of our gravel pit by one J. Engle, the carter. I went to a tavern in Second Street, where P. Ozeas and two other gentlemen were settling a dispute between John Grau and Ch. Stoltz, to give them some information.

July 22.—Forenoon, agreeable to appointment, met the Commissioners in Sixth Street to view the new pavement between Market and Chestnut Streets. From thence we went to Elbow Lane and to Dock Street. At one o'clock my wife and I set out for the Falls to Captain Von Heer's. There met and dined with Captain N. Boys and wife, Captain A. Geyer and wife, Peter Kraft and wife, John Purdon and wife, William Richards, and Alexander Miller, who, with his wagon and horses, conveyed seven of the Commissioners to said place and back to Philadelphia.

July 26.—Agreeable to appointment, met the Commissioners at the new common sewer in Fifth Street, near the Workhouse; from thence we went to the board house, that stands in Filbert Street, at the request of Mr. Henderson, who lives next door. In the afternoon attended with Peter Kraft in Sixth Street near Race Street.

July 28.—Before breakfast took a ride with Colonel Timothy Pickering to my lot, he riding a bay horse of Mr. John Lawrence, which he bought for $50. In the afternoon met the Commissioners and Regulators at James McCutcheon's, in order to prepare an estimate of the projected common sewer in Cedar Street, to be laid before the Magistrates at the appointed meeting to-morrow.

July 29.—In the afternoon met the Magistrates, Regulators, Street Commissioners, and a Committee from the people of Southwark, at James McCutcheon's tavern, where it was agreed that a common sewer of ten feet wide and eight feet high in the clear be built in Cedar, or what some call South Street, to begin west of Fourth Street near the Playhouse down to the River Delaware. Its beginning and ending is to be two sewers of a smaller size, for a small distance only. The people of Southwark agree to pay their proportion toward it, as they will be much benefited. At the same time two estimates were produced of what the sewer will cost, one by the Regulators of £4350, the other by the Street Commissioners of £4792. The length of said sewer from its beginning to Delaware is 1920 feet. The gentlemen present were :—

William Shippen, John Gill, Joseph Wharton, William Rush, William Pollard, Lewis Weiss, *Magistrates.*

James Pierson, Gunning Bedford, Thomas Nevill, John Conolly, Josiah Matlack, *Regulators.*

Nathan Boys, Andrew Geyer, John Purdon, William Richards, Peter Kraft, Jacob Hiltzheimer, *Street Commissioners.*

M. Fisher, Elias Boys, Thomas Penrose, Joseph Marsh, Hugh Lenox, *Committee of Southwark.*

August 1.—This evening it was so cool that we drank tea by the fire ; at night met at Court House.

August 2.—We breakfasted by the fire. In the afternoon met Commissioners Boys, Geyer, and Richards at the sewer Fifth Street, from thence we went and viewed several bad places in Cedar, Pine, and Spruce Streets, and at the same time we went to the Hospital, found it clean and neat.

August 4.—Afternoon attended with Mr. Geyer the works in Sixth Street near Race Street, and the common sewer near the Workhouse.

August 5.—Met all the Street Commissioners except Peter Kraft, who is sick, in the morning at Dock Street, between Third and Walnut

Streets, where we have just begun to pave. From thence we went about two miles to a place called Mrs. Master's White House, to a dinner given by William Govitt, David Schaffer, William Hall, George Bickham, Leonard Jacoby, and Israel Whelan, City Wardens, for raising the shambles in Market Street, from Third to Fourth Street. Present: Isaac Howell, John Gill, William Pollard, and William Craig, four Magistrates; Hugh Roberts, carpenter, and John Brooks, two County Commissioners; Nathan Boys, Andrew Geyer, John Purdon, William Richards, and Jacob Hiltzheimer, five Street Commissioners; Pearson, Bedford, and Matlack, Regulators, and a number of other reputable citizens.

August 7.—Began to plow in Seventh Street, near Walnut, and hauling the earth to the sewer adjoining the Workhouse wall. Took a ride with Peter Kraft to William Standley's place.

August 9.—Lewis Weiss, Esq., had my servant girl brought from the Workhouse, and asked her if she would go back to her master and behave as she ought to do. She answered, " No," upon which he ordered her back for another thirty days.

August 11.—This afternoon went with Joseph Dobbins to Alexander Wilcocks, Esq., and got him to undertake to settle a dispute that is between us.

August 12.—Forenoon went with Joseph Dobbins to Mr. Wilcock's again, and he settled the dispute between us.

August 14.—Went to the sewer near the Workhouse to see our laborers; from thence to the pavers in Dock Street, between Third and Walnut Streets, and afterward went to the gravel pit, where Wartman's and Miller's teams were hauling gravel.

August 16.—Attended the laborers in Seventh Street. Went with Messrs. Boys, Geyer, and Kraft to Pine Street, and fixed on the spot where Morton is to lay the trunk in this street. It is about midway between Fifth and Sixth Streets.

August 18.—In forenoon went to Dock Street, where the pavers are at work ; from thence went to the gravel pit, where four teams were hauling gravel. In the evening went with my wife to the meadow ; at night met at the Court House.

August 19.—In the afternoon four of the Commissioners, Geyer, Boys, Kraft, and myself, agreeable to appointment, met at the corner of Ninth and Vine Streets, William Masters, Esq., and Mr. Jacob Souder, two of the Regulators for the Northern Liberties, to confer with them concerning a house a certain Jew, as we are informed, is going to erect in the road on the north side of Vine Street, right opposite Ninth Street. The Regulators told us that the Jew had applied to them to lay and stake out his lot ; they refused, and told him they would not lay out a lot in the road for him or any other person without orders from higher authority. Mr. Souder then showed us a plan of the road and lots adjoining, by which plan we saw that the road exactly leads in to Vine Street, facing Ninth Street ; therefore, the road ought not to be obstructed in that place. From thence we went down Vine Street, opposite Fifth Street, where John Harrison had just been raising six houses, and dinner being on table, we were invited to partake.

August 21.—In the morning attended the plow and laborers in Fifth Street and Pine Street. Began to dig my cellar adjoining our present kitchen.

August 22.—My son Thomas and daughter Kitty set out to their Uncle Clayton's, in Chester County. In the morning and evening attended the workmen in Pine and Fifth Streets, laying a trunk in Pine Street.

August 23.—This morning —— Haffner, the bricklayer, began the cellar wall, back of our wooden kitchen. In the evening gave my wife a ride round by the banks of Schuylkill.

August 24.—Attended the workmen in Eighth Street morning and evening. Took a ride with my wife to William Standley's place. My son Thomas and daughter Kitty returned home. Went with Mr. Franck to the Workhouse, who there spoke to my servant maid

Rosina (being her countryman). She promised to behave better, upon which took her home, after paying £1 19s. 6d. for her lodging and board for forty-eight days.

August 25.—Attended with Peter Kraft the teams and laborers in Eighth and Arch Streets.

August 27.—Went with my wife to Germantown to Matthew Clarkson's, and there spent the day.

August 30.—In the afternoon three of the Street Commissioners met me at my house by appointment, when we went and viewed Minor Street and agreed that it be plowed and the earth hauled to the new arch, east of Fifth Street.

September 2.—Forenoon met three of the Street Commissioners agreeable to appointment: Boys, Geyer, and Purdon ; and two of the Regulators, Pearson and Conolly, at the drawbridge, in Front Street, concerning the foot pavement being raised on the west side of the street near the bridge.

September 3.—In the afternoon went to the burial of John Switzer, a printer, from thence to church. After church went with A. Hertzog and Daniel Sutter to see P. Ozeas, who is sick.

September 5.—In the afternoon went with John Cornman to the burial of Whitehead Humphreys, from his house in Seventh Street to the Friends' graveyard in Arch street; from thence I went to Carpenters' Hall, and there met four of the members of the Society of Agriculture.

September 8.—At night met the Street Commissioners at the Court House, and from thence Guyer, Boys, Richards, and myself went to Geiss's in Market Street and drank a bottle of Rheinish wine.

September 9.—In the morning attended the laborers in South Street near Front Street.

September 12.—Sent my boy Lapsley to Gravel Hill to bury our bitch, that died yesterday. She was a very remarkable dog, attending our cows day and night, in the stable as well as in the field. In the summer of 1779 she settled herself with my cattle at pasture, and did not leave there for a long time. At last she would come with the cows to the corner of Chestnut and Seventh Streets and then go back and wait for them. Some time afterward, perhaps eighteen months, she would come to the stable and go back with the cows, which she has done ever since, except the month of May, 1782. She went with some cows I sold to Mr. Randle Mitchell near Trenton, and there stayed till I ordered her brought down in one of Mr. Hunt's shallops. We never could tell what she lived on while she remained at the pasture. It was thought she sucked the cows, but no one ever saw her do it, though often watched.

September 14.—In the afternoon met the Magistrates and Regulators in Pear Street. Present: Fleeson, Howell, Wharton, Bedford, Matlack, Conolly, Wetherill, Boys, Richards, and myself, when it was agreed that the street be lowered eighteen inches at the pump. From thence four of us went out to see the troops exercise. Mr. Howell and Captain Boys drank tea at my house.

September 15.—Part of the forenoon attended with Mr. Kraft in South Street. Afterward went to Front Street, where Hoffner's man was preparing to repair the steps from Front to Water Street, near Arch Street.

September 18.—Mounted my horse and went to see the several water courses in Market and Fourth Streets ; the four receivers were full, but it did not swell so as to reach the houses: the trunk across Fourth Street, near South Street, is not large enough ; Eighth Street still wants raising on each side of Arch Street before the water that collects there can be drawn off.

September 19.—Dined with General Mifflin at his house in Race Street. Mrs. Mifflin concluded to move to their house in Market Street above Seventh. Forenoon attended plowing in Minor Street.

September 20.—Attended the sale of city lots at the Coffee House, at twelve o'clock. Andrew Geyer and I attended the laborers and teams in Seventh and Spruce Streets.

September 21.—Attended the plowing of Seventh Street between Walnut and Spruce Streets, and in the evening took a ride with my wife to William Standley's place. Our horse went very lame.

September 24.—In the forenoon went to church in Race Street. In the afternoon went with Mr. William Standley to St. Paul's Church, on Third Street, to hear the Rev. Mr. Pilmore preach. He has an excellent delivery, and speaks with a smile on his countenance; in the evening we heard him again. His text was Isaiah, chapter lx, 1 v.

September 25.—Attended the teams and laborers in Seventh and Spruce Streets, and in the afternoon went on horseback to Mr. Standley's place at Point. Sold my servant-maid, Rosina Schaeffer, to August Will for £20, and signed her over to him before Justice Farmer.

September 29.—Attended the public works as yesterday. Took dinner to my people at the meadow with my wife; at night met at the Court House.

September 30.—Attended the workmen part of the day. Had Messrs. Pearson, Bedford, and Conolly to lay out for General Mifflin, Daniel Rundle, Franks, Lardner, and myself the several lots in Chestnut Street lately bought of the State.

October 2.—Forenoon, attended the laborers in Seventh and Spruce Streets; afternoon, met the Vestry at our school-house and from thence went to McCutcheon's tavern to meet the Street Commissioners.

October 3.—In the morning attend in Seyfred's Ally, where our laborers are preparing the ground for paving. At night went to the Court House; Abraham Hunt, walked with me from my house to the Indian King, where he lodges.

October 4.—Forenoon attended with Messrs Kraft, and Geyer in Vine Street between Fifth and Sixth Streets, regulating the water courses.

October 5.—Went to the State House; there attended as a struck jury-
man on a cause between Thomas Green Pollard, plaintiff, and
Samuel Garrigues, defendant, until ten o'clock at night.   Took Mr.
Edward Duffield home with me, who was one of the Judges.

October 6.—After breakfast Mr. Duffield and I went from my house
again to the State House and joined our ten colleagues on the same
cause, and here follows their names: Philip Price, John Vandever,
John Swift, Nathan Levering, John Ferree, Noah Townsend, Benjamin Cotman, George Bringhurst, Evan Thomas, and Edward Heston,
all of them from the county except myself.   Counsel for the plaintiff
were James Wilson, Alexander Wilcocks, and William Bradford;
on the other side John Cox, William Lewis, Rawle, and Ingersoll.
These gentlemen kept us from ten o'clock in the morning until ten
at night, notwithstanding the Hon. Judge McKean limited them to
forty-five minutes each to speak, but I wished that he had limited
the number of speakers on each side likewise, for one on each side
would have been enough.   We went to the tavern opposite the
State House and there stayed.

October 7.—We agreed on our verdict, which was one moiety of the
land possessed by Samuel Garrigues, the defendant, to Thomas
Green Pollard, the plaintiff.

October 9.—In the afternoon went with my wife to William Henderson's place, late Joseph Woods's, but now belonging to the
estate of General John Cadwalader.   In the evening met the Street
Commission at Nathan Boys's.

October 10.—Forenoon, the Street 'Commissioners met at my house,
where we settled our yearly accounts.   In the afternoon went to
the meadows with my wife and found that they are again over-
flowed.

October 11.—This morning about two o'clock a number of gentlemen
came to my door and informed me that I was elected one of the
Representatives for the City of Philadelphia.   In the afternoon

went with Colonel Timothy Pickering in my chair to show him the meadows below the city.

October 14.—This afternoon went over Schuylkill to Isaac Warner's fish-house and dined with about forty gentlemen: Richard Penn, Robert Morris, Gouverneur Morris, Samuel Morris, Tench Francis, Arthur St. Clair, F. Johnson, Captain Barry, James Craig, Theodore Forrest, William Hall, John Baker, Samuel Nicholas, William Gray, Joseph Ogden, Senior and Junior, Robert Roberts, Joseph Rakestraw, Israel Whelen, James White, John Patton, and a number of others.

October 15.—After breakfast set out with Mr. Hunt and my wife for Trenton. Dined at Mr. McElroy's, at Bristol, and drank tea at Mr. Hunt's at Trenton.

October 16.—After dinner left Trenton with my wife and arrived at Peter Gordon's, Esq., Hopewell.

October 20.—In the afternoon went with Mr. Hunt, his wife, and my wife in his light wagon to General Philemon Dickinson's; there drank tea with George Clymer, Esq., and wife, old Mrs. Lambert, the Widow Dagworthy, two Mrs. Cadwaladers, Mrs. DeKue, and the General's family. He was sick and could not appear.

October 21.—After breakfast left Mr. Hunt's, Trenton, dined at Bristol, and arrived at my house in Philadelphia at sunset. We crossed Delaware ferry with Mr. and Mrs. Clymer, Miss Cadwalader, and Miss Dickinson.

October 23.—In the afternoon attended for the first time in the House of Assembly, and only twenty-four members being present, we adjourned to three o'clock to-morrow. Spent the evening with General Mifflin at his house on the south side of Market Street between Seventh and Eighth Streets.

October 24.—No quorum being present in the House, we adjourned again to three o'clock to-morrow. In the evening I met twenty-one members opposite the State House and had a consultation concerning the business to come before the House.

October 25.—There being no quorum, the House again adjourned to three o'clock to-morrow. Spent the evening with General Mifflin, his wife, and Captain Falkner and. wife.

October 26.—Attended at the State House, and there being present just a quorum, the House elected General Thomas Mifflin their Speaker again, Peter Z. Lloyd their Clerk, Jacob Shallus Assistant Clerk, Nicholas Weaver, Sergeant-at-arms. General Muhlenberg, one of the Executive Council, administered the oath to the Speaker, who did the same to all the members, three several oaths, and every member signed his name to each.

October 27.—Forenoon the House met. Messrs. Whitehill, D. Clymer, and myself waited on Council, agreeable to order, and informed them that the House was ready to receive such business as they may have to lay before them. At night went with General Mifflin and Matthew Clarkson to hear a Mr. Jones lecture upon agriculture at the college.

October 31.—In the forenoon the House proceeded to select delegates to Congress. Arthur St. Clair, William Irvine, of Carlisle, Charles Pettit, Samuel Meredith, and William Bingham were elected.

November 1.—Forenoon attended as yesterday, when the House appointed Michael Billmeyer their printer of the minutes in the German language, and Hall & Sellers to print them in English.

November 2.—Forenoon attended as yesterday, and spent the afternoon with General Mifflin. The House elected Thomas Bradford their printer of the laws and bills for consideration.

November 3.—Forenoon attended at the Assembly, where fifty members met and went to business. Spent the evening with the Street Commissioners at the Court House, where Isaac Howell, Esq., administered the oath to Samuel McLane, who is to serve for the remainder of my term—to October next.

November 4.—In the afternoon met the Assembly in their room, where the Executive Council attended and proceeded, with the members of Assembly, to the election of President and Vice-President. Benjamin Franklin was unanimously re-elected President, and Charles Biddle re-elected Vice-President. He had thirty-six votes and Peter Muhlenberg thirty-three votes. After the election every member of Council and Assembly certified the election by signing their names each to a seal on a piece of parchment. We then walked in procession to the Court House steps, proclaimed the officers just elected, and then returned to the State House. David Rittenhouse was unanimously re-elected State Treasurer. Went with my wife to Gravel Hill, and there met Peter Trexler, Esq., and other gentlemen.

November 6.—Forenoon went to General Mifflin's at the Falls. He and Dr. William Smith and his son William came, after I arrived, from over Schuylkill. I remained to dinner, after which the General came to town with me in my chair. At three o'clock attended the House, and spent the evening, with fourteen members of Assembly, opposite the State House.

November 7.—In the morning attended at the State House, went into the committee room with Messrs. George Clymer, Whitehill, Findlay, and Richard Willing, to agree on the report we are to make to the House on the petition referred to us from the non-resident landholders of the counties of Bedford, Northumberland, and Westmoreland. We agreed that the owners have leave to appeal until the middle of April next, and that the sale of the lands be put off until the 1st of June following. The House elected Timothy Pickering Register of Wills and Recorder of Deeds for the county of Luzerne; the office of Prothonotary for the county he lately received from the Executive Council. In the evening met at Carpenters' Hall the Society of Agriculture, where Mr. John Sellers produced a model of a bridge that is to be erected over the Schuylkill, and will cost £25,000. At the same time was exhibited a drill plow, just from England, that cost £19 sterling, besides the freight.

November 8.—Attended at the Assembly. John Coxe, Esq., was appointed the law officer, whose duty is to attend the committees of the House, to draw laws and bills for them, for which service the House will allow him, at the last session at the end of the year, a reasonable compensation. In the afternoon went with my wife to William Jones's meadow.

November 10.—Attended the House, where, on the second reading of the report from the committee on the petition of non-resident landholders, as mentioned in this journal on the 7th instant, Mr. Whitehill moved for an amendment to said report, which occasioned a long and smart debate for and against the amendment. The speakers were: Robert Morris, Thomas Fitzsimmons, Daniel Clymer Whitehill, and Findlay. The amendment was lost.

November 13.—In the afternoon the House met, two new members, Mr. Brackenridge and another, being qualified, petitions and reports read; no other business before the House, it adjourned. In the evening met eight of the members at the tavern opposite the State House.

November 16.—Forenoon attended at the State House until the members' names were called and the minutes of yesterday read, then went with Joseph Rakestraw five miles up Schuylkill, to John Vandever's, who is, as observed by his friends, a little out of his mind. We dined with him; then he, Mr. Howell, a surveyor; John Barry, Joseph Rakestraw, and myself went and viewed the new projected road over Roxborough Hill, in compliance with an order of Court of General Quarter Session, bearing date 20th of September last, but for want of the other three gentlemen, William Macpherson, Robert Morris (Miller), and Isaac Worrall, named in the order of Court, we could not make a report, as the order requests us to.

November 17.—Forenoon attended at the State House. The report was read again about removing the seat of justice to Harrisburgh, but was determined to remain where it is.

November 18.—In the forenoon attended at the Assembly, at which time the petition of Gunning Bedford and others was read, praying to be allowed the balance of their accounts due to them for erecting the triumphal arch in Market Street in 1784. It appears by the journals of the House that £1600 was voted for that purpose, but the managers exceeded that sum, which occasioned a great debate for and against the allowing any sum above the limited sum. The speakers in favor of the petitioners were Robert Morris, George Clymer, Thomas Fitzsimmons, and George Logan; against, Messrs Brackenridge, Whitehill, and Findlay.

November 19.—Snow last night. Being unwell, I remained in the house all day.

November 20.—In the afternoon attended at the State House; afterward went with William Will and George Logan, as a committee, to Captain Stiles's, concerning the powder-house, of which Stiles is the officer.

November 21.—Forenoon attended as usual in the Assembly Room. The order of the day was called concerning the report of a committee which was to bring in a bill to alter or correct an error in that part of the law that affects the Court of Admiralty, of which the Judge of Admiralty, Francis Hopkinson, complains, setting forth that it must have been altered by an unauthorized person, as the words in the late volume do not agree with the original in the rolls office, and thereby make the presence of the Judge of Admiralty in the Court unnecessary, but agreeable to the original it could not be held without that officer. This occasioned a long debate between Messrs. Brackenridge and Daniel Clymer, and finally the report was committed to Messrs. Thomas Fitzsimmons, H. Brackenridge, and Daniel Clymer.

November 22.—Forenoon attended at the State House. The bill for suspension of sales of lands for taxes next month, as advertised, until the 1st day of June next, occasioned some debate concerning the expense that will attend the five days' appeal in April next. It

8

was determined that the expense should be paid by the non-resident landholders, for whose use the said appeal is ordered. The bill was enacted into a law.

November 23.—Forenoon attended at the State House, at which time the report had a second reading concerning Rutter & Ingize's account of £112 for making the State arms over the seat of justice in the State House. The speakers for allowing the bill were—Messrs. Fitzsimmons and Daniel Clymer; against it, Messrs Whitehill, Brackenridge, and Findlay. Was determined it could not be allowed by the House. Dined at General Mifflin's with the following gentlemen : James Hockley and George Ross, Esq.; Richard Peters, Mr. Beard, and two strangers.

November 24.—General Mifflin, Speaker of the House, and Messrs. Ross and Hockley breakfasted with me, after which we went to the State House together. The several gentlemen, Messrs. George Clymer, Fitzsimmons, and William Robeson, on the one side, Messrs. Whitehill, Findlay, and Brackenridge on the other, debated concerning the division of Bedford County, and to have the seat of justice for the new part fixed at the crossing of Juniata. Afternoon took a ride with Norton Pryor to the meadows.

November 25.—Forenoon attended at the State House, but very little business coming before the House, it adjourned before eleven o'clock. In the afternoon took a ride with Townsend Whelen, Esq., to my lot to look at my large cow and steer.

November 26.—Forenoon went to church, after which had to dine with me the following gentlemen : Israel Whelen and his brother Townsend, and Daniel Clymer.

November 27.—In the afternoon attended at the State House. In the evening met seven of the members of Assembly at the tavern opposite the State House, where we conversed about the new road to be laid out from the Schuylkill to the westward, and which way the money is to be raised to make it a turnpike. The bridge over

Schuylkill, and the most suitable place for it, was likewise a subject of conversation.

November 28.—Forenoon attended at the State House. At ten o'clock the House set out, two and two, to the House of Mr. Helm, in Race Street near Second, the lodgings of the late Samuel Atlee, Esq., a member for Lancaster County, who died suddenly, last Saturday, in the street, before he could reach his lodgings. The funeral set out from Helm's house, up Race Street, down Third and Arch Streets, then down Second Street to Christ Church, where the services were held by the Rev. Mr. Andrews. The corpse was then taken out of church again to the yard, and there buried. The Executive Council likewise attended the funeral, with their Vice-President, Charles Biddle, Esq, the President, Benjamin Franklin, Esq., not being in health to attend.

November 29.—Forenoon attended at the State House. Some debate about the report on the Western Road, but the matter postponed until this day week. In the afternoon met the vestrymen at the Reformed Congregation schoolhouse, and there distributed £32 2s. 9d., which was contributed last Sunday for the poor of the congregation.

December 1.—Forenoon attended at the State House, where a debate ensued concerning the receiving certificates equal to specie in payment of debts due to this State for lands, before a certain day in 1776. The speakers for receiving the certificates were Mr. Whitehill and Mr. Findlay, against receiving them, Messrs. Robert Morris, George Clymer, Thomas Fitzsimmons, William Robeson, and Mr. Hugh Brackenridge. On putting the question, it was determined that certificates are not to be received for that purpose.

December 5.—Forenoon attended the State House, when came on the order of the day concerning the reduction of the expenses of the Government. The speakers on the subject were Messrs. Morris, Fitzsimmons, Daniel Clymer, George Clymer, Logan, Wynkoop, Robeson, Brackenridge, Findlay, and Whitehill. Spent the evening at the Court House with Messrs. N. Boys, Geyer, Ozeas, Pancake, Richards, and McLane, Street Commissioners. Mr. E. Boys and Mr. Latimer were also present.

December 6.—Forenoon attended the Assembly. The order of the day was brought forward, concerning the new road to be made from the middle ferry on Schuylkill to Lancaster. All the speakers in the House debated upon it for some time, and then the report was recommitted. My son Robert and daughter Kitty went with Rebecca Morris and A. Johnson in sleigh to General Mifflin's place up the Schuylkill.

December 7.—Forenoon attended as usual; another order of the day came on concerning lands.

December 8.—Forenoon attended the State House; no debates. The House adjourned at eleven o'clock. Dined at Mr. Israel Whelen's, on Market Street, near Sixth, with the following gentlemen : Messrs. Moore, Rawlston, Willing Evans, and Townsend Whelen, Chester County members of the Assembly, and S. Morris, William Govitt, William Hall, Mark Wilcock, and Colonel J. Hannam.

December 9.—Forenoon attended at the Assembly, when came up the report concerning the contested election in Bedford County. The dispute is, whether Mr. Powell or Mr. Cable be admitted as third member for said county. Messrs. Whitehill, Findlay, and Piper spoke in favor of Mr. Powell's admittance. Messrs. Fitzsimmons, George Clymer, Daniel Clymer, Robeson, and Brackenridge were the speakers on the other side, and their opinion is that " neither of the two can be admitted, without more substantial proof than what was offered." The House agreed that the speaker write to the officers of the county for all the vouchers they may be able to collect, and to forward them to this House by a certain day.

December 11.—In forenoon went in sleigh with William Standley and my son Robert to Standley's place at Point to look at our five partnership cattle. In the afternoon attended at the State House, when a dispute happened between General Mifflin, Speaker, and Daniel

Clymer, Esq., about Mr. William Findlay and Mr. Isaac Gray. They both got up to speak at the same time. The Speaker said that Mr. Findlay was first; Mr. Clymer claimed that Mr. Gray was. After a considerable altercation, it was determined that Mr. Findlay be heard first by the Speaker. They spoke about actual, legal, and continuate settlements of lands.

December 12.—In the forenoon attended, as yesterday. Several petitions and reports were read. Likewise, some bills, among which was a bill called for by Mr. Brackenridge, concerning the incorporating of a Presbyterian congregation at Pittsburgh. Mr. Brackenridge moved to omit the words " Presbyterian congregation," and in their place insert the words " religious society of Christians." This occasioned a surprise among 'some of the members, and some debate ensued, but, nevertheless, the last-mentioned words took place. Mrs. Matthew Clarkson spent the afternoon at our house, and after tea Mr. Hunt, my son Robert, and myself took Mrs. Clarkson home in sleigh.

December 13.—Attended at the State House forenoon and afternoon. The report was read, recommending that a bill be brought in to restore the charter of the bank, with provisions of limiting its time and capital. A debate ensued. The speakers in favor of the bank were Messrs. Robert Morris, Fitzsimmons, George and Daniel Clymer; against it, Mr. Findlay and Mr. Whitehill. Mr. Brackenridge argued different from either side ; he contended that the charter the Assembly first granted the stockholders of the bank was still in force, and that no succeeding House had a right to take it away without a trial by court and jury. Therefore he insisted that the present House ought to put the stockholders of the bank in possession again of every privilege their first charter gave them. The yeas and nays being called, the report was adopted. I must confess that Mr. Brackenridge's argument exactly agreed with my ideas, which will appear by my vote on the journals of the House of this day. Mr. Matthew Clarkson came from the State House with me to my house; afterward my son William took him home in sleigh.

December 14.—Forenoon attended at the House of Assembly. This afternoon Mr. Stoneburner and his son-in-law, William Rush, likewise P. Burchhalter and P. Trexler, Esqrs., came to see me. I observed the bricklayers at work running up the gable ends of the house, Mr. Robert Morris is building at the corner of Minor and Sixth Streets, notwithstanding the uncommon severity of the season.

December 17.—Forenoon went to church. In the afternoon Townsend Whelen and Richard Thomas, Esqrs. spent the afternoon with me.

December 18.—In the afternoon attended at the State House, when Mr. Barclay, from Bedford County, was examined by General Mifflin, Speaker of the House, concerning the late contested election in that county. From thence I went to Mr. A. Kintzing's to see my wife home.

December 19.—Forenoon went to the Assembly as usual, but the Speaker being very sick, could not attend, and the House adjourned to the morrow.

December 20.—Forenoon attended the House. The Speaker not being able to attend, the House adjourned without transacting any business. Went to Gravel Hill in my sleigh with Townsend Whelen, Esq., and my son William. Had to dine with me the following gentlemen: William Findlay, Esq., Gerardus Wynkoop, Esq., Townsend Whelen, Esq., Matthew Clarkson, and Captain N. Falkner.

December 21.—Forenoon attended at the State House. The Speaker being not well enough to attend, the House adjourned. Went with my wife and daughters Mary and Hannah to Mr. Standley's place, at Point, in sleigh with a pair of chestnut horses.

December 22.—Forenoon attended at the State House. General Mifflin still not well enough to attend. The resignation he sent by me to the House yesterday was read to-day and accepted, whereupon the House proceeded to the election of another Speaker. Gerardus

Wynkoop, Esq., was elected; he received forty-five votes. Daniel Clymer, Esq., escorted the new Speaker to the chair, after which Mr. Evans, a member of Council for Chester County, administered the oath, and then the House proceeded to business. In the afternoon the House met again. The bill for holding an election in the county of Luzerne, was enacted into a law. The election is to be the first day of February next.

December 23.—Forenoon attended at the Assembly as usual. The bill was read the second time and debated by paragraphs locating the seat of justice at Hannas Town, in the county of Westmoreland. Dined at Matthew Clarkson's with William Findlay, Robert Rawlston, Esqrs., Messrs. Jennings, John Wharton, and Mr. Clarkson's two sons-in-Law, Bringhurst and Rawlston.

December 25.—Christmas day, clear and cold. Forenoon went to church in Race Street. My wife and I dined at General Mifflin's with his family, and the Hon. Gerardus Wynkoop, Capt. N. Falkner and wife. My son William brought Capt. Falkner and wife to the General's in a sleigh and took them home.

December 26.—Forenoon went with General Mifflin to the State House. About noon the Hon. Gerardus Wynkoop resigned his office as Speaker, after which General Mifflin was again elected by ballot, and then was escorted to the chair by the ex-Speaker. It was then moved by some members, that the new Speaker be again qualified, although he has been out of office only since Friday last. This occasioned much debate, but at last it terminated in his not taking it.

December 28.—Attended at the State House. The bill concerning the bank had a second reading, and was debated by paragraphs, which lasted till 9 o'clock at night; it was finally carried that the Stockholders of the Bank be furnished with a charter.

December 29.—Attended at the State House. The bill was read a second time and debated by paragraphs, laying a duty on particular articles manufactured in foreign countries and imported into this State, which took up almost the whole day. In the evening met

thirteen members of the Assembly at the tavern opposite the State
House, and there fixed on the seven Commissioners that are to be
appointed to meet the Commissioners from other States at Philadelphia, in May next.

December 30.—In the forenoon attended at the State House as usual,
when came on the election of the following gentlemen: Thomas
Mifflin, Robert Morris, Jared Ingersoll, George Clymer, Thomas
Fitzsimmons, James Wilson, and Governor Morris, to meet the
Commissioners above mentioned, to revise the Federal Constitution.
At the same time the bill was agreed to, which lays a duty of six
pence on a bushel of salt and one penny on a pound of coffee. In
the afternoon attended again at the Assembly room. The contested
election of Bedford County was called up again, which occasioned
a long debate. The conclusion arrived at was that the Speaker
write letters to the officers of the County concerned in the election,
and send them by a special messenger. I reported to the *House
that the committee, Mr. Lilly, Mr. Findlay, and myself, had affixed
the seal to certain laws. After which the House adjourned until
the third Tuesday in February next. Then the orders were
signed and handed to each member by the Speaker, for their pay;
my order is for 69 days at 15 shillings.

December 31.—Forenoon went to church. James Hockley and Townsend Whelen dined with me.

1787.

January 1.—Forenoon went to church; in the afternoon met the
vestry and settled the quarterly accounts. From thence went to
the Widow Mathews's, in Market Street, and met fourteen of the
members belonging to the Amicable Fire Company.

January 2.—Forenoon my son William and I went with General
Mifflin from my house to his, and there we signed our names to two
deeds as witnesses, which the General, his wife, and the two Miss

Morris's conveyed to each other. In the evening went with Leonard Stoneburner to Carpenters' Hall, and there met about twenty-four members of the Society of Agriculture. General Mifflin wrote some instructions concerning the late Bedford election, agreeable to resolve of the House last Saturday, and sent off Mr. John White with the same.

January 3.—My son Thomas came from Trenton, upon the Delaware, on the ice. In the afternoon took a walk up Second Street, near Vine, to Mr. John Baker's, and coming back, I stopped at Colonel Miles's and Colonel Morgan's store.

January 5.—The ice on the Delaware is so much reduced, that about twenty sail of vessels came up to the city this day. I am very unwell.

January 6.—Doctor Kuhn came to see me and ordered me bled, which was performed by Rudolph Nagel. In the afternoon Mr. John Baker came here, and we settled Mr. Von Phul's book, as treasurer to our congregation.

January 8.—Dr. Kuhn came to see me, and General Mifflin called at the same time, and so did Mr. Bernard. At night I got very bad, but in less than an hour got better.

January 9.—Dr. Kuhn paid me a visit. I am now in a good way.

January 13.—Took a walk as far as General Mifflin's, and afterwards to Mr. Barges.

January 14.—Went with General Mifflin on horseback to his place at the Falls of Schuylkill. Mrs. Mifflin and the two little girls went in their carriage.

January 18—In the afternoon I was overset by a cow, running suddenly out of my yard with a dog after her, and was much bruised thereby.

January 20—In the forenoon went to Mr. George Clymer's in Fourth Street south of Walnut Street, concerning the nine tons and upward of hay, he mentioned to my wife yesterday, which I stand charged with in the late Reese Meredith's book, August 11, 1777. I do not recollect anything of it. In the afternoon took a ride in search of one Michael Lutz, who it seems was tenant on Mr. Meredith's place at the time the hay was had.

January 22.—Mr. George Nelson came to see us and we looked amongst the public accounts to find whether we had any hay of the late Mr. Reese Meredith, in the year 1777, and found that we had for public use, six loads in July, 1777. Mr. Nelson stayed to dinner after which I went to meet the Vestry at the German Reformed schoolhouse.

January 26.—I spent the evening yesterday at Capt. Nathan Boys's, in Front Street below the Bridge, with Andrew Geyer, Mr. Pancake, Peter Ozeas, Samuel McLane, William Richards, Street Commissioners, John Purdon, Peter Kraft, Michael Hartman, Alexander Miller, and George Honey.

January 27.—Took a walk down to Market Street Wharf, and coming home stopped and drank tea at Mr. Barges, and when I came home, Mr. John White was at my house, just returned from Bedford County with three boxes of tickets concerning the late contested election in said County.

February 1.—Forenoon went to George Clymer, Esq., and showed him the letter from William Simmons, at New York, which certifies that the money had been paid to Mr. Clymer, for hay the public had of the late Mr. Meredith, his father-in-law, in August 1777, and the money paid in September, 1778.

February 4.—Forenoon went to church on Race Street. Last night General Mifflin sent his coachman down from his farm near Reading, with a sleigh, and this morning he returned with Miss Rebecca Morris and Emily Johnson.

February 6.—To-night went with Matthew Clarkson from my house to the Society of Agriculture at Carpenters' Hall.

February 7.—Mr. Hunt's negro Tom came here with a wagon and two horses; went away after breakfast to take a load of goods out of his master's shallop, which cannot get up on account of the ice in the Delaware.

February 9.—My daughter Kitty went in a sleigh to Abington with Eda Lukin. Forenoon went in my sleigh with Mr. William Standley my son Robert and daughter Hannah to Mr. Standley's place at Point.

February 10.—Col. J. Wadsworth breakfasted with us and in the afternoon Mrs. Matthew Clarkson, my wife and I went in my sleigh to Mr. Edward Duffield's; overtook Mrs. Duffield and her son Edward four miles from town; took her in with us, one of her horses being lame.

February 11.—About 12 o'clock it began to rain, which made us leave Mr. Duffield's. Put down Mrs. Clarkson at her house in Arch Street, and wife and self reached our home at half-past one, just one hour and a half going thirteen miles, and it rained the whole way.

February 13.—Spent the afternoon at General Mifflin's on Market Street, with himself, Mr. Samuel Potts, and Colonel Mentges.

February 14.—After breakfast went with General Mifflin to his place at the Falls, on horseback; Mrs. Mifflin, and Sarah Morris in their chariot. After dinner I came home.

February 16.—My son Thomas brought down from Mr. Hunt's a pair of bay horses for Mr. Edward Tilghman.

February 17.—Went with General Mifflin to his place at the Falls, and crossed the Schuylkill at Righter's, and went to look at the farm he bought last summer, about a mile from the river. After dinner I came home, and went to the burial of William Standley, Jr's., wife. Walked with Baltus Clymer.

February 19.—In the afternoon went to Mr. Josiah Hewes and got an order from him to admit Simon Holler into the hospital to get his leg treated, which is, and has been for some time past, very painful to him.

February 20.—After dinner went to General Mifflin's, and from there he and I called at Mr. Robert Morris's, and after taking a few glasses of wine we went to the State House together.

February 21.—Forenoon attended at the State House, but there being no quorum present, the House adjourned until to-morrow. In the evening met Mr. Pollard, Jonathan Penrose, Esq., and Richard Renshaw at the Rivers' Tavern, being referees appointed by the Court to settle a partnership account between Abraham Kintzing and Joseph Pemberton. Agreed to meet again at the same place on Friday evening next.

February 22.—Attended at the State House, but no business being brought forward, the House adjourned till half past nine o'clock to-morrow.

February 24.—Attended at the Assembly Room in the forenoon. Mr. Powell from Bedford County was qualified and admitted to his seat. The reason of his not being admitted to his seat before, was owing to the election being disputed, which dispute was not decided until now. After the House adjourned, I went with the Speaker, General Mifflin, to his place at the Falls, and after dinner returned home.

February 25.—Colonel Wadsworth drank tea at my house, and in afternoon I went to church.

February 26.—Colonel J. Wadsworth came to my house, and he and I went and breakfasted with General Mifflin. After that I went to the State House to meet the committee concerning the Rev. Mr. Marshall's memorial praying to repeal a certain law passed in September last. In the afternoon met the House; from thence I went to Mr. Jacob Barge's to attend my wife and Mrs. Dunlap.

February 27.—Forenoon attended at the State House, and the order of the day was called, which was to improve the four following roads: from Philadelphia to Lancaster, from Philadelphia to Reading, from Philadelphia to Allentown, from Newman's Creek, through Philadelphia to —— Ferry over Delaware, in Bucks County. The Speaker put the question whether these roads shall be made and kept in repair at the charge of the State at large. Yeas and nays being taken, 29 for it and 36 against it, when the report fell.

February 28.—Forenoon attended at the State House. The bill imposing a duty on salt and coffee was read. The first paragraph, which mentions six pence a bushel on salt, was for a long time debated by Messrs. Morris, Fitzsimmons, G. Clymer, and Mr. Brackenridge; against it, Mr. Logan, Mr. Whitehill and Mr. Findlay. The question being put, was lost, and of course the bill failed. Affixed the seal to four laws.

March 1.—Forenoon attended the Assembly. Dined at General Mifflin's, with the following gentlemen : Colonel J. Wadsworth, Colonel Pickering, Hugh H. Brackenridge, Richard Willing and Samuel Wheeler, Esqs, and Mr. Joseph Harrison.

March 2.—After dinner took a ride to Gravel Hill; afterwards went with my wife, Mr. and Mrs. Dunlap, and John Mease, to John Everhart's slaughter house in Eighth street, to see the beef of our cow killed yesterday. At four o'clock went to the State House, and there met the committee appointed by the House on the memorial of the minister, elders, trustees and others of Scot's Presbyterian Church of Philadelphia, praying the House to repeal or suspend a law passed in September last. The committee that met numbered fifteen members, two only absent. We heard both parties, and agreed, 13 against 2, that the law ought not to be repealed or suspended.

March 3.—This morning at three o'clock, J. Hiltzheimer and Timothy Matlack weighed the cow killed by Mr. Everhart, which Hiltzheimer raised and fed:

		Pounds.	
The fore quarters weighed, ...	326		
	328		
	——	654	
The hind quarters, ...	282		
	289		
	——	571	
The neat beef, ...		1225	
The hide, ...	111		
The head and heart, ...	49		
The belly and feet, ...	72		
Feck, ...	35		
Tallow, ...	163		
Entrails not weighed			
	——	430	
The whole weight exclusive of the entrails, ...		1655	
The rump, ...	77		
The above weights were taken by me,		T. MATLACK.	

March 5.—In the afternoon attended at the State House. The bill had a third reading concerning the German College that is to be erected at Lancaster.

March 6.—Forenoon attended at the State House. The order of the day was on the laying out of a town opposite Pittsburgh.

March 7.—In the afternoon took a walk with General Mifflin to Mr. Habacher's and Captain Falkner's; from thence went to the State House; there met the committee on the same business as on 2d inst., and again agreed, as on that day, twelve against the law being repealed, and only two for suspending it, which two were Messrs. Wheeler and Mawhorter.

March 8.—Forenoon attended as usual at the State House. The order of the day was concerning a dispute between our Western inhabitants and the Spaniards about trading down their river, as they call it. Mr. Brackenridge spoke long upon it; finally the report was postponed. Mr. Lilly and I affixed the seal to five laws.

March 10.—In the forenoon attended at the State House. The House got through with the bill they left unfinished yesterday. Mr. Lilly and I affixed the seal to five more laws, among which was one co-operating with the State of Massachusetts Bay, agreeable to the articles of confederation, in apprehending the proclaimed rebels, Daniel Shay, Luke Day, Adam Wheeler, and Eli Parsons.

March 12.—Afternoon attended the State House, and after the House adjourned about fourteen of us spent the evening at the tavern opposite.

March 13.—Forenoon attended at the State House. The report was read for receiving three-fourths in certificates, and one-fourth of the money made in 1781—money due for land before the year 1776. The question was put, shall the report be adopted, and it was adopted.

March 15.—Forenoon, attended at the State House. Mr. Lilly and I affixed the seal to three laws, among them was the laying out a road through this State, from the waters of the Potomac, to the Ohio. In the afternoon, took a ride on horseback. My son Robert returned from James Hockley's, being sent yesterday by several members of the Assembly, begging Mr. Hockley to come down to the House, as the incorporation of the bank is to come up to-morrow.

March 16.—Forenoon, attended at the Assembly. The order of the day was the bill to revive the incorporation of the bank. Two blanks were filled up in the bill; the first, with fourteen years in the room of an unlimited time; the second, was $2,000,000, in place of $10,000,000. The number of members for passing this bill were 35, and against its passing, 31. In the afternoon took a ride with my wife in chair down to the meadows, afterwards went with Mr. Fitzsimmons, Mr. A. Hunt, and his son Pearson, to Eberhart's slaughter house in Eighth street, to look at my large steer, Ned, that was killed yesterday.

St. Patrick's Day, in the morning. Jacob Hiltzheimer and Timothy Matlack, weighed the great steer killed by Mr. Eberhart (five years old):

		Pounds.
Fore quarters	406	
" "	399	
		805
Hind quarters	284	
" "	276	
		560
Neat beef,		1365
Hide,	156	
Tallow,	83	
Head and heart,	63½	
Feet,	34	
Belly,	36	
Feck.	33½	406
Whole weight exclusive of entrails,		1771

Height on the rump, 18 hands wanting only 4 inches.
" on the shoulder 17 hands 1⅜ inches

	Feet.	*Inches*
In girth round the body close to the forelegs,	8	4
" " at the navel,	8	7
" " across the hips in a straight line,	2	4
In length from the nose to the end of the tail,	16	10
" " from the forehead to rump,	9	5
Head,	2	5¾

Weighed and measured in presence of

TIMOTHY MATLACK.

Marmaduke Cooper's steer, also 5 years old, slaughtered on the same day, measured by Mr. Cooper, was 17 hands and 1 inch high on the shoulder and 00 feet 00 inches round the girth behind the forelegs.

	Pounds.	
Fore quarters, ...	380	
" "	378	758
Hind quarters, ...	263	
" "	262	525
Neat beef, ...		1283
Hide, ...	150	
Tallow, ...	102	
Head and heart, ...	64½	
Feet, ...	34	
Belly, ...	27	
Feck, ...	33	410½
Whole weight exclusive of the entrails, ...		1693½

Mr. Cooper's steer was uncommonly high before and low and light made behind.

TIMOTHY MATLACK.

The difference in length of these two cattle when hanging in the boxes was only one inch—Mr. Hiltzheimer's was longest.

The measurements of the cow were as follows:—

	Hands.	Inches.
In height on the rump, ...	15	3¼
" " on the back over the loins	15	2⅜
" " on the shoulder, ...	15	1½

	Feet.	Inches.
In length from the nose to the tail extended, ...	15	2
" " from the nose to the ridge of the horns, . . .	2	1½
" " from the forehead to the rump, ...	8	6
In girth round the body behind the forelegs, ...	8	1½
" " at the navel, ...	9	0½
" " across the hips in a straight line, ...	2	6¼
From the ground to the dewlap, ...	1	6

The same day we measured St. Patrick, a three-year old of the same blood, 15 hands 3½ inches on the shoulder. He was unruly and we could not measure him behind, without difficulty.

TIMOTHY MATLACK.

9

March 17.—Forenoon attended at the State House. Mr. Lilly and I affixed the seal to the law that passed the House yesterday; I mean the act to revive the incorporation of the bank of North America, which has been a bone of contention these two years in the House of Assembly, but it is now to be hoped that the minds of the people will be quiet for the term of fourteen years.

March 20.—In the forenoon attended at the State House. The bill for establishing a Court of Admiralty Session had its third reading and ordered to be engrossed. The Episcopal Academy of Philadelphia and the Academy of Washington County had the second reading and ordered to be transcribed and printed for public consideration.

March 21.—Forenoon attended at the State House, when Mr. George Clymer moved that the committee appointed a few days ago to bring in a bill to move the seat of government to Harrisburg be discharged, and they were discharged.

March 22.—Forenoon attended the Assembly. Several congregations were incorporated, and the bill had a third reading and ordered to be engrossed which gives John Fitch an exclusive right for fourteen years to make and vend steamboats.

March 23.—Forenoon attended at the State House. The bill was brought forward for receiving funded certificates for the arrearages due on lands before the Declaration of Independence, which was postponed until to-morrow.

March 24.—Forenoon attended as usual. The House elected as Delegate to Congress General John Armstrong, in the place of Charles Pettit, Esq., whose term expires next month. The bill passed the House which was before the House yesterday.

March 26.—In the afternoon attended at the State House. Several bills had a second reading, and one a third reading, which was to give Oliver Evans an exclusive right for fourteen years of making and vending machines to convey flour from the lower to the upper floor in mills.

March 28.—To day the House finished with the bill confirming to certain persons called Connecticut claimants the lands within the County of Luzerne. The House appointed the following gentlemen Commissioners for the purpose: General Peter Muhlenberg, Timothy Pickering, and Joseph Montgomery, at 20 shillings per day each. The Honorable Benjamin Franklin was added to the seven members elected 30th of December last to sit in the Federal Convention to be held in this city in May next, as the law will show that was enacted this day in his favor. Dined with General Mifflin and so did Captain N. Falkner; in the afternoon attended again at the Assembly.

March 29.—Forenoon attended at the State House and made a report that Mr. Lilly and I, being two of the committee appointed to affix the seal to such laws as might pass this session, had affixed the seal to thirty-nine. Received from the Speaker my order for thirty-eight days' pay, being £28 10s. The House adjourned to the first Tuesday in September next.

March 30.—Forenoon went with Townsend Whelen, Esq., and drank punch with William Will, Esq., son-in-Law to Mr. Metzger, who has married Will's daughter.

March 31.—Forenoon attended my people hauling earth out of my lot in Chestnut Street near Seventh. In the afternoon went to Mr. Samuel Nichols's, Sign of the Waggon, and there met John Lowne, and William Gray, referees appointed by the Court to settle a dispute about a quantity of hay between James Tulman and Aaron Middleton. Tulman's account says nine tons and Middleton's account says seven tons fourteen hundred. Middleton produced vouchers in support of his account, Mr. Tulman did not. Therefore we, the referees, gave in our verdict that the plaintiff Mr. Tulman, hath no cause of action.

April 1.—Before breakfast went to Gravel Hill with two of my daughters. Forenoon went to church, and in the afternoon Timothy Matlack came to see me concerning the settlement between A. Kintzing and Joseph Pemberton.

April 2.—Before breakfast went with two of my daughters in chair to the upper end of the town; there looked at some red cedar posts that came down the Delaware and were for sale.

April 5.—Went with Edward Shippen, Esq., and paid him £25, one year's rent, for Mr. Tilghman's lot, due the 14th of March last. In the afternoon went with my wife to Mr. Standley's place up the Ridge Road. Frederick Paul finished the garden fence to my lot in Chestnut Street a little west of Seventh Street.

April 7.—Before breakfast went with two of my daughters to Gravel Hill; in the afternoon took a ride with my wife around by the banks of Schuylkill, below the city.

April 9, Easter Monday.—Forenoon went to church. The Hon. Samuel Meredith breakfasted with me.

April 10.—Forenoon went with Mr. William Standley in my phaeton and pair of sorrel horses to his place on Ridge Road; in the afternoon took a ride with my wife to William Jones's meadow and brought home an elder bush and planted it in our garden.

April 11.—Before breakfast went with two of my daughters to Samuel Meredith's place, two miles from town, and dug up several roots and planted them in our garden in Chestnut Street. In afternoon went with my wife to Jonathan Roberts's.

April 12.—Forenoon went to Mr. Adgates' concert in the Reformed church in Race Street.

April 13.—I went down to the meadow on horseback; in the afternoon took a ride with my wife; in the forenoon she went with Mr. Bernard and my son Robert to look at George Gray's garden, at his ferry on Schuylkill.

April 15.—Forenoon went to church and after church went with General Mifflin to his place at the Falls and there dined, and so did Joseph and Matthew Hasserow, likewise a young English gentleman.

April 19.—After breakfast set out with my gray horse Camillus and chair toward Trenton ; at Pennypack bridge met four of the Street Commissioners, Boys, Geyer, Ozias, and Pancake, who were making a contract for a large quantity of building stone, 6 shillings a perch, to continue the common sewer this season in Fourth Street, beginning about 150 feet south of Market Street. They concluded to go with me to Trenton, so we sat out and dined at McElroy's, at Bristol. There I was informed by Mr. Bernard that Mr. Hunt and my son Thomas had gone to Philadelphia, upon which we all turned back.

April 20.—In the afternoon fire broke out at the steel furnace in Eighth Street, consumed the same, with the house, kitchen, and stables of the Widow Russ.

April 25.—After breakfast Jacob Barge and I went about the city to ask such gentlemen as have money due them from John Baker, Treasurer, for serving on juries, to give the same to the Widow Russ, to rebuild her house that was consumed by fire on Friday last, and met with very good success. In the evening Mr. Mayo, from Virginia, came to see me.

April 26.—Forenoon went about the city with Mr. Barge on the same business as yesterday. In the afternoon took a ride with Mr. Mayo in my chair to show him the meadows, and in the evening met at the Widow Matthews's, Isaac Howell, Esq., Mr. Barge, Mr. Weed, Mr. Keen, and Mr. William Gray, concerning the rebuilding the Widow Russ's house.

April 28.—In the afternoon went with my wife to Gravel Hill and Mr. Standley's place, called Primefield. Brought home a few cabbage plants, and planted them in our garden in Chestnut Street, made this spring.

May 1.—Forenoon took Mr. Peter Kraft in my chair and went to C. Breton's place, on the banks of Schuylkill, and there met the following gentlemen by appointment: N. Boys, A. Geyer, W.

Richards, S. McLane, P. Ozeas, Pancake, John Purdon, and Mr. Forbach, and dined there.

May 2.—In the afternoon went with my wife to Mr. Standley's, at Point; after we returned I went to the raising of the Widow Russ's house, which was built by subscription.

May 5.—In the afternoon went with my wife to Thomas Roberts's, about six miles, and drank tea there.

May 7.—In the afternoon went with my wife to Gravel Hill, from thence down toward Schuylkill, and to where the artillery battalion were exercising, of which General Mifflin was newly elected colonel, and this day commanded ·for the first time. In the evening met the fire company at the Widow Matthews's, close by, in Market Street.

May 12.—General Mifflin came to our house and told us that Rebecca Morris, who was married two days ago, set out to-day with her husband, Mr. Talbot, to his farm on the North River in York State.

May 13.—Went twice to church. This evening his Excellency General Washington arrived in the city from his seat in Virginia. The City Troop of horse received him at Mr. Gray's ferry; the artillery company saluted with firing their cannon.

May 22.—In the afternoon went with Mr. Jacob Barge to the burial of David Erwin's wife. She was taken from Robert Erwin's house in Sixth Street and buried in the Friends' graveyard.

May 26.—Dined at Robert Erwin's, Jr., who lately set up as tavern-keeper in Market Street, in the new house his uncle built last summer, with the following gentlemen: Matthew Clarkson, Edward Milnor, Richard Footman, John Cornman, Jacob Barge, Captain Langhaar, Joseph Rakestraw, Reynold Keen, and Robert Erwin, Sr.

May 28.—In the afternoon went with my wife to both meadows. General Pinckney had my pair of sorrel horses the first time.

June 4.—In the afternoon went with my wife to Mr. Standley's at

Primefield, and in the evening my wife and I went to Market Street gate, to see that great and good man, General Washington. We had a full view of him, and Major Jackson, who walked with him, but the number of people who followed him on all sides was astonishing. He had been out on the field to review Captain Samuel Miles with his troop of horse, the light infantry, and artillery. Mr. Samuel Vaughan, Captains Boys and Geyer, drank tea at our house.

June 5.—My wife and I went to Mr. Matthew Clarkson's and there drank tea with his wife, Mrs. Gross, Mrs. Barge, Mrs. Keppele, Mrs. Bache, Miss Clifton, and a very little English woman who came with Mrs. Bache.

June 8.—In the morning I called on General Pinckney, from South Carolina, and showed him two bay geldings, now in his carriage, six years old, the one belonging to Colonel Jacob Morgan the other to Colonel Thomas Forrest. The General agreed to take them, price £55 each.

June 14.—Took a ride with Mr. Meade to try a horse, and then went to Primefield with my wife and daughter Hannah.

June 16.—This afternoon Matthew Clarkson and Samuel Miles came to see me; we had punch and tea, which my wife and daughter provided.

June 17.—Went twice to church. Mr. Robert Morris went with General Washington in the General's carriage to dine at Mr. John Ross's country house over Schuylkill.

June 19.—Son Robert took his sister Kitty to Primefield early this morning, and in the afternoon went with my wife and daughter Hannah to Gravel Hill, and from thence to Mr. Standley's and drank tea there.

July 2.—In the afternoon met the Vestry at the German Reformed schoolhouse, and in the evening the fire company at Robert Erwin's, Jr., the Sign of the White Horse, in Market Street. Said

Erwin was this evening elected a member into our fire company, and he had this day a son born.

July 3.—Before breakfast went with my daughter Hannah to the meadow, where I found three men mowing the five-acre piece. On returning we met his Excellency General Washington taking a ride on horseback, only his coachman Giles with him.

July 4.—Went on horseback to Captain Von Heer's, at the Falls of Schuylkill, and there dined with the following: Andrew Geyer, Nathan Boys, William Richards, Samuel McLane, Peter Ozeas, Philip Pancake, Street Commissioners; Peter January, Peter Kraft, John Purdon, George Latimore, and —— Sneider. Coming home I overtook a company of gentlemen who had dined at Mrs. Keepler's country seat. Colonel Jacob Morgan asked me to go with him to Funk's Tavern. There had good punch, after which we parted and I got home before ten o'clock. My wife and two daughters, Kitty and Hannah, went to Primefield and there drank tea.

July 8.—Went twice to church to-day.

July 9.—Went to Gravel Hill in my chair and from thence to General Mifflin's at the Falls. Brought Mrs. Mifflin home in my chair. Went with my wife to William Jones's meadow.

July 11.—Yesterday Colonel Pickering was here and took his leave, as he was about setting out with his family for the town of Northumberland; I wished him success in all his undertakings, knowing him to be a gentleman and a very useful member of society.

July 14.—This evening watered the street before my houses in Seventh Street and our yard with the Amicable Fire Company engine.

July 17.—In the afternoon went with my wife, Matthew Clarkson, and Mr. and Mrs. Barge to Mr. Gray's ferry, where we saw the great improvements made in the garden, summer houses, and walks in the woods. General Washington and a number of other gentlemen of the present Convention came down to spend the afternoon.

July 21.—After breakfast set out with my wife and two youngest daughters to Thomas Clayton's, and arrived there a little before three o'clock.

July 22.—In the afternoon put my two horses in the wagon, and went with my wife and daughter Mary, Thomas Clayton and wife, to Caleb Brinton's, who is the talk of all Chester County, on account of his riches, industry, and nearness in making bargains. He received us kindly and treated us well. He lives in a neat house on a high hill, with a garden in the front inclosed with a stone wall, about 600 yards from the Brandywine, where General Washington and General Howe had an engagement in September of 1777. After tea we returned to Clayton's again.

July 23.—In the afternoon T. Clayton and my daughter Mary went on horseback to visit several of his neighbors, and I took a walk about the plantation.

July 24.—After dinner put my gray horse, Camillus, and one of my pair of sorrels in the wagon and with my wife and daughters set out for home. We took Marcus Hook in on our way, because we had not visited there before, and arrived at home about seven o'clock.

July 27.—Gave the Hon. General Pinckney, of South Carolina, and a member of the present Convention, a list of the best public houses on the road to Bethlehem, where he is going to visit for a few days, as the Convention has adjourned for ten days.

July 28.—After dinner went to see Colonel Sam Miles, who has been confined with a cut in the right hand these five weeks, and afterward took a ride with my wife.

July 31.—Went to Colonel Lewis Farmer, in Market Street, and had the Dutch woman I bought on the ship from Hamburg, bound for five years, commencing the 14th instant. Her freight to Ross Vaughan is £17.

August 3.—This evening John Gill, Esq., Colonel John Shee, and Colonel Bull drank tea with us; about the same time came from Trenton Mr. Abraham Hunt and his son Pearson, and they likewise sat down with us.

August 12.—Went to church fore and afternoon. My daughter Kitty went with Mr. William Standley to Oxford Church to hear Mr. Pilmore preach.

August 14.—This evening went with General Mifflin to the Society of Home Manufacture at the Academy in Fourth Street.

August 15.—Forenoon went with five of the Street Commissioners to Thompson's in Fourth Street and took a drink of punch. They told me that they expect to complete the common sewer along Fourth Street in four weeks. Spent the evening on Third Street with Messrs. Boys, Geyer, and Pancake.

August 18.—My son Thomas went back to Trenton. In the afternoon . went with my wife up Germantown Road and across by old Mrs. Lawrence's place, and across Frankford Road near the bridge, to Mr. Standley's place at Point.

August 19.—Went with my wife and daughter Hannah to Germantown to Mr. Stoneburner's, and with Mr. and Mrs. Barge went with William Rush and his wife in his wagon. The Rev. Mr. Pilmore came there from Whitemarsh Church, when we all dined.

August 28.—Last evening I was sent for by the Street Commissioners to Robert Erwin, Jrs'., tavern, and spent the evening with Messrs. Boys, Geyer, Richards, and Pancake; Isaac Howell and Joseph Wharton, Magistrates, and Mr. Connelly, Regulator.

August 29.—Was requested by the Street Commissioners to spend the evening with them at Robert Erwin's, where, besides the Commissioners, were Isaac Howell, William Pollard, Lewis Weiss, Alexander Todd, William Rush, and Robert McKnight, Magistrates ; James Pearson, Thomas Nevil, Gunning Bedford, and Mr. Connelly, Regulators.

September 1.—In the afternoon Leonard Stoneburner and his son-in-law, William Rush, came to see me and drank tea with us.

September 3.—In the afternoon went with my daughter Betsey to Mr. Pines's to instruct her in drawing. In the evening met the Amicable Fire Company at Robert Erwin's tavern.

September 4.—Had to breakfast with me General Mifflin and Captain Dayton, from Elizabethtown, N. J., both members of the Convention now sitting in this city. In the evening went with Leonard Stoneburner to Carpenters' Hall, and there met about ten members of the Society of Agriculture, and from thence we went to the Academy in Fourth Street and voted for managers of the Manufactory Society.

September 5.—Took a ride with the Hon. Mr. Langdon in his phaeton. In the afternoon met the Assembly at the State House, in the lower room, and adjourned to meet to-morrow at half past nine o'clock in the upper room, leaving the lower room as before to the gentlemen of the Convention.

September 6.—Forenoon met the Assembly at State House in the upper room. In the afternoon went with the Hon. Mr. Langdon, and Hon. Mr. Sherman down to the banks of the Schuylkill; had a drink of punch, and then took a small round home.

September 7.—Forenoon went to the State House as usual, and nothing of importance being offered, the House adjourned at twelve o'clock to meet to-morrow at half past nine. Dined at General Mifflin's with George Ross and Richard Willing.

September 8.—Attended at the State House; nothing of consequence; the House adjourned at twelve o'clock to meet on Monday. After dinner took my wife to Primefield and walked over to Mr. John Dickinson's place to look at some hay he offered me.

September 10.—In the afternoon attended at the State House, when five engrossed bills were signed by the Speaker.

September 12.—Went to the State House as usual, heard the cry of fire, and was informed that it was Mr. Corman's sugar-house, near the Bettering House. On my way home on horseback from

Gravel Hill my horse struck me in the face with his head and quite stunned me for several minutes.

September 15.—In the morning went with General Mifflin to see the camel in Shippen's Alley, between Walnut and Spruce Streets, and then attended at the State House. In the afternoon went with my wife to General Mifflin's, at the Falls of Schuylkill.

September 17.—In the forenoon gave Mr. John Luken a ride in my chair to Mr. Ogden's ferry. He told me that he had not been so far from his house in twelve months. In the afternoon attended at the State House, when a communication from our delegates in the Convention was read, informing the House that the Convention had adjourned, and that they would be ready to-morrow to lay before the House their proceedings of a four-months' session.

September 18.—Forenoon attended the Assembly as usual. Our delegates to the Convention brought into the Assembly the proceedings of said Convention, signed by thirty-nine members, as appears in the said Constitution read by our Speaker, Thomas Mifflin, to the House this day.

September 19.—Forenoon attended the Assembly, when the bill passed the House to erect part of Bedford County into a new county called Huntington.

September 22.—Forenoon attended the Assembly. The bill for regulating auctions and vendues was on its third reading. A considerable debate ensued—Fitzsimmons, Clymer, and Robinson on one side, Dr. Logan and Robert Whitehill on the other side. The bill was postponed.

September 23.—In the morning went with Townsend Whelen, Esq., to the burial of Joseph Ogden, Jr., who was shot through the leg last Thursday, his gun going off by accident in the boat in which he was with Benjamin Scull. The doctor cut off his leg, but could not save him, owing, as is said, to his losing too much blood. The corpse was taken from the Middle ferry to the Friends' graveyard, followed by an uncommon large number of people.

September 28.—Forenoon attended at the Assembly. It was proposed by Mr. George Clymer that this House recommend to the people to choose a convention as soon as convenient to deliberate and to confer on the Federal Constitution as recommended by the late honorable Convention. This occasioned a long debate; the speakers in favor of it were the two Clymers, Fitzsimmons, Robinson, and Brackenridge; against it, R. Whitehill and William Findlay. On the votes being taken forty-three were for it and nineteen against it: the House then adjourned to four o'clock in the afternoon. Half an hour after the Speaker took the chair, and the members' names being called, it was found that eighteen of those who had voted against the Convention stayed away, and one of the forty-three, Mr. Antes; Mr. Bower was the only one who appeared in the House that voted against it in the forenoon, therefore, no quorum being present, the House adjourned to half past nine to-morrow.

September 29.—Forenoon attended the Assembly. When the Speaker, General Mifflin, took the chair, two members were wanting to make a House, although there are twenty members about the city that stayed away on purpose that the public business—I mean that the report which recommended the choosing a Convention to confirm the late made Federal Constitution—should not be adopted, but the spectators, being much displeased that a matter of so much consequence should be left undone for want of two members, they hunted up two—Claymont and Miley—and brought them to the House. After that the report was adopted, which is that the several counties elect the same number of delegates to serve in Convention as they do for the Assembly the first Tuesday in November next, to meet in Philadelphia in two weeks after the House adjourns. I gave in a report that the Committee affixed the seal to twenty-six laws passed this session. Went with my wife to Gravel Hill and to Primefield.

October 2.—In the afternoon went with my wife to General Mifflin's place at the Falls. Mr. Falkner, Mr. Lyon, and Miss S. Morris came there in a light wagon.

October 3.—In the afternoon went to the Bettering House, east wing; there took part in a dinner with a large number of gentlemen given by George Gray, Hugh Roberts, and Peter Brown, County Commissioners, which was for the raising of the Court House at the corner of Sixth and Chestnut Streets.

October 5.—In the afternoon the following members of Assembly met at my house—Fitzsimmons, George Clymer, and William Robinson. Afterward went down town to take leave of the Hon. General Pinckney, who is setting out for South Carolina.

October 9.—In the afternoon went with my wife to both meadows, and after we returned I walked to the State House and gave in my vote for Assemblymen and other officers. Afterward went to young Robert Erwin's and had some punch and a lunch with William Gray, Andrew Bonner, William Govett, Stephen Paschal, Jr., Thomas Potts, and Mr. Bartholomew.

October 12.—Last night met at Patrick Byrns's, in Front near Walnut Street, the following gentleman: Jonathan Penrose, Esq., Wm. Pollard, Esq., and Richard Renshaw, arbitrators, reappointed by the Court, since the death of Joseph Pemberton, to settle the account between the Pemberton estate and Abraham Kintzing, formerly partners in meadow lands.

October 13.—After dinner had my gray horse Camillus, five years old, put in the chair; wife and I set out toward our place in New Jersey. Went up Old York Road fourteen miles, turned to the right for two miles, and arrived at Jonathan Balderstone's, in Montgomery County, where we were well received and stayed all night.

October 14.—After breakfast we set out, crossed the Delaware at Coryell's, went on to Ringold's Tavern, kept by Robeson, and there dined, and then went eleven miles further to my place, occupied by Isaiah Coles, in all fifty-one miles.

October 15.—After breakfast viewed the house on my place and agreed to lay out £13 in repairs on it. Left Coles's and went to our old friend Peter Gordon, Esq., in Hopewell.

October 16.—Mr. Gordon, his next neighbor, Nathaniel Stout, and myself went to see Mr. N. Stout, on the Hill, and observed that his house, barn, and fences were all in bad order. After Mr. Gordon and I returned to his house, we found Mr. Stout, from the Hill, there, waiting for us. We had some talk about exchanging places; he has about 240 acres and I 200 acres; he valued his at £1200, and I mine at £700. The difference was more than I would give, so we parted.

October 17.—After breakfast left Mr. Gordon's and went to Mr. Ralph Phillips's, in Maidenhead. Colonel Joseph Phillips called and spent the evening with us.

October 18.—Mr. R. Phillips, his wife and little daughter, my wife, and I set out to Princeton and Scudder's Mill.

October 19.—After breakfast we left Mr. Phillips's and came to Mr. Abraham Hunt's, in Trenton. Mr. Hunt had gone to Philadelphia, but we were well received by Mrs. Hunt. Mrs. Mayo, her brother and sister, DeHart, were there and on their way to Richmond, in Virginia. At all the different places we were exceedingly well treated. I went down to Lamberton to see my son Thomas, who returned with me to see his mother.

October 20.—After breakfast we left Trenton and went down to Lamberton, our son Thomas with us. We stayed at his shop a short time, and then went on to McEllroy's, in Bristol, and there dined. We reached home before dark.

October 22.—In the afternoon the General Assembly met, but not enough members present to make a House.

October 24.—In the morning went with General Mifflin to his place at the Falls, called at Mr. Standley's place, and dined at the General's.

After dinner we came to town and went to the State House, and, forty-six members being present, the General was chosen Speaker.

October 25.—Attended at the State House in the forenoon. P. Z. Lloyd and J. Shallus were rechosen Clerk and Assistant Clerk yesterday; to-day James Martin was chosen Sergeant-at-Arms in the place of Nicholas Weaver, and Joseph Fry, Doorkeeper.

October 26.—Attended at the State House in the forenoon, and in the afternoon went to the meadows with my wife.

October 27.—After breakfast went with General Mifflin to the State House, and in the afternoon the General's sister-in-law, S. Morris, came to my house in chair for my wife and I to go up to his place at the Falls, which we did, and drank tea there. My wife and I returned; they remained.

October 29.—In the afternoon attended at the State House. At midnight heard the cry of fire. Found that it was an old building on the east side of Third Street between Market and Chestnut Streets, next to the Harp and Crown Tavern.

October 31.—In the afternoon attended at the State House as usual, where was elected by Council and Assembly his Excellency Benjamin Franklin, President of the State, and the Hon. Peter Muhlenberg, Vice President. In the afternoon went with my wife to Primefield.

November 3.—Forenoon attended the Assembly. The House having no business on their file, and Tuesday next being the day for electing members to serve in a State Convention which is to meet in this city on the third Tuesday in the present month, according to law, the House adjourned to next Wednesday. Went with my wife to the meadows, and on our way down we saw a small frame house on Fifth Street near South, which was consumed by fire this forenoon.

November 6.—This day was the election for five delegates to serve in the State Convention, viz., Thomas McKean, James Wilson, Benjamin Rush, George Latimer, and Hilary Baker. In the evening I went with Mr. Pickering, Samuel Miles, and Matthew Clarkson from my house to the Agriculture Society at Carpenters' Hall.

November 7.—Forenoon went to the committee room and there was met by the members of the Grand Committee on Claims, and in the afternoon attended the Assembly.

November 8.—Forenoon attended as usual at the State House. Had to dine with me the following gentlemen: Honorable Thomas Mifflin, Richard Peters, Richard Thomas, Townsend Whelen, Mr. Clingan, Mr. Davison, Mr. Schott, and Colonel Pickering, all members of the present Assembly except the last mentioned. At five o'clock I met again the Grand Committee, and at seven o'clock fifteen of the members at Hasall's Tavern, to name the Delegates for Congress to be elected to-morrow. Armstrong, Irwin, Meredith, and Bingham, who are in Congress now, and Wayne, to take the place of St. Clair, whose time is up.

November 9.—Forenoon attended the House of Assembly, and afternoon met the Committee of Claims.

November 10.—Forenoon attended the State House, in the afternoon went with my wife to Mr. Standley's place and afterward to General Mifflin's at the Falls, where we drank tea and returned home.

November 11.—Forenoon went to church, then took Thomas Clingan in my chair and went to General Mifflin's, where we dined with the following gentlemen: George Clymer, Richard Willing, Thomas Clingan, J. Paul Schott, members of Assembly, and Colonels Brodhead and Pickering.

November 12.—Forenoon met the Grand Committee of Claims at the State House, and afternoon the Assembly.

November 13.—Forenoon attended the Assembly, and in the afternoon met the Grand Committee of Claims.

November 15.—Forenoon attended the Assembly, and afternoon met the Grand Committee at the State House in the committee room.

10

November 16.—Forenoon attended the Assembly, and made three reports, on John Penn, Jr., and John Penn's memorial on Colonel Mentges, for an allowance for services done to the State, and on Devereux Smith's sufferings as Magistrate. The Luzerne Bill had its second reading. The speakers in its favor were Messrs. Fitzsimmons, Lewis, G. Clymer, Peters, and Robinson; against it Messrs. McLane and Findlay.

November 20.—Forenoon attended the Assembly. Dined at Erwin's Tavern with the following gentlemen : General Mifflin, Richard Peters, Richard Willing, Samuel Evans, Townsend Whelen, William Lewis, John Paul Schott, Richard Thomas, and Francis Johnson, all members of Assembly except the latter.

November 21.—Forenoon attended the Assembly. The State Convention met yesterday afternoon in the upper room in the State House, but only thirty-eight members appearing, they adjourned until this afternoon.

November 22.—Attended the Assembly both fore and afternoon. The Luzerne Bill was before the House all day and did not get through with it. We had a very warm debate about an amendment of Mr. Findlay's. Messrs. Lewis, Clymer, Fitzsimmons, and Peters spoke against it; but, after all, the amendment was adopted.

November 23.—Forenoon attended the Assembly. The Luzerne Bill was brought up again and postponed, in order to examine at the bar of the House the three Commissioners of that county concerning the disposition of the people with regard to the law the House passed last March. The Commissioners were Colonels Pickering, Montgomery, and Balliet. In the afternoon met the Committee of Claims at the State House; after that I went to see Mr. J. Barge.

November 24.—Forenoon attended the Assembly. The Luzerne Bill came up again, and after debating all the morning on it, part of it was committed, and the House adjourned to meet at half past nine o'clock on Monday morning.

November 25.—Forenoon attended church, and then went with my wife to General Mifflin's, at the Falls, and there dined; after dinner Mr. Hockley and Robert Hiltzheimer came in.

November 28.—Attended the House of Assembly twice. In the afternoon the Luzerne Bill, that occasioned such long debates, and indeed, sometimes confusion, was brought up again and finally postponed. I wish this may not renew the trouble in that county.

November 29.—Forenoon attended the Assembly. Mr. Findlay called up the Luzerne Bill that was postponed yesterday, in order to amend the clause he introduced last Thursday, by striking out the words " Legal Representatives," and insert " Heirs and Assigns," but it was negatived. Therefore this bill, which is a supplement to an act passed last March concerning the Connecticut claimants, notwithstanding so many attempts have been made to get it through the House, remains on the file unfinished. The House adjourned to meet on the 19th day of February next.

November 30.—Forenoon went to the State House and heard the debates in our State Convention. The speakers in favor of its adoption were Messrs. McKean, Wilson, Rush, Yates, and Hartley; against it, Messrs. R. Whitehill, Findlay, and Smilie.

December 2.—Went to church twice. Mr. Matthew Clarkson spent the evening with us.

December 4.—Went with Captain N. Falkner, in my chair, to William Lesher's in Germantown. Then I went out and brought to the house Leonard Stoneburner, a number of the inhabitants and landholders of Philadelphia County, to consult concerning the offering to cede a part of the county to the Federal Government for their residence and exclusive jurisdiction. Mr. Matthew Clarkson was called to the chair and Mr. William Hall made Secretary, and after some debate it was agreed that the question be put. The Chairman told the gentlemen present that those who are in favor of making Congress the offer should show their assent by holding up their

hands, which was done by all in the room.   A number of blank petitions were then handed to gentlemen residing in different parts of
the county to get them signed.   A number of gentlemen signed at
the table.

December 6.—Went to Gravel Hill on horseback.   This day the Depu-
ties of Delaware ratified the new Federal Constitution by a unani-
mous vote.

December 9.—Forenoon went to church ; in the afternoon Mr. Arndt,
a member of the Convention, and Mr. Afflick came to see me.   Two
of my daughters went to Oxford church.

December 12.—To-day our Convention ratified the Constitution of the
United States ; votes in its favor forty-six, against it twenty-three.

December 18.—In the afternoon Matthew Clarkson went with me in
my chair to Gravel Hill.   In the evening went to the Court House,
there supped with eighteen gentlemen, being invited by the Street
Commissioners, N. Boys, A. Geyer, P. Ozeas, P. Pancake, J. Jones,
and Hallowell.

December 20.—General Mifflin and Captain N. Falkner dined with us.

December 21.—At twelve o'clock went to Captain N. Falkner's in Race
Street and there dined ; then we set out in my chair with gray
horse Camillus and called on General Mifflin at the Falls.   The
General and his sister-in-law, S. Morris, in his phaeton with a pair
of young horses, set out with us toward his farm near Reading.   At
Vanderen's Hill he got stalled, and after some trouble I got his
horses and carriage up; after that they went very well for that day.
We arrived at Norrington, and stayed at Shannon's Tavern for the
night.

December 22.—Had breakfast and set out by eight o'clock.   The first
hill, which is near the town, the General's horses stopped again.
However they both got out of the carriage, and after some labor we
got them up and they went on very well until we reached the
Perkiomen Creek, when they refused again to pull.   A wagon with

four horses coming after us, the driver hitched two of his horses to the General's and hauled them up on the level. We then went on to Pottstown and there dined. There the General borrowed a horse of Colonel F. Nicholas, to put in the place of his worse horse ; at two o'clock crossed Schuylkill at the White Horse, went over Flying Hill, and arrived at the General's house about an hour after sunset.

December 24.—The General, Falkner, and I went to the town of Reading, and returned to his house to dinner.

December 25.—Christmas. We three went to Reading by invitation of General D. Brodhead and dined with him. There were nine at the table : Mr. C. Read, Mr. Dundass, Mr. D. Clymer, Mr. Moore, General Mifflin, Captain Falkner, and myself.

December 26.—In the forenoon the General, Falkner, and I went to see Jacob Kurtz, a new neighbor, in order to inspect his extraordinary barn, 100 feet long, with three thrashing floors over each other. In the afternoon the General and I drove to Reading.

December 27.—After breakfast Captain N. Falkner and I set out with my horse and chair from General Mifflin's. When we reached Pottstown we were called by Colonel Francis Nicholas, who insisted on our staying to dine with him, as he would have only a few friends, with all of whom he knew we are acquainted. We stayed and dined with Mr. Samuel Potts and three sons, Mr. Thomas Rutter, two sons and son-in-law Walker, and my son Robert. After dinner we were joined by Mr. Jesse Potts and a son of John Potts, just from Jersey. Captain Falkner and I lodged with our good friend, Colonel Nicholas.

December 28.—Colonel Nicholas, Captain Falkner, and I walked about a mile to Mr. James Hockley's, at Glassgow Iron Works, and breakfasted with him. We visited the forge, where I saw them make pig iron into bars. We dined with Mr. T. Rutter, eleven ladies of the Potts' and Rutter family, and seventeen gentlemen, all in one room. Captain Falkner and I went home with Colonel Nicholas, there supped and lodged.

December 29.—Took our leave of that generous man, Colonel Nicholas, went one mile, and breakfasted, according to promise, with Mr. Samuel Potts; then went on to Shannon's and there dined. We arrived at home half an hour after sunset.

December 30.—Snowing the greater part of the day, so stayed in the house all day.

1788.

January 1.—Forenoon went to church. In the evening met the Agricultural Society at Carpenters' Hall.

January 4.—Had to dine with me the following gentlemen: General Daniel Brodhead, of Reading; Colonel Francis Nicholas, of Pottstown; Dr. George Slough, of Lancaster; Captain Nathaniel Falkner, and Matthew Clarkson, Esq.

January 10.—Went to the burial of James Budden, from his house on Chestnut Street between Tenth and Eleventh, to the Church ground on Arch Street. Captain Miles's troop of light-horse, of which he was a member, paraded.

January 17.—Went to Ogden's Ferry and there met Richard Humphreys, Nathan Gibson, James Bartram, and Philip Price. Daniel Rundle was not well enough to attend. We were directed by order of Court of December 11th last to lay out a road from Market Street, to begin on west side of the Schuylkill to the County Line, to meet the road recently opened through Chester County. We proceeded along the course to Cobb's Creek, near which the present road crosses near John Sellers's mill. We dined at James Worrell's, where we met J. Ogden, John Sellers, Nathan Sellers, T. Harrison, and Jones. We returned home by Ogden's.

January 21.—Matthew Clarkson dined with me, after which we went to the State House to settle the estate of Alexander Russel.

While there, Mr. Powell, Miles, and Whelen desired me to remain to receive the votes for the officers to be elected for the Society for Encouraging Manufactures and Useful Arts. The following gentlemen were elected: Thomas Mifflin, President; David Rittenhouse, George Clymer, Samuel Miles, and Samuel Powel, Vice-Presidents; Joseph Hilborn, Treasurer; Dr. Casper Wister and J. B. McKean, Secretaries; John Wharton, John Wilcox, John King, Robert Hare, George Fox, H. Kammerer, Tench Coxe, William Rawle, William Brigham, William Robeson, M. Lewis, and Hillary Baker, Managers.

January 24.—This morning when our maid came down-stairs she found that the house had been robbed, an entrance having been effected through one of the windows. Closets and drawers were ransacked, and with the exception of a sword belonging to General Mifflin, but little of value was taken.

February 1.—Went to the burial of the daughter of Levi Hollingsworth, who was drowned while crossing Darby Creek in a sleigh. I walked with Thomas Morris to Friends' meeting house, corner Second and Market Streets, where William Savery and Nicholas Waln spoke. The corpse was then taken to Friends' ground on Arch Street. Drank tea with my wife and daughter at Matthew Clarkson's.

February 6.—Went down to the wharf to see the ice in the Delaware; there met Tench Francis, who came home with me and spent the evening.

February 13.—Daniel Rundle and I took a ride over Schuylkill to view the new road from William Hamilton's place to Cobb's Creek. We called at John Sellers's and dined there.

February 18.—Called to see Matthew Clarkson and there read in Dunlap's newspaper that Massachusetts had adopted the Federal Constitution on the 6th inst.

February 27.—General Dickinson, Townsend Whelen, and Timothy Matlack drank tea at my house.

February 29.—Breakfasted with me General Mifflin, S. Meredith, G. Wynkoop and Mr. Dubois, after which we went to the State House. In the afternoon went to the burial of the wife of William Richards in the meeting-house yard on Spruce Street.

March 2.—Visited General Mifflin at the Falls. We crossed the ice and walked to Richard Peters's place, where we dined.

March 4.—Attended the Assembly, and in the afternoon went to the burial of Mrs. John Lukens. Walked with Tench Francis.

March 6.—The House went into Committee of the Whole. Mr. Edward Tilghman appeared for the City Wardens, who are opposed to the bill vesting the rights of the Middle Ferry on Schuylkill to the subscribers for the building of a permanent bridge.

March 7.—Mr. Fisher, counsel for the bridge company, spoke for nearly two hours and a half in their behalf.

March 10.—After the Assembly adjourned, General Mifflin, Captain Falkner, and Colonel Mentges came home with me and drank tea.

March 15.—The memorial of Dr. William Smith was read concerning the College, on which a long debate ensued, when it was finally decided that a committee be chosen by ballot next Tuesday to consider it.

March 17.—A remarkably fine day for St. Patrick to come to town. In the Assembly this afternoon the report amending the penal laws was debated and agreed to.

March 28.—In the House the bill for the gradual abolition of slavery was on its third reading. After dinner I went to Mr. Erwin's and drank a glass of wine with General Mifflin and his cousin, Warner Mifflin, who attended the Assembly with other Friends to urge the passage of the bill. The House met again in the afternoon and the bill was passed.

March 29.—General Mifflin and Dr. William Smith breakfasted with me. The Assembly adjourned to September next.

March 30.—Forenoon went to church, after which I took Colonel Irwin, of the Assembly, in my chair and went to General Mifflin's at the Falls, where we dined with James Morris, Colonel Thomas Craig, Collison Reed, John F. ¡Mifflin, Daniel Mifflin, Colonel Francis Mentges, and Dr. William Smith.

March 31.—James Wilson, Esq., is to rent my house at Southwest corner Seventh and Market Streets at £ 75 per annum.

April 17.—General Mifflin with Susannah Morris in his chair, and I with Captain Falkner, attended the burial of John Vanderin at Friends' ground, Germantown, where Nicholas Waln spoke. We returned to the General's for dinner, after which Edward Milnor and his son-in-law, Donaldson, called and we all went down to the Schuylkill to see the fishermen haul in their net with shad. I brought two fine ones home with me.

April 19.—My wife went to market for the first time in six weeks, owing to her illness. General Mifflin dined with us, after which he set out for the Falls.

May 6.—Samuel Meredith drank tea at my house, after which we attended a meeting of the Society of Agriculture.

May 10.—Went to Mr. John Penn's stables by request to value his pair of carriage horses and also a saddle horse. He told me that Mrs. Penn and he would set out for England in a few days, and that young John started the 30th of last month.

May 22.—I rode out to Cunningham's Centre House to hear the famous Jemima Wilkinson preach, and in the room where formerly a billiard table stood I saw and heard her. She spoke much in the New England dialect. She appeared to be about twenty-five years of age, her hair was dressed like that of a man, and she wore a black gown after the fashion of church ministers.

June 4.—Took James Wilson, Esq., in my chair to the Falls and there breakfasted with General Mifflin, agreeably to his invitation. John F. Mifflin, Dr. Redman, Captain Zeigler, and an English gentleman on his travels were present. At two o'clock dined with Captain N. Falkner on Race Street, with General Mifflin, Captain Samuel Morris, Charles Biddle, Josiah Hewes, and William Hall.

July 4.—The Federal procession of to-day was in honor of the ratification of the Constitution of the United States. I was busy superintending the horses and carriages on the way to Mr. Hamilton's at Bush Hill.

July 6.—Went to church twice. The Rev. Mr. Schneider, of Albany, New York, preached an excellent Federal sermon in the morning.

July 7.—Met the Church Vestry at the schoolhouse, and after the meeting Mr. Daniel Sutter took four of us home with him and prepared a bowl of good punch.

August 3.—I left to-day with my wife, daughter Betsey, and Mrs. Barge, in a light wagon, for a two weeks journey through the country.

August 17.—Returned home with my family after visiting Lancaster, Wright's Ferry, Lititz, Ephrata, Reading, Allentown, Bethlehem, Christian's Spring, Nazareth, and Easton.

September 2.—Attended a meeting of the Agricultural Society and reported the result of my experiment in planting twenty grains of Cape wheat in my garden.

September 6.—Forenoon attended the Assembly, and in the afternoon went with a number of members to Mr. Hollingsworth's store to see the model of Rumsey's waterworks set in motion by steam.

September 25.—After the Assembly adjourned, had to dine with me. General Mifflin, Richard Peters, D. Whelen, Mr. Edward Troxler, with Colonel Pickering, Matthew Clarkson, and Captain Falkner. In the evening about twenty-five members met at Hassell's tavern to consult on the selection of two Senators to represent this State.

September 29.—From the State House a large number of members went to Hassell's tavern, when it was determined to run Robert Morris and William Maclay for Senators.

September 30.—Robert Morris and William Maclay were elected Senators. In Committee of the Whole, Oswald's memorial against the Judges, McKean, Atlee, and Rush, was under consideration. Mr. Lewis spoke in their favor and Mr. Findlay for Oswald.

October 3.—A long debate ensued on the resolution offered by George Clymer and another by Mr. Findlay. The latter was rejected and Mr. Clymer's adopted, which was that the charges of Oswald, the printer, were not proven, and therefore there was no ground for impeachment.

October 9.—Colonel Pickering breakfasted with me, after which I took him in my chair to Mr. Standley's and to Mr. Meredith's, close by.

November 1.—Attended the Assembly, and a quorum being present, the Clerk read the returns of the late election, after which we elected Richard Peters, Esq., our Speaker. Gerardus Wynkoop and I had the honor of conducting him to the chair, when he was qualified by General Mifflin.

November 3.—Attended at the State House, when the usual committees were appointed. I was reappointed Chairman of the Committee on Claims.

November 4.—Had to breakfast with me Major William Macpherson and J. Salter. Speaker Peters and General Mifflin called after breakfast and we all proceeded to the State House. After dinner took a ride with my wife to General Mifflin's at the Falls to see the alterations he is making to his house.

November 5.—The Assembly unanimously elected General Thomas Mifflin President of the State, and Mr. George Ross was elected, by a majority of twenty votes, Vice-President.

November 6.—After the House adjourned a number of the members went to Christ Church, where Bishop White read the service and Mr. Blackwell preached the sermon.

November 11.—Owing to the continued illness of the Speaker the House adjourned. From the State House walked down to the wharves and found them covered by water from Market Street to the drawbridge.

November 26.—His Excellency President Mifflin dined with me. Went to the State House and voted for eight Representatives to serve in the new Congress, viz., F. A. Muhlenberg, Henry Wynkoop, Thomas Hartley, George Clymer, Thomas Fitzsimmons, Peter Muhlenberg, Daniel Hiester, and Thomas Scott.

November 28.—My daughters had a frolic at home, his Excellency General Mifflin and several young men being present.

December 11.—Dined with General Mifflin at the Falls and the following gentlemen: George Ross, a French Colonel, Captain Samuel Morris, Captain Awl, Captain Falkner, Captain Simmons, Captain Joseph Anthony, William Hall, Joseph Rakestraw, Andrew Tybout, John Baker, Philip Wager, Leonard Jacoby, John Wharton, and Francis Mentges.

December 21.—Attended the burial of Andrew Doz at Fifth and Arch Streets; walked with Thomas Fitzsimmons.

December 26.—After dinner went to the Lutheran schoolhouse and there met the German Society. They elected me one of their Vice-Presidents. From thence went to Colonel Farmer's house on Market Street to supper. About twenty-four gentlemen sat down, all Germans except William Rawle and Mr. Barton, two lawyers.

December 31.—Took Richard Peters, Esq., to Weed's ferry and saw him safely over, when I returned home.

1789.

January 7.—Went to the State House and voted for ten Presidential Electors, who are to meet next month in Reading.

January 9.—Dined at Captain Falkner's on Race Street, with General Mifflin, President; George Ross, Vice-President; Richard Willing, Samuel Miles, Z. Potts, members of Council.

January 16.—After breakfast took my wife and daughter Hannah in sleigh to Matthew Clarkson's, at Germantown.

January 17.—Went down to the wharves and found the ice fast, and was told this is the second time this season.

January 24.—Put my horses in the sleigh and called for John Luken, Robert Erwin, Sr., and Joseph Rakestraw. We drove along the banks of the Schuylkill to Mr. Briton's at the sign of the Swan, there dined, and reached home before dark. Mr. Luken had been laid up with the gout for a long time.

January 31.—Snow fell last night and this morning and is nine inches deep. Went with General Mifflin and my daughter Elizabeth in my sleigh to his house at the Falls of Schuylkill. Returned to town with John Mifflin, his sister, the Widow Archer, in his sleigh, and his brother Joseph's daughter in mine.

February 1.—Took my wife and daughter in my sleigh to Mr. Clarkson's at Germantown; there met Michael Hillegas and daughter, Joseph Anthony, Jr., and wife. Mr. Hillegas returned in my sleigh, the weather exceedingly cold at the time.

February 2.—Very cold. In the afternoon called for Mr. Barge, when we proceeded to the burial of John Wister at Friends' ground, [Germantown] just back of his garden. He was eighty-one years old; came from near Heidelberg, Germany, sixty years ago, as he told me this day one week ago, at which time I spent above an hour at his house, talking about our own country.

February 3.—The ice is fast in the river for the third time this season. Went to the State House in the afternoon, but no quorum present. Then took my wife and two youngest daughters a sleigh ride along the Schuylkill. Attended a meeting of the Agricultural Society at Carpenters' Hall.

February 4.—Went to the State House, but for want of four members no business was done.

February 5.—A quorum present; accordingly, the House proceeded to business.

February 8.—Peter Trexler, Conrad Ihrie, and Stephen Balliet, members of the Assembly from Northampton County, went with me in my sleigh to Hon. Richard Peters's, Speaker of the Assembly, at Belmont, where we dined.

February 9.—Met in the Assembly Room; no debate, only petitions and reports read. From there went to Hassler's tavern, where the city members and the Speaker met to discuss the bill for incorporating the city.

February 10.—We passed a bill that enables aliens to purchase and hold real estate in this Commonwealth until January 1, 1792, at which date the act expires.

February 14.—Forenoon attend the House. At noon set out from my house with President Mifflin and General Neville for the Falls, to dine with nineteen members of the Assembly. Dr. William Smith, formerly of the College; the President of the German Society; , Kennedy, of the Land Office; Colonel Mentges, and Mr. Harris were also present.

February 19.—The bill for incorporating the city had its second reading and was ordered to be printed.

February 20.—Snow thirteen inches on a level; very cold.

February 21.—Attended the Assembly, when the bill to take off the tax on chairs and light wagons had a second reading. The debate was long, but when the question was taken a majority was in favor of it. After we adjourned I took Gerardus Wynkoop, J. Chapman, and a member from Bucks in my sleigh to President Mifflin's, at the Falls, where we dined with a number of gentleman.   ·

February 28.—Had to breakfast with me Dr. Gregg, Dr. Chapman, and Gerardus Wynkoop from Bucks County, Alexander Lowrey, General Neville, and Joseph Carson, after which we all went to the Assembly.

March 3.—Breakfasted with me Jonathan Roberts, of Montgomery, and Obadiah Gore, from Luzerne County. In the afternoon met the City Wardens and Street Commissioners at the State House concerning incorporating the city.

March 4.—Forenoon attended the Assembly. The bill passed a third reading and was ordered engrossed, restoring the College of Philadelphia to the trustees, provost, vice-provost, and masters of the Academy, an incorporated body prior to November 27, 1779.

March 6.—Weighed the steer raised by me, five years old last August, called St. Patrick—net meat, 1417 ℔s. He was killed by George Hassell and weighed in the presence of David Seckel, Tench Francis, Andrew Tybout, John Wharton, and William Govitt.

March 11.—The bill incorporating the city became a law.

March 13.—The report of the Committee on Ways and Means considered. Mr. Lewis spoke three hours in favor of repealing a part of the Funding Bill passed in March, 1785. In the afternoon the House heard Robert Wells on behalf of John Fitch, and Mr. Fisher is to be heard on Tuesday on behalf of Rumsey with regard to the steamboat privileges passed in March of 1787.

March 15.—On my way home from church this afternoon George Clymer called me to come in, where I found the following gentlemen seated around the table with wine before them: James Wilson, General P. Dickinson, Dr. Jones, Colonel Lambert Cadwalader, Mr. Clymer's two sons, and General Dickinson's son.

March 19.—By appointment about thirty members met to-night at the City Tavern and agreed to an address to the people at large to call a Convention for altering and amending our State Constitution.

March 22.—Went to the burial of William Shaw. His body was brought from Chester and buried from the house of Samuel Shaw on Market Street, in Friends' ground. Walked with William Turner.

March 26.—At 8 o'clock this evening my daughter Kitty was married to Jacob Cox by Bishop William White, in the presence of Thomas Mifflin, President of the State; Richard Peters, Speaker of the Assembly; Mr. Cox, his wife, son, and five daughters; Pearson Hunt, William Lawrence, Mrs. Clark, Robert Crozier, and all my family.

March 27.—My daughter and son-in-law set out for Maryland.

March 31.—Messrs. John Wilcox, Samuel Hodgdon, and Andrew Tybout, a committee appointed by the citizens of Middle Ward, waited on me to know whether I would serve as an Alderman of the city under the corporation if elected. Thanked them kindly and told them that I knew my abilities were not equal to the office, and therefore they must excuse my accepting. Met the officers of the German Society.

April 4.—Attended my men digging the garden in Chestnut Street.

April 7.—His Excellency Thomas Mifflin and Timothy Pickering breakfasted with me. In the afternoon went to the State House and voted for fifteen Aldermen to serve seven years.

April 12.—My daughter and son-in-law returned from Maryland.

April 20.—At Bristol (on my return home from Trenton) heard the great guns fire in Philadelphia to welcome his Excellency George Washington, President of the United States, from Wilmington. He dined at the City Tavern with the principal gentlemen of the city and members of the troop of light-horse. At night fireworks were exhibited at Market and Ninth Streets.

April 21.—About ten o'clock the President set out for New York with Colonel Humphrey and Charles Thomson. Captain Bingham, with part of his troop, followed, and at Frankford his Excellency thanked them and begged that they would turn back, as it was raining. Captain James Thompson with the County Troop went on further.

May 1.—With Messrs. Stoneburner and Hunt went to Robert Erwin, Jr.'s, and had some punch, after which I went on horseback over Schuylkill to Isaac Warner's Fish House and there dined with about forty gentlemen, among whom were George Ross, Benjamin Chew, the elder, Richard Peters, William Lewis, Jonathan Penrose, Josiah Hewes, I. Wheeler, and Tench Francis. It was their opening day.

May 7.—My wife, two youngest daughters, and myself drank tea with my son-in-law Cox at his house, Market and Fourth Streets.

May 12.—Breakfasted with General Mifflin, as did Colonel Mentges and a young Englishman named Lowe, who has been recommended by General Gates to General Mifflin.

May 22.—About two o'clock Lady Washington came to town, on her way to New York.

May 25.—Lady Washington and Mrs. Morris set out for New York to join their consorts.

May 27.—Joseph Ogden and I went in my chair to Robert Morris's place, called the Hills, where we valued all the stock and farming utensils for William Crouch, who was formerly overseer, but now rents the place.

May 29.—Tried two pair of horses in my phaeton—one pair for James Tilghman, Esq., the other for Mrs. Montgomery.

May 30.—Daniel Rundle, Joseph Ogden, Peter Dehaven, Richard Humphreys, and myself, a jury on road from Middle Ferry to the Darby Road, met on the ground. John Sellers ran two lines, a straight one, the other with an angle. We agreed to meet on Monday to determine the course.

June 5.—The road jury met, with John Sellers, who run for us another course. Afterward we went to George and Robert Gray's and had some punch in the garden.

June 15.—Went out to Crouch's at the Hills and brought home a little pig imported by Mr. Morris from the East Indies.

11

June 30.—Cut the barley of a single grain planted in my garden last September and counted the yield, 3900 grains. This appears to be beyond belief, but it is a truth.

July 7.—Cut the wheat of a single grain planted last September, and found the yield to be 2816 grains—Cape wheat.

July 14.—To-night attended the Agricultural Society at Çarpenters' Hall, twelve members present, and produced before the Society the several sorts of grain I raised in my garden, the product of a single grain.

August 29.—Attended the Assembly; in the afternoon went to Isaac Warner's Fish House and dined on turtle with Richard Peters, William Lewis, Reynold Keen, Colonel Patton, J. Wharton, F. Johnson, William Gray, and others, about thirty in all.

August 31.—Twenty-seven members of the House met at Hassell's to consult about calling a Convention in October to alter our Constitution.

September 4.—Met the Committee appointed by the House to view the young mulberry trees which had come up from the seed this spring, in the Ridge Woods belonging to N. Aspinwall.

September 5.—Went to Schuylkill Falls and dined with General Mifflin, Rev. N. Colin, Richard Peters, William Lewis, A. J. Dallas, Francis Johnson, and James Morris.

September 8.—Met the Committee to consider the petition for and against dividing Chester County. We gave a hearing to both parties and then agreed to make a verbal report to the House.

September 9.—Robert Lollar was elected by the House Register and Recorder for the County of Montgomery, vice F. A. Muhlenberg, resigned. The House then went into Committee of the Whole, Mr. Hoge in the chair, to consider the calling of a Convention.

September 15.—Attended the Assembly, when the report was adopted to call a Convention to meet in this city the fourth Tuesday in

November next. The petitioners were 10,682 in favor to 556 against calling it. My man Stephen planted in my Chestnut Street lot two rows of barley, two of speltz, two of red-bearded wheat, two of white-bearded wheat, two of red spring wheat, two white spring wheat, two of common red wheat, and four of Cape wheat, five grains in each row.

September 25.—The bill to divide Chester County was passed—the new part to be called Delaware County.

September 29.—Had to breakfast with me, General Mifflin and Messrs. Fowler, Atlee, and Davison.

September 30.—The House adjourned at noon—the members have been together forty-four days.

October 12.—This forenoon five wheelbarrow men were hung for killing a man in a house on Market Street near Broad.

October 15.—Helped to carry my neighbor, John Luken, to the Friends' graveyard.

October 21.—In the evening a Miss Brailsford, of South Carolina, was brought to my house. She was thrown out of her carriage on Seventh Street and very much injured. Doctors Jones, Rush, Shippen, Wister, and Dunlap are attending.

October 22.—The mother and sister of the injured lady remained at my house all night. About eleven o'clock Dr. Jones ordered her to be carried to her lodgings, at Hunter's, up Market Street, as they have no hope of her recovery.

October 23.—This morning I was informed that Miss Brailsford died last night.

October 24.—Three of my daughters, two sons, and myself attended the burial of Miss Brailsford to the Church ground in Arch Street. I walked with John Lawrence, and my two sons helped to carry the coffin.

October 26.—I attended the burial of the wife of Samuel Coates from northwest corner Front and Walnut Streets to the Friends' ground.

October 28.—Dined with William Lewis, Esq., at southwest corner Third and Walnut Streets, and the following gentlemen: Richard Peters, Francis Gurney, Lawrence Seckel, Richard Willing, and Frank Johnson. After dinner we went to the State House, but found only thirty-three delegates present.

November 2.—In the afternoon went to the State House. Fifty-five delegates present, who chose Richard Peters their Speaker, after which Thomas Mifflin, President of the State, administered to him three oaths, and then the Speaker qualified the delegates, which, with each delegate signing his name to each oath, made it late in the evening before adjournment.

November 5.—With Richard Peters and several members of the Assembly went to David Rittenhouse's and there looked through his telescope at the sun and observed a black spot on it.

November 11.—After breakfast attended the Assembly. The election of President and Vice-President, jointly with the Executive Council, being in order, Thomas Mifflin and George Ross were unanimously elected. We then proceeded to the Court House at Second and Market Streets, where they were proclaimed, and then returned to the State House. In the evening fireworks were exhibited opposite the President's house on Market Street.

November 13.—The House elected Christian Febiger Treasurer of the State, in the place of David Rittenhouse, resigned.

November 15.—Attended the funeral of Adam Geyer, but finding he was to be buried at Kingsessing, could not go, being unprepared for that distance.

November 24.—This day the Constitutional Convention met here. The Committee on Message for Council relative to the Health Officer met at State House, where attended Doctors Jones, Rush, and Hutchinson. They enlightened the Committee with regard to diseases brought here by ships from foreign countries, occasioned largely by stowing too many passengers in one vessel. They found on record that in 1729, there was an alarming sickness here, that in 1762, the yellow fever was in the city, and that in 1784, only by the stoppage of a vessel at the Pest House was a second epidemic averted.

November 26.—Last night a fire broke out in a house next door to the Bunch of Grapes Tavern, on Third Street, between Market and Arch Streets; a woman and two children were burned to death.

November 27.—Assembly went into Committee of the Whole, Mr. Wynkoop, in the chair. The amendments to the Constitution of the United States were under consideration; the first two articles postponed, the remaining ten adopted.

November 30.—The two articles postponed on 27th inst were debated at much length by Messrs. Peters, Rawle, and Kennedy, and again postponed.

December 10.—Went to the State House to listen to the members discuss the altering and amending the Constitution of the State—the speakers were James Wilson, William Lewis, David Redick, Addison, William Findlay, and John Smilie.

December 14.—Went with General Mifflin on horseback to Mr. Peters's, and thence to the General's place, about a mile distant; crossed the Schuylkill at Righter's Ferry, and rode to the Falls, where we dined. Returned to the city about dark.

December 19.—Dined with a number of gentlemen at General Mifflin's, on Market Street—William Findlay, General Watts, Rev. N. Colin, Charles Biddle, Dr. Hutchinson, and others.

December 25.—Attended Christ Church, with General Mifflin, George Ross, General Hand, General Irvine, and Hans Graff, of the Convention; the Rev. Dr. Smith preached.

December 26.—Met the German Society at the Lutheran schoolhouse; elected Hon. F. A. Muhlenberg president, and Peter Miller vice-president. About thirty members then went to Lewis Farmer's, on Market Street, and had supper, which broke up at eleven o'clock.

December 31.—Attended the Convention. The debate was whether Senators shall be chosen by the people or by electors, Mr. Wilson in favor of the people and Hare and Pickering against.

1790.

January 1.—From church went to Reading Howell's, on Fifth Street ; paid him 7 shillings 6 pence subscription for his map of this State, which he is now about completing.

January 6.—Went to the new Catholic Church of the Holy Trinity, at corner of Sixth and Spruce Streets, the foundation stone of which was layed in the summer of 1788. Shortly after being seated a gentleman came over to me and very politely asked me to take a pew nearer the altar, and took me to one in which was the Rev. Mr. Blackwell. When the collection plate was handed around, we put on a dollar each. In addition to the officiating priests there were twelve boys and fourteen girls, dressed in white, each with a candle. I counted ninety-eight candles burning.

January 12.—Attended the Agricultural Society at Carpenters' Hall, seventeen members present. I proposed Abraham Hunt, of Trenton, for membership.

January 13.—Met at Carpenters' Hall, Hon. T. Pickering, S. Miles, Robert Milligan, and William Rush, a committee of the Agricultural Society to examine the several claims for premiums of the Society.

January 26.—Twenty-one members of the Agricultural Society met at usual place to taste two parcels of cheese, one from Rhode Island the other from Massachusetts, the premium of the Society for that article being claimed. We awarded it to Rhode Island.

January 27.—General Mifflin and I went to John Duffield's on Front Street, and dined with General D. Brodhead, Dr. Glentworth, Dr. McKnight, of New York, John Taylor, and my son Robert. We were excellently entertained.

January 28.—Went on horseback to Metz's tavern, a mile below the city, and dined with Abraham Kintzing, William Rush, William Jones, Jonathan Penrose, William Trotter, Richard Renshaw, and others.

January 29.—Doctor McKnight, of New York, came to see me and conversed with my wife concerning her health. Doctor Gibson, who has been attending her, gives us great hopes of her recovery.

February 5.—A quorum of members of the Assembly being present, we met up-stairs in the State House, the Convention being in session on the first floor. With several members, went to the burial of Rev. Mr. Duffield, of the Pine Street Meeting — I walked with Richard Peters.

February 14.—My wife was very ill last night but is somewhat better to-day. General Mifflin called to see her.

' February 21.—Dined with General Mifflin and Anne Powell; Mrs. Mifflin ill and confined to her room. In the evening attended the Friends' meeting on Market Street and heard Scott, a New England man, preach to a full house. He was so much in earnest that he took off his coat and stood in his waistcoat; his discourse, however, was very good.

March 4.—My wife is so ill I did not attend the Assembly this afternoon. Colonel Pickering drank tea with us.

March 5.—Sat up with my wife all last night. This afternoon she became very ill and continued so to ten o'clock, when she became easier and rested fairly well. My daughter Hannah and I sat up, one on each side of her bed. Our friends are exceedingly kind.

March 6.—Remained at home all day, my wife very low.

March 7.—Sat up with my wife last night. Remained in the house all day. Nurse Elton came to wait on my wife.

March 9.—Attended within hearing of my wife, who was very low at three o'clock this morning. In the afternoon she became worse and at nine o'clock died, aged forty-nine years, nine months, three days.

March 11.—Snow fourteen inches deep. At five o'clock in the afternoon I was called to attend the funeral of my wife. My friends advised me to stay at home, but I had determined to go. President Mifflin took my arm and walked with me to the grave in Friends' graveyard, Fourth and Arch Streets. He likewise returned home with me, as did the Hon. Richard Peters. My faithful and beloved wife had a very long illness. It commenced on October 7, 1787, at the time we visited my farm in New Jersey. She then complained of a cold, which occasioned her to frequently cough, which gradually increased to the day of her death.

March 12.—Numbers of my friends called to see me, and Timothy Matlack remained all day.

March 16.—Am not feeling very well and kept my room all day, Mr. Barge, Peters, Pickering, Gurney, Paul, Vaux, and Rev. Dr. Smith called to see me.

March 17.—At the desire of several of my friends, attended the Assembly in the forenoon.

March 21.—After church called to see Matthew Clarkson, and was told he was very ill last night. Mr. Duffield and wife and Mr. Taylor and wife called to see me.

April 2.—Took a ride with General Mifflin to his place at the Falls of Schuylkill. He ordered his fisherman to give me a fine shad, which I took home for dinner.

April 5.—Started out for an early walk, and as I passed near General Mifflin's saw a number of people about his door; when on inquiry was told that a baby wrapped in a blanket was found on the steps.

April 9.—Went to my meadow and from there to the Upper Ferry, where Joseph Rakestraw and I had some punch. The Hon. Richard Peters came down the Schuylkill in his boat and joined us.

April 21.—In the afternoon went to the State House, and from there the members of Council and eight members of the Assembly, with our Speaker, Mr. Peters, proceeded to the house of Dr. Benjamin Franklin, who died last Saturday night, in the eighty-fifth year of his age. The body was conveyed to Christ Church ground on Arch Street. I never saw so many people attend a funeral before.

May 13.—Dined with General Mifflin and Miss Morris; Mrs. Mifflin still very ill. Later visited the lot purchased by the Executive Council of Colonel Patton, on Walnut Street near the Schuylkill, on which the Powder house is to be erected.

June 6.—Dined at Mr. Barge's. Perhaps the reader may wonder at my dining so often with this gentlemen and his wife, and perhaps some may call it sponging. This I abhor, and those who are acquainted with me will not charge me with it. They ask me more times than I can accept, and when I do it is for the sake of their good company. They are growing old—approaching seventy years—and have no children, are wealthy, very generous, and can well afford to entertain frequently a few of their select friends, of which they say I am one.

June 8.—Mr. and Mrs. Barge, my daughters, and self rode out to Harrowgate, where we drank tea, and then returned by Turner's Lane.

June 10.—Dined at Mr. Barge's with Margaret Chevalier. It was so cold we had to sit by the fire.

July 2.—Went to the funeral of Israel Whelen's daughter at Friends' ground, Fourth and Arch Streets. Walked with William Gray.

July 7.—This morning I applied to Samuel Lewis for a permit to have Mary Clayton, aged 40 years, buried in Friends' grave-yard, which he kindly granted after asking me a few questions. Thomas Fisher also signed it.

July 9.—Attended the burial of Isaac Melcher (whose body was brought from his farm in Horsham), at German Reformed ground.

July 10.—Took Mr. Barge in my chair, Mrs. Barge, Mrs. Whelen and the children in light wagon, and drove to the Widow Miller's, eleven miles, to breakfast. Mr. and Mrs. Barge go to Lancaster, and Mrs. Whelen and children to her father's, Mr. Downing.

July 17.—Attended the commencement at the Hall on Fourth Street, William Smith, Provost. In the afternoon the Indians from the South, about thirty in number, with Alexander McGilloray, arrived on their way to New York, to Congress.

July 27.—Called at General Mifflin's to inquire after his wife, who is very ill. Breakfasted with the General, the Widow Archer, and Jonathan Mifflin. Visited Mr. Barge, who has a bad attack of the gout. In the evening the members of the Assembly from the city met at Mr. Rawle's on public business—we remained to supper. Mr. Lewis did not meet us.

July 31.—Was present at the raising dinner of the high house on the north side of Market Street, between Fifth and Sixth Streets, belong-ing to Henry Seckel. A little way below the play-house, a table 100 feet long was prepared, around which collected fully 200 people, who had plenty to eat and drink. I took old Mr. Seckel home in my chair.

August 1.—Mrs. Mifflin, the wife of Thomas Mifflin, President of this State, died at nine o'clock A.M., after an illness of six months.

August 3.—At nine o'clock my daughter Molly and I went to the burial of Mrs. Mifflin, from her house in Market Street to the Friends' ground on Arch Street. Raining at the time.

August 4.—Took Captain Falkner in my chair to the Falls to see General Mifflin.

August 8.—This morning went to the Falls to inform General Mifflin that Mrs. Talbert with her baby and step-daughter had arrived last night from Albany, to visit her sister, Mrs. Mifflin, not knowing of her death.

August 23.—John Arndt, member of the State Convention from Northampton County, breakfasted with me. At ten o'clock attended the burial of Rev. Mr. Weinberg, pastor of the German Reformed Church on Race Street for about twenty-seven years.

August 26.—Met Messrs. Powell, Coxe, Fisher, Latimer, and Dunlap, a committee of the City Corporation, to consult about raising funds to erect the Federal [President's] House.

August 28.—Forenoon attended the Assembly; in the afternoon Mr. Barge and I went to the burial of Samuel Nicholas in Friend's ground, Arch Street.

September 2.—Attended the Assembly. At ten o'clock walked in procession from the State House to the Court House in High Street, the Corporation, the Convention, the Council, the Assembly and others, to hear the new Constitution proclaimed. At four o'clock I dined at the city Tavern with His Excellency the President of the United States, who arrived to-day from New York.

September 3.—Had to breakfast with me Messrs. Wynkoop, Rea, Chapman, and Johnson, of the Assembly, and Mr. Findlay of the Convention. Attended the Assembly, which adjourned after appointing a committee to ascertain whether the new Constitution proclaimed yesterday dissolves the Assembly.

September 4.—The committee, several judges and gentlemen of law, agreed that the Assembly was dissolved, and we accordingly dispersed.

September 7.—The Rev. Mr. Winckhouse was elected pastor of the German Reformed Church, in the place of the late Mr. Weinberg.

September 15.—Paid a man half a dollar for putting up the numbers to my house and lots on Market Street, Nos. 224, 226, 228, and 230.

September 20.—Went to the burial of Dr. Gerardus Clarkson, from his house on Spruce Street to St. Peter's Church yard. I walked with Philip Benezet.

September 22.—Visited General Brodhead and drank some old Hock, a wine I am very fond of. Mr. Tudor, of this city, and Mr. Horsfield from Bethlehem called.

September 23.—My son Robert had to dinner, General Daniel Brodhead, Thomas Bond, Harry Clymer, Mr. James, an Englishman, and Mr. Potter. After dinner came in Colonel E. Blaine, Dr. George Slough, and Richard Peters, Esq.

October 11.—Went to the Lutheran Church to hear the new organ, made by David Tanneberger of Lancaster County.

October 16.—Went over Schuylkill to Isaac Warner's Fish House and dined with S. Morris, Governor of the Company, F. A. Muhlenberg, Robert Morris, Samuel Powell, Richard Peters, Thomas Willing, Richard Willing, William Bingham, Francis Gurney, William Lewis, Tench Francis, and about forty more.

October 24.—After Church General Brodhead went with me in my chair to General Mifflin's place at the Falls to dinner. There were present six Seneca Indians, Complanter, Half Town, Great Tree, John, William, and James Huxhing, also Charles Biddle, Dr. Gregg, Z. Potts, Thomas Proctor, Dr. William Smith, Mr. Butler, and three strangers.

October 31.—At four o'clock this morning Hare's brew house was burned—the third time in twelve years.

November 7.—In the afternoon went to the burial of Isaac Pennington, from his house on Carpenter Street to Friends' graveyard on Arch Street.

November 9.—Went to the burial of Joseph Howell, in Church Alley, to Friends' ground.

November 10.—Planted some of the American Sugar Tree seed given by Henry Drinker to the Agricultural Society.

November 27.—This forenoon the Honorable, the President of the United States, George Washington, arrived here from his seat in Virginia, and proceeded to the house of Robert Morris on Market Street, provided for him by the city corporation.

November 29.—The Hon. F. Van Borckel came here from New York and put his five horses in my stable.

December 8.—The first meeting of the Assembly under the new Constitution was held yesterday. To-day William Bingham Esq. was chosen Speaker viva voce.

December 18.—Colonel Wadsworth, member of Congress from Connecticut, and his daughter, Mr. Trumbull and his daughter, and Mr. John Trumbull breakfasted with me at my house.

December 27.—This evening a member of the German Society waited on me and informed me that I have been elected their vice-president, and he was also requested to say, that the members desired that I would take supper with them. Accepting the invitation, we went to Geisse's tavern on Third Street between Market and Arch Streets, where I met about thirty members, with F. A. Muhlenberg, who had been re-elected president.

December 31.—Had to breakfast with me William Findlay, Thomas Lilly, William Macpherson, members of the House, and Michael Smyser, of the Senate.

1791.

January 8.—At 11 o'clock, the members of Congress and the Assembly attended a concert in the Lutheran Church, on Fourth Street. The President of the United States with his lady were present.

January 20.—Attended the Assembly. The House went into committee of the whole, Mr. Montgomery in the chair, to discuss the resolution that our Senators in Congress be instructed to oppose the Excise Bill now before that body.

January 23.—Went to the Falls [Schuylkill] with Governor Mifflin, and dined with Colonel Gunn, a Senator; General Jackson and Judge Burke, from Georgia, the two latter members of the House; State Senator Joseph Hiester and other gentlemen.

January 24.—In the afternoon attended the Assembly, and from thence went to Mr. Henry Hill's on Fourth Street, where we, with George Clymer and J. B. Bordley, a committee appointed by the Agricultural Society, reported adversely on the application of an anonymous person for the premiums advertised by the society.

January 26.—Met twenty-one members of the Assembly at Geisse's tavern, in Third Street, to discuss the subject of dividing the State into a number of districts for choosing eight members to represent the State in Congress.

January 30.—This afternoon attended the funeral of George Bryan, Esq., fourth judge of the Supreme Court, with a number of members of the Assembly.

February 7.—This evening Tench Francis called on me and requested that I accompany him to the State House (up-stairs) to organize a society for improving roads and inland navigation. There I met about twenty gentlemen, with Robert Morris in the chair. We ' agreed that a memorial be prepared and a copy sent to the Senate and House.

February 11.—Dined with Governor Mifflin, Judge Burke, M. C., Speaker William Bingham, Francis Gurney and a number of other gentlemen.

February 16.—General Neville, and Colonel Ritchie took breakfast with me. Attended the Assembly. In the evening met the Agricultural Society, at the new Dancing Academy in Chestnut between Sixth and Seventh Streets. Jacob Morgan, William Rush, and I went in the adjoining room and had some punch.

February 26.—Mr. Maclay, and McDowell, of the Assembly, and Mr. Barge called to see me. Dr. Jones attended me, as Dr. Kuhn buried his wife yesterday and could not come. I feel much better to-day.

March 17.—The bill granting £4000 for the defence of the frontier, with the Senate Amendment, was passed.

March 20.—Had to dine with me, Messrs. J. Carson, from Dauphin, D. Stewart, from Huntington ; O. Gore, from Luzerne and Colonel John Irvine, of Westmorland.

April 9.—Forenoon attended at the State House. By invitation went to Metz's tavern, below South Street, and there dined with Judge James Biddle, Daniel Clymer and other gentlemen.

April 12.—The Hon. Albert Gallatin, took breakfast with me, after which we attended at the State House.

April 13.—The Legislature adjourned to August 23d, next, and I received an order for my attendance as a member of the House for 128 days at 15s. per day.

April 21.—Dined at Governor Mifflin's with Mr. Casno, from Holland, General Brodhead, Colonel R. L. Hooper, Mr. Gallatin, Jonathan Mifflin, and others ; Colonel Clement Biddle came in afterwards.

May 29.—Went to church ; afterwards in my chair to the Falls, where I dined at Governor Mifflin's with Miss S. Morris, Ruth Potts, and two other ladies; Edward Fox, Colonel Oswald, Dr. Joseph Redman, young Mr. McClanahan and my son Robert. After dinner

drove over to Germantown to L. Stoneburner's, and on my way
home called at Bringhurst's. Between Bringhurst's and Philadelphia, I overtook and passed sixteen carriages; some disputed the
road with me but without success. My horse Camillus did not
choose to swallow the dust of other carriages.

June 2.—Jacob Krug, of Lancaster, breakfasted with me. Dined by
invitation of General Brodhead at Mr. Thompson's Indian Queen
on Fourth Street, with Governor Mifflin, his Secretary, Mr. Dallas,
Francis Johnson, David Kennedy, John Dunlap, James and Charles
Biddle, Sharpe Delaney, and several others.

June 19.—Mr. Barge and I went to the burial of Robert Roberts on
Market Street—his death was caused by drinking a draught of cold
water while overheated.

June 23.—Took Governor Mifflin with me in my chair to his place at
the Falls and had dinner, Mr. and Mrs. Barge, Mr. and Mrs. Otto,
Reuben Haines, Mr. Marbois, a French gentleman, and Israel
Whelen being present.

June 24.—With Captain Hysham went to burial of Dr. Jones, from
Mr. Clark's on Market Street to Friends' ground. Governor Mifflin
called at my house and over-persuaded me to accompany him and
family to Cape Henlopen. About noon we embarked on Captain
Michael Dorson's boat, at Church's Wharf—the Governor, his two
daughters, the widow Ritchie, a little girl named Maria, and John
Mease's daughter. At 4 o'clock we reached Marcus Hook and
anchored. We discovered that a chicken pie prepared at home for
our dinner had been left behind, which gave rise to many reflections.
At 9 P. M. we proceeded down the river.

June 26.—Below Reedy Island a gust coming on, we returned to the
island and anchored. After the gust we sailed for Port Penn, where
we landed and passed the night at Captain Reed's tavern. We
found the landlady neat and a good housekeeper.

June 27.—Wind N. W.; weighed anchor and proceeded down the bay.

The weather was squally, and the water so rough, that I was not able to keep on deck. Near the lighthouse we anchored for the night, it being too rough to go on shore.

June 28.—All went on shore. The captain walked with us to the house of Mrs. Fisher, in Pilottown, where we took lodgings. Breakfasted and at 11 o'clock I had a drink of good punch which put me to rights again after three days of sea-sickness. After dinner Samuel Rowland, who is 72 years old, took the Governor, the four girls and myself to the seashore, where our captain and his crew met us, and watched them make four hauls with a seine. We returned to Mrs. Fisher's, drank tea, and soon after I got into a very clean bed, and had an excellent night's rest.

June 29.—Early this morning went with two of Mr. Maule's sons to Lewestown Creek, fishing. After dinner walked to Lewestown and called on Mrs. Horsman, and drank tea with Colonel Hall and wife and George Hazard.

June 30.—The Governor, Major Mitchell and Daniel Rodney of Lewes went fishing in Captain Dorson's boat, but the water was so rough they did not return until late at night—minus any fish. Mr. Hazard and I, in two chairs, took the ladies a seven mile ride in the country. Returned to Mrs. Fisher's for dinner, after which I went to Lewes with Mr. Hazard and drank tea at Colonel Hall's.

July 1.—Dined at Daniel Rodney's, after which his younger brother walked with me to the lighthouse, through the deep sand. This building is of elegant stonework, almost square, and from the base to the top, where eight copper lamps hang, is 117 steps. The lamps are lighted every night and consume about sixty gallons of oil a month. What surprised me was a well fifty feet deep, in a sand hill, containing clear, cool and excellent water, of which I drank freely.

July 2.—Wind northeast, and cool. The Lewes gentlemen made up a party to visit Rehoboth Bay, to dine on oysters, which are un-

12

commonly large and fine flavor. In addition to the Governor's party were Mrs. Sykes, her daughter, her husband's sister, Mrs. Moore, Mrs. Rodney, Mrs. Bell, Mrs. Day, Colonel Hall, Dr. Hall, Dr. Neill, Major Mitchell, Mr. Rodney and George Hazard.

July 3.—Wind northeast, and so cold that we put on winter clothing. The Governor's party with George Hazard visited the seashore, where Captain Dorson seeing us came ashore, and accompanied us to Mrs. Fisher's to dinner.

July 4.—Wind northeast and cold; cannot set out for Philadelphia to-day. This being Independence Day, the Governor invited several of the neighbors to dine with him; after having drank some wine the conversation turned on the late war.

July 5.—The Governor and I breakfasted with Mr. Rowland (a Quaker) wife and daughter. Besides coffee and tea there was enough food on the table for six men besides us.

July 6.—Wind still northeast and cool. In the afternoon we all packed up and went aboard our vessel. The wind changing to west, we set sail for Philadelphia.

July 7.—In the afternoon anchored off a marsh near Cohansey Creek, when some of us went on shore. The Governor took his gun, but found no game. At 9 P. M. we got under way, a good south-westerly wind blowing.

July 8.—At seven o'clock this morning we arrived at South Street wharf.

July 17.—In the afternoon went to the burial of Timothy Matlack's wife, from his house on Front above Arch Street, to the graveyard on the west side of Fifth near Spruce Street. I walked with Andrew Geyer.

August 6.—Colonel Wadsworth, of Hartford, Connecticut, took break-fast with me and afterward looked at his lots to the west of Tenth Street.

August 7.—Mr. Barge and I went to the burial of Amos Foulke—a little rain at the time.

August 9.—Set out this afternoon for Bethlehem with my daughter Hannah, where I will leave her at school.

August 13.—At 8 o'clock went to church, where my daughter appeared in the new dress provided for her by the Sisters. Attended a love-feast in the afternoon, and after the service took leave of my child in her school room, and then left Bethlehem for Philadelphia.

August 18.—This evening fireworks were exhibited on Market Street, opposite the door of President Washington.

August 23.—Received a letter from Mr. Van Vleck, of the school at Bethlehem, that my daughter desires to return home, which agrees with one I also received from her.

August 24.—The Assembly met to-day—in the forenoon I attended.

August 28.—At night a fire broke out in Stable Lane, Spruce between Second and Third Streets and consumed Richard Waln's stable.

September 5.—This afternoon went to the President's house on Market Street and there dined with him and his lady, and four members of his family, besides the following members of the House: Hon. William Bingham, Speaker, Messrs. Wells, Gurney, Seckel, from the city; Macpherson, Lilly, Gardner, Tyson, Reed, Stewart, Hoge, Montgomery, Maclay, White, Findlay, Baird, Eyerly, Lerch, Mulhollan, Tannehill, and Peter Lloyd, our clerk. I cannot help remarking that President Washington is an unassuming, easy and sociable man, beloved by every person.

September 14.—In the afternoon Governor Mifflin, his two daughters, my daughter Molly and myself went to Gloucester Point. Went to Hassal's tavern in the evening, and met the following gentlemen who are interested in making a turnpike road from the city to Vanderen's Mill: Robert Morris, Samuel Powell, John Nixon, William Lewis, Walter Stewart, Rev. William Smith, Mr. Fischer and Tench Francis. Mr. Morris was chosen chairman, and Messrs.

Smith, Fisher, Francis and myself were appointed a committee to ascertain the expense of construction.

September 17.—I took Mr. Francis in my chair to view the road, from Vine Street to Vanderen's Mill, six miles, which it is proposed to turnpike.

September 19.—Dined with the Hon. William Bingham, as did also a number of members of the Assembly.

October 5.—The Governor called for me and I dined with him, James and Charles Biddle, John Collins, Ex-Governor Rhode Island, and Major Struben.

October 8.—After breakfast took a walk with the Governor to Mr. Rittenhouse's and to view some lots out Market Street. Attended the burial of Adam Cornman, at the Moravian ground on Vine Street.

October 12.—Met the Committee on erection of the house for the use of the President of the United States, at corner Ninth and Market Streets.

October 22.—Breakfasted with Governor Mifflin at the Falls and from thence we crossed at Righter's ferry to Jones's Lane on Lancaster road and to John Sellers's. He returned with us to the Black Horse where we dined. Returned and nighted with the Governor.

October 25.—At noon President Washington went to the Congress at corner Chestnut and Sixth Streets, and delivered his address— yesterday being the first day of meeting of the Second Congress.

October 29.—Had to breakfast with me Governor Mifflin and Mr. Coleman and Ege from Lancaster. The Governor and I went in my chair to the Falls, where we dined. James Biddle called, who returned home with me.

December 31.—General Lincoln, of Massachusetts, breakfasted with me. In the forenoon attended the Assembly ; in the evening met the German Society.

1792.

January 9.—In the forenoon met the Committee on the subject of dividing the county of Bedford.

January 10.—Attended in House, and met the Committee on Claims. In the evening went to meeting of the Society of Agriculture.

January 14.—Spent the evening at Robert Erwin's with J. Rakestraw, Tench Francis, John Lawrence, William Jones, and other friends.

January 15.—Dined at the Falls with the Governor, General Irvine, Judge Bryson, and Dr. Wilke, from Pittsburgh. The Governor returned to the city with me in my sleigh.

January 19.—Very cold. This afternoon took my three daughters and son Robert sleighing down to the widow Marshall's at the Point House.

January 25.—Attended the House. Miers Fisher argued two hours against the report of the Committee, that the prayer of Thomas Leiper for a canal on Crum Creek cannot be granted. In the afternoon R. Wills spoke in favor of the report.

January 26.—Took my daughters, Betsey and Hannah, with Mollie Ogden, in my sleigh and went down to the Point House. From there we crossed the Delaware on the ice, followed by Colonel Marsh in his sleigh, and drove to Sparks's tavern, where we had a quart of hot wine prepared by Betsey Marshall, who accompanied Colonel Marsh. On our return to the Point House we called for hot coffee, and here my horses ran off, but were caught without damaging the sleigh or injuring themselves.

January 27.—Leiper's report was again called up in the House, when Mr. Gallatin argued about an hour in favor of it, which he did in a masterly manner. The report was almost unanimously adopted.

January 28.—Took Mr. Gallatin and General Brodhead in my sleigh to Metz's and there dined with Robert Erwin, Tench Francis, J.

Rakestraw, William Jones, Andrew Tybout, J. Ash, Donaldson, R. Haines and Henry Miller.

February 14.—Dined at the Hon. William Bingham's, in his new well-furnished house on Third Street near Spruce, with the following gentlemen: Miers Fisher, B. Morgan, and other members of the Assembly.

February 20.—Dined at the Governor's on Market Street with F. A. and Peter Muhlenberg, J. Ross, Edward Bird, T. Craig and others.

March 12.—After roll-call, a motion prevailed that the House adjourn to four P. M., to enable the members to listen to the debate in Congress concerning the disputed election between Generals Wayne and Jackson of Georgia.

March 21.—No quorum present this afternoon, owing to so many of the members attending the Indian funeral from the Hotel on Chestnut Street to the Presbyterian ground on Arch Street.

March 27.—When I returned home this afternoon, I found Complanter's son, Jack, and other Indians at my house, who called to see me.

March 28.—Dined with the Hon. William Bingham and a number of members of the Assembly.

March 31.—Attended at the State House. Finished with the bill for the turnpike between Philadelphia and Lancaster. Had to breakfast John Sellers and H. Lloyd from Delaware County.

April 4.—Breakfasted with the Governor and so did Richard Wills, Francis Gurney, Joseph Rakestraw and General Irvine, after which we all went to the lot recently purchased at the corner of Ninth and Market Streets, on which to erect a house for the President.

April 10.—The Governor, Mr. Wills, Mr. Gurney, Rakestraw, Williams and myself went to the corner of Market and Ninth Streets, to select the site for the President's house and at the same time to notify the tenants to move immediately, as they had been warned some time ago. In the afternoon attended at the State House, when both houses adjourned, after sitting 127 days.

April 12.—Am troubled with a swollen face. In the afternoon had James Pearson, Thomas Nevell and W. Matlack regulate the lot at Ninth and Market Streets, Mr. Wills, Mr. Gurney, J. Rakestraw, and Williams present.

April 15.—Dined with Mr. Barge, as did Michael Keppele and Mr. Weidman. After dinner Mr. Barge and I took a ride to Gravel Hill.

April 17.—Andrew Clymer began to dig a cellar for the frame house General Brodhead is going to put up on Market Street.

April 18.—This afternoon Edward Wills and I attended the burial of the wife of B. Scull on Market Street.

April 19.—Set Michael Hogan, laborer, at work to take up a fence at the corner of Ninth and Market Streets, at £4 10s. per month.

April 20.—Attended at the President's house lot, and in the afternoon Mr. Barge and I went to Hoppel's, in Camptown, to see the large beef of Lawrence Seckel—live weight 2380 pounds, dressed 1494 pounds.

April 21.—My son Thomas had to dine at my house, Hon. Richard Peters, F. Johnson, Daniel Brodhead, Doctor Slough, Jacob Barge and Jacob Cox. ·After dinner, Francis Gurney, J. Rakestraw, and I staked off the cellar for the President's house.

April 23.—This morning set Michael Wartman digging and hauling the dirt out of the cellar for the President's house.

April 24.—With Mr. Barge went to the burial of Mr. Robson, a gentleman from Virginia, who was buried in the graveyard at the old chapel.

April 26.—Engaged Jacob Meyer to work at the President's house at £6 per month.

April 28.—Took Mr. Stoneburner in my chair to Robert Morris's stone quarry, to look at the stone.

April 29.—Went to Gravel Hill before breakfast. Dined at Mr. Barge's with Michael and Henry Keppele. Went to Church in the afternoon.

April 30.—Set out for Trenton to meet, according to appointment, Timothy Baker. Visited my friend Abraham Hunt there.

May 1.—Mr. Baker did not bring the whole amount of money and therefore did not give him the deed for the farm I sold him some time ago.

May 2.—Breakfasted with Mr. Hunt and then set out for home. Came down the west side of the river to Thomas Richie's. Stopped at the sign of General Washington, where Colonel Lambert Cadwalader overtook us and all dined together. Arrived at my house about 7 o'clock.

May 5.—My two men, Stephen and James, took my big steer to Mr. Penrose's hay scales, where it weighed 2104 lbs. We went to the ferry and drank coffee with George Emlen, R. Rundle, Mr. Clay, and Mr. Cox.

May 7.—At eight o'clock met at the President's house lot the Governor, Mr. Wills, Mr. Gurney, Mr. Rakestraw, and Taylor. Mr. Gurney, Taylor, and myself went to Morris's stone quarry to inspect the stone we are to use in the building.

May 10.—This afternoon Benjamin Taylor, mason, set the corner stone of the President's house. Governor Mifflin arranged it and gave the stone a stroke with the mason's hammer, and directed the hammer be put in the stone. Richard Wills, Francis Gurney, and myself, the three Commissioners, each gave the stone a knock. The Governor ordered sixteen dollars worth of drink, with bread and cheese, for the people present.

May 14.—Attended the public works. Colonel Williams and I went over Schuylkill to see William Hamilton, but did not find him at home.

May 16.—In the morning attended at the President's house, and in the afternoon went down to Metz's tavern and there dined with William Jones, who gave the dinner on account of the bricklayers raising his house on the south side of Market Street near Fifth, intended for his son Robert. The following gentlemen were present: R. Keen, Francis Johnson, James Ash, Israel Whelen, Colonel Williams, William Hall, William Gray, Joseph Gray, B. Scull, William Sheaff, Hugh Roberts, Nathan Boys and others. Colonel Williams and I left before dark and went to the building of the President's house.

May 18.—Attended at the President's house. Colonel Williams and I went up town for timber and bought a load of stone of Conrad Ott at 6 s. 6 d. per perch.

May 21.—B. Taylor and I went to Robert Morris's stone quarry to select some particular stone for the President's house.

May 22.—Attended at the works. Went to Governor Mifflin's at the Falls, dined with him and Susanna Morris and Blair McClanachen.

May 24.—Attended at the public works. Colonel Gurney, R. Wells and I went to Miller's to engage stone-cutters.

May 25.—Colonel Gurney and I went in my chair to David Rose's brick-kiln and agreed with him to deliver common brick at 32 s. 6 d. per 1000; stock brick at 100 s. per 1000, for the President's house. From there we went down to Colonel Williams's, at corner of Second and South Streets, and drank punch with him. He was married last night. In the evening went to the ferry and met Mayor Clarkson and R. Keen.

May 26.—Attended at the works. B. Taylor and I went in my chair to Ott's and bought stone; from thence to Robert Morris's quarry on the Schuylkill. Dined at old Mr. Robert Erwin's with R. Keen, John Baker, Israel Whelen, Edward Wells, William Gray, Charles Jervis and Andrew Tybout.

May 29.—Went to Morris's quarry and ordered more stone. Colonel Gurney and I went to Reynolds's brick yard and agreed with him to deliver at the President's house, as wanted, 20,000 stock bricks at £5 per 1000, and 400,000 common at 32s. 6d.

May 31.—Went to the quarry for more stone. My man Stephen and the President's man took three of his horses down to my meadow.

June 1.—Took Colonel Williams in my chair to the works and then called to see Colonel Gurney, who was taken ill yesterday.

June 6.—Early this morning took the Governor's daughter Fanny in my chair and drove to the Falls to breakfast. The Governor with his daughter Emily set out for Black Point.

June 7.—Went with Colonel Williams to John Reynold's and Alexander Miller's brick yards and bespoke a particular kind of brick for the President's house.

June 8.—My daughter Molly with Mr. Simons set out for New York in the stage.

June 15.—After breakfast the Governor and I, in my chair, visited several places, and afterwards drove to the Falls.

June 16.—My men hauled in the hay at Gravel Hill, and from thence I drove to George Ogden's at the upper ferry, and had some good punch.

June 19.—Breakfasted with the Governor, attended at the President's house and at noon Mr. Barge and I drove to the Governor's, at the Falls, where we dined.

June 24.—Went to church twice. Dined at Mr. Barge's with Michael Keppele, after which I gave my daughter Betsey and my grandson a ride.

June 28.—William Jones, Hutchinson, and myself dined at the Widow Marshall's, at the ferry.

June 29.—Mr. Barge went with me in my chair to Governor Mifflin's, at the Falls, where we dined with Mrs. Barge, Miss Rebecca Cox, my two daughters, Jacob Cox and wife, General Brodhead, Joseph Rakestraw, William Williams, Colonel Gurney, Robert Crozier, and my son Robert.

July 1.—Very warm. Before breakfast took a ride along the banks of the Schuylkill. Went to church and then dined with Mr. Barge. In the evening Mr. Barge and I in my chair, General Brodhead and a young man in his chair, drove to Breton's tavern on the Schuylkill, where we had some punch and wine.

July 2.—The carpenters are putting down the floor in the President's house.

July 4.—At noon went to the President's house and opened it to allow the gentlemen of the artillery to go in out of the rain, until they fired the salute of fifteen guns in honor of Independence day. Dined at home.

July 7.—Attended at the President's house and at six o'clock P. M., the carpenters, bricklayers, and stone-cutters were treated to a round of beef, ham, and punch, to celebrate the putting down of the first floor.

July 8.—Dined with Mr. Barge, after which, we drove down to George Weed's at Gray's Ferry and had some punch, and from thence to the Irish track Lane and home.

July 9.—Attended at the President's house. In the evening drove down to my meadow and to the ferry house, where I met the Governor and his daughters.

July 11.—The Governor and I in my chair drove to the Swedish Church to see the Rev. N. Collin. The President and his family set out on their journey.

July 13.—Breakfasted with the Governor and afterwards took him in my chair to several places where he had business. In the evening drove with Mr. Barge to my meadow and the ferry, where we met Colonel Gurney and Mr. Smith with his family.

July 14.—Owing to the rain on the 4th inst., the fireworks were exhibited to-night at the Potter's Field.

July 15.—Mr. Barge and I drove to Hesser's tavern and had some punch. On our way home we met Mr. Stoneburner and family returning from White Marsh Church, where Bishop White preached, who insisted on our going home with them to dinner.

July 20.—Drove down to Mrs. Marshall's, where Colonel Gurney met me and we had breakfast. We took Betsey Marshall and Ann Rowan with us, crossed the river to John Marshall's, ten miles, and directed him to send up the scaffold poles for the President's house. Dined in Haines's tavern in Woodbury, and arrived home at three o'clock.

July 31.—Attended at the building. Dined in town with the Governor, after which we went in my chair to his place at the Falls.

August 3.—Attended at the building. In the afternoon the Governor and his daughter, Emily, in his chair, Mr. Barge with me in mine, went to the Point House where we had coffee. Jonathan Penrose and wife joined us at the table.

August 7.—B. Taylor and I went to Ross's brick yard, concerning the stock bricks for the front of the President's house. In the evening drove to Point House, where I took a swim.

August 8.—Attended at the President's house. Dined at Mr. Barge's with the following gentlemen from Lancaster: General Hand, Adam Reigart, Andrew Graff, Abraham Witmer, and Thomas Boude.

August 9.—Had to breakfast with me Adam Reigart, Andrew Graff, Abraham Witmer, and Thomas Boude. At eight o'clock set out for Chester with Mr. Barge, Mrs. Grim from New York, and my three daughters, in a hired carriage.

August 11.—This morning went to D. Ross's brick yard with B. Taylor; afterwards with Colonel Williams to the old fort near the Swedish Church, after scaffold poles. Lost my pocket book with $35 in it.

August 15.—After breakfast set out for the seashore with Governor Mifflin and his two daughters with their maid. Dined at Bristol, where the Governor sent back his hired carriage—he took one of his daughters in his chair, and I took the other with her maid in mine. We nighted at Douglas's Tavern in Crosswix.

August 16.—We left Crosswix after breakfast for Monmouth, where we dined ; and from thence to Shaffto's, at the seashore, where the Governor took lodgings. I went to Chantlers and Harbert.

August 17.—Spent the day about my lodgings, and went twice into the salt water.

August 18.—Bathed twice to-day. I went in my chair over to the Hon. William Bingham's place to dinner (twelve miles) by invitation of Mrs. Bingham, who received me very kindly and made much of me. Mr. Bingham had not arrived from Philadelphia, but was expected hourly.

August 19.—The Governor came and dined with me—there were fourteen gentlemen at the table. After dinner we went to Green's, where Colonel Febiger, Mrs. Butler and John Wharton board, and where the Governor's daughters dined.

August 20.—William Jones and I went to where the Governor boards and breakfasted with him, after which we started for home. We dined at Monmouth, with Colonel Febiger and family, Mrs. Butler, Mrs. Duncan, and John Wharton. We all nighted at Douglas's in Crosswix, where we met Samuel Morris, Andrew Tybout, Joseph Donaldson, and Peter Brown, who set out for Trenton.

August 21.—After breakfast we set out for Bordentown, and from thence to Burlington, and dined at Hogland's. Crossed the ferry and drank coffee at the Sign of General Washington, and arrived home at 7.30 P.M.—two light wagons, three chairs and two servants on horseback. I led the way with my gray horse, Camillus.

August 22.—Attended at the President's house; dined with Governor Mifflin, and accompanied him to the Falls.

August 24.—The Governor and I in my chair went to several places about the city, and to D. Ross's brick yard. William Jones and I went to the Governor's place at the Falls, and there dined with Colonel Febiger and wife, General Butler's widow, Mrs. Duncan and John Wharton.

August 26.—Before breakfast took my daughter in chair to meadows and ferry house, and while we were there the chimney took fire. We stopped the flames before any damage was done to the house. Went to church twice, and gave my grandson a short ride.

August 28.—This afternoon the Governor and I in my chair went down to Gloucester Point gunning. Drank coffee at Mrs. Marshall's.

August 30.—Breakfasted with Governor Mifflin and Colonel William Williams. In the afternoon the Governor and I went down to · Gloucester Point gunning.

August 31.—At eleven o'clock I met at Robert Erwin's the following gentlemen, a jury of valuation : Joseph Rakestraw, John Wharton, William Van Phul, William Sheaff, John Harrison, Henry Keppele, Benjamin Davis, William Gray, Joseph Ogden, Peter Baynton and William Kinley. We valued for the Honorable Richard Peters 132 feet of ground where Mr. A. Markoe's house stands, in Market Street, 306 feet deep, £3150, which sum the State is to pay Mr. Peters in place of the lot the State sold, and likewise £220 for a thirty-three feet lot at the southeast corner of Market and Seventh Street from Schuylkill, and 306 feet deep. The gentlemen chose me their foreman.

September 1.—Before breakfast took Susanna Morris from Ann Powell's, in my chair, up to General Mifflin's place at the Falls.

September 5.—Mr. Mayo from Virginia breakfasted with me. Dined with the Governor and Reuben Haines.

September 7.—This afternoon gave the carpenters at work on the

President's house a lunch, on account of their putting down the second floor.

September 12.—Colonel Gurney and I went in my chair to the stonecutter's and to Ross's brick yard and notified them to attend at the President's house at twelve o'clock. Dined at Mr. Barge's with Peter Wager and wife, John Hubley, from Lancaster; Mr. Strepper, from New York; Mr. Bartow and Michael Keppele.

September 16.—Before breakfast Jacob Cox and wife drove to Gloucester Point with me. Went to church. I was informed that John Penn, ex-Governor, and his brother-in-law, Andrew Allen, arrived last night from England.

September 22.—Attended at the President's house. Dined at Jacob Meyers's on turtle soup, with Colonel William Williams, Joseph Rakestraw, William Jones, Jacob Barge, and Edward Laskey.

September 27.—Had my boy, Franz Peter Keaman bound by Colonel Lewis Farmer for four years and seven months, for which time I paid Mr. Bohlen £20 2s. od. Met the officers of the German Society.

September 30.—Went to church, after which Mr. Barge and I went to the Falls and dined with the Governor, Generals Harmer and Brodhead, Mr. Holker, Dr. Wilkey, a captain of the Federal army and Mr. Dallas.

October 8.—Visited the President's house. Dined with Mr. Barge and so did F. A. Muhlenberg and Mr. Weidman. In the afternoon Colonel Gurney and I went to John Reynolds's brick yard and ordered more bricks, and from thence to the meadow to feed my ox, when Colonel Pickering with two friends from New England came to see my cattle.

October 11.—This afternoon Mr. Ebert and wife and Mr. Levering and wife, from Bethlehem, drank tea with us. My daughter Betsey returned from New York where she has been visiting over a week.

October 19.—Dined at the Governor's with the Lancaster turnpike Commissioners, General Hand, Adam Reigert, Andrew Graff, Jacob Graff, A. Witmer and Thomas Boude, and Philip Wager and Captain Falkner, of this city.

October 25.—More bricks are needed for the President's house. Had a beefsteak dressed at the corner of Market and Ninth Streets, and supped with Mayor Matthew Clarkson, Tench Francis, Judge J. Biddle, Colonel Williams, Joseph Rakestraw and William Jones.

October 27.—Went to the President's house before breakfast. Set out for Trenton and arrived at Abraham Hunt's before sunset. At night my son Thomas was married to Miss Emley, a niece of Mr. Hunt's, by the Rev. Mr. Frazer; after the ceremony the company partook of a bountiful supper.

October 28.—Wilson and John Hunt, sons of Abraham, came with me to Philadelphia. At the sign of General Washington, dined with a Congressman from South Carolina, returning from a visit to Boston.

November 2.—Attended at the President's house, and toward evening we had a cut of beef and some punch on account of the carpenters finishing the third floor. Richard Wills, Colonel W. Williams, Joseph Rakestraw, E. Taylor, and William Preston were present. The journeymen carpenters had their lunch at their workshop.

November 5.—Took Mr. Dallas, the Governor's secretary, in my chair and drove down to the sign of the Buck, to view the road laid out from Bracton's gate across the fields to the road leading to State Island ferry, which new road meets the road at Simes's place, a little below King's, now Abraham Kintzing's. After our view we retuned to the Buck tavern, kept by Daniel Burchart, and had a cut of a round of beef and some punch. The Governor, Mr. Dallas, and I came home, and I dined with the former, as did Colonel Mentges.

November 6.—Attended at the President's house. About noon fifteen guns were fired at corner of Ninth and Market Streets, because the President delivered his address to Congress, which met yesterday.

November 13.—My son Thomas and his wife, from Trenton, came to visit me.

November 15.—I had to dine with me General Brodhead, Mr. and Mrs. Barge, Mr. and Mrs. Simons, Jacob Cox and wife, Moses Cox and daughter, Rebecca Hunt, Pearson Hunt and wife, Wilson Hunt; and after dinner Colonel Francis Gurney, Colonel William Williams, John Connelly, Mayor Clarkson, Judge James Biddle, Miss De Hart, Miss Spencer, Joseph Rakestraw, Michael Keppele, and William Jones. My friends called it a wedding supper for my son and his wife.

November 18.—Dined at Mr. Barge's with Michael Keppele, and in the afternoon went with Mr. Swanwick to the German Catholic chapel at the northwest corner Sixth and Spruce Streets. After the service I took a walk with Joseph Cowperthwaite, James Ash, and Captain Craig.

November 29.—Attended at the President's house. The carpenters began putting on the fourth floor, and we had for them a cut of beef and some punch.

December 1.—The carpenters put on the fourth floor and some rafters at the President's house. We had about one hundred and eighty people at the raising supper, with Mayor Clarkson, Judge James Biddle, Gunning Bedford, and Richard Wills.

December 3.—Spent part of the afternoon with the Governor, Albert Gallatin, Mr. Terrance, Mr. Bradford, Mr. Smilie, Secretary Dallas, and Colonel Gurney at the President's house. Went to the play with my daughters.

December 4.—Had to breakfast with me, Colonel Wadsworth, Mr. Gallatin, Mr. Bradford. Went to the State House; forty members present, and adjourned to ten o'clock to-morrow.

13

December 5.—Went to the State House, and Gerardus Wynkoop was chosen Speaker. Attended at the President's house.

December 7.—Went to my meadow, spent an hour at the President's house and from thence to the State House. Dined with Mr. Barge and Michael Keppele at the house of the latter's mother, corner of Fourth and Arch Streets.

December 12.—Dined at the Governor's with Messrs. Smith, and Smilie, State Senators ; Gerardus Wynkoop, Powers, Morton, Rhea, Gallatin, and Oliver, of the House; A. J. Dallas, Colonel Febiger, Dr. Hutchinson, and Mr. Swift.

December 14.—Attended at the House. The matter of electing a United States Senator came up, Mr. Hare in the chair. Debated until two o'clock; Messrs. Morgan, Forrest, and Evans for a concurrent vote ; Mr. Swanwick and Gallatin for a joint vote. Mr. Gallatin's argument was very forcible, and I think will prevail, as it did last year. In the afternoon attended at the President's house.

December 15.—Attended in my place in the House. It was ordered that a committee be appointed to bring in a bill to elect a Senator by a joint vote of both Houses.

December 18.—The Dauphin County contested election case was the order for the day. Mr. Brown the sitting member, Mr. King the contestant. The House proceeded to the election of a committee, as the law directs. *First*, all the members present were called and their names put down. *Second*, their names on a small piece of paper were rolled up and put in a box, shut up and shaken. Then the Clerk took them out one by one and put them into three boxes alternately, then shook each box, then took them out one by one alternately and handed them to the Speaker, who read them aloud and asked the parties, Mr. Brown, sitting member, and Mr. Potts, acting for Mr. King, if they had any objections to the number just called, and repeated the same until seventeen names were drawn.

No objections were made to any of the names. The Clerk then proceeded to take the remaining names out of the boxes and handed them to the Speaker, to see that no member had absented himself since the beginning of the investigation. Then the first drawn seventeen members was handed to each party, and a member appointed Mr. Forrest, when he and the parties withdrew into the Committee room, and each party struck off of the list four members, which reduced the committee to nine members, who were sworn by the Speaker, that they will faithfully and truly try the contested election between Mr. Brown and Mr. King, according to the evidence.

December 20.—In the afternoon attended at the President's house, when the committee appointed by the House came to inspect the building, to report how much money will be needed to complete it.

December 21.—Attended the House. Messrs. Paul, Chapman, Eyerly, Gallatin, Potts and Oliver, a committee appointed, visited the Hospital, and found it neat and clean in every department, much to their satisfaction. The managers present were Mr. Hewes, S. Coates, B. Wister, Mr. Barnes, Mr. McMurtrie, Mr. Perot, and Dr. Hutchinson.

December 25.—Breakfasted at the Point House, and afterward William Jones assisted me in calculating the number of bricks Alexander Miller delivered at the President's house.

December 26.—At one o'clock sixteen Indians and three squaws arrived from the westward and were received by the firing of cannon at the corner of Ninth and Market Streets. At eight o'clock P. M. went to H. Eppele's on Race Street and supped with fifty members of the German Society.

1793.

January 2.—After the House adjourned, I went to hear the members of Congress debate on the question of reducing the expenses of the War Department.

January 6.—William Jones and I finished the account of bricks delivered at the President's house: John Reynolds, 549,150; Alexander Miller, 446,400. David Ross's account is unfinished.

January 8.—No frost in the ground; saw a man plowing yesterday and to-day. In the evening the Committee of the House met the Mayor and Aldermen at the Court House, corner Fifth and Chestnut Streets, with regard to alterations in the incorporation act.

January 9.—With three of my daughters and some of their friends, went on the roof of the small building Southwest corner Ninth and Market Streets and saw Mr. Blanchard take his aerial flight out of the prison yard. Cannon fired from daylight to the time of his departure, between ten and eleven o'clock A. M. In the evening I was informed that he landed a few miles from Woodbury, forty-six minutes after ascending.

January 15.—At one o'clock the doors of the new play house at Northwest corner Sixth and Chestnut Streets were opened to receive the Governor and Legislature, and we found the beautiful building nearly ready for performances.

January 19.—Colonel Wadsworth breakfasted with me. Dined with the President of the United States on Market Street, with our Speaker and eighteen members of the House. I cannot help remarking the ease and great sociability shown to all by the President.

February 9.—Dennis Whelen, Esq., took breakfast with me. Dined with Samuel Powell, Speaker of the Senate, and Messrs. Hoge, Montgomery, Hanna, Smith, Hiester, Eddie, Thomas, Scott, Gallatin, Evans, Johns, Shoemaker, Postmaster-General Pickering,

Treasurer Febiger, Alderman Hillary Baker, and William Findlay, M. C.

February 10.—John Hannum, of Chester County, breakfasted with me. Dined with Mr. Barge, and afterwards attended the funeral of the wife of William Standley. Walked with Israel Whelen.

February 14.—The report relating to the State Bank and Loan Office was debated the whole forenoon. Dined at the Governor's with Messrs. Brown, Hanna, Gardner, Hockley, Cannon, Kemmerer, Will, Falkner, Benezet, and Willets. After dinner William Jones and I took a sleigh ride.

February 15.—Had to breakfast with me Mr. Brown, Hanna, Stewart, Turner and Gardner. Went to the State House, and the State Bank report came up again. After a long debate the vote was taken, 43 for the bank, 19 against it.

February 19.—Attended the State House. Dined at the Governor's with General Irvine, M. Slough, Abraham Witmer, J. Fisher, Messrs. Stokley, Allen, Williamson and Ellicot.

February 21.—The report of the Committee on Ways and Means was read a second time, which among other things provides £5000 to finish the President's house. Mr. Gallatin made a motion to strike out that item and to insert, "to sell the house and lot in its present state." This unreasonable motion did not prevail, and £2500 were added to the £5000.

February 26.—After dinner walked down toward the President's house, when the Governor called me into his house, where I found about eight gentlemen of my acquaintance drinking wine. The Governor and D. Bradford came home with me and drank coffee.

February 28.—Attended at the State House. At high noon the members of the House met the Senate, when both elected Albert Gallatin, by 45 votes, United States Senator. Henry Miller received 35, and General St. Clair and General William Irvine each one vote.

March 15.—Attended at the State House. Mr. Swanwick brought the news that the King of France was beheaded, January 21st last.

March 16.—Mrs. Matthew Clarkson visited my family and I took her home in the evening. Stayed to supper with Mr. Clarkson and their youngest son.

March 24.—Benjamin R. Morgan and I went to Colonel Forrest's in Germantown, and dined with Colonel Lutz, Mr. Grosskopf, Stoneburner, Dr. Leib and his brother, and Mr. Budd.

April 2.—John Swanwick, Jacob Morgan, and Charles Biddle were elected by the House directors of the Bank of Pennsylvania, and Kearney Wharton, Samuel Fox, and William Miller by the Senate.

April 5.—The Report of the Ways and Means Committee was debated. Mr. Gallatin spoke for near three hours against the item relating to the Comptroller General. The next House will miss him very much, as he will take his seat in the Senate of the United States at their next meeting.

April 7.—Dined at the Barge's with Michael Keppele and young Sergeant. Received news that war was actually declared between France and England.

April 11.—Attended at the State House twice; the House adjourned to August 27th next, after being in session one hundred and twenty-nine days.

April 17.—John Hubley, Mr. Barge and I breakfasted at the Governor's house with his daughter Fanny; he was taken ill during the night and could not come into the city this morning. In the afternoon went to the corner of Market and Thirteenth Streets to see Mr. Ricketts perform some extraordinary feats of horsemanship. We paid one dollar each.

April 19.—Had to breakfast with me Lewis Farmer, and George Frey from Middletown. The President's mare was taken to my meadow.

April 24.—Before breakfast my son William and daughter Hannah took a ride in chair; after dinner Mr. and Mrs. Barge and my three daughters went to Rickett's circus. General Washington and family were present.

April 30—Took two men down to the meadow to repair fence and gate-posts, and while there President Washington came to see his mare. Went to buy some wood, but found none at the wharves.

May 1.—Dined with Mr. Barge, after which we drove to Gravel Hill and the Point House, to see the French man-of-war come up the Delaware.

May 2.—Went down to the old fort this afternoon, and as the French frigate passed they fired fifteen guns; our people fired the same number at Market Street wharf.

May 4.—Allen McLane took breakfast with me. Drove to the meadow and found that the President's mare had been taken away and his two horses left in her place.

May 8.—Sent two men with my large ox, five years and nearly five months old, to Penrose's, and he weighed 2576 pounds, which is 220 pounds more than this date last year.

May 21.— Waited on Mrs. Horry agreeably to a letter received yesterday from her brother Charles Cotesworth Pinckney, of Charleston, S. C., concerning a pair of horses.

May 23.—In the afternoon met R. Wills and Francis Gurney, Commissioners of the President's house, Mr. Williams and Mr. Rakestraw, carpenters, and William Preston, bricklayer. Although we have but £300 in our hands, we concluded to go on with the building, run up the chimneys, and finish covering the roof.

May 31.—Visited the farm of William West, in Delaware county, and dined with his family. He showed me his new barn, and his fields of clover, which are very fine. On my return home stopped to see Richard Willing.

June 20.—Mr. Barge and I attended the burial of William Jones's wife in Friends' ground.

June 25.—Dined at Mr. Barge's with Mr. Oster, French Consul at Richmond, and Mr. Bohlen, of this city.

June 28.—Tench Francis and I went to see Robert Erwin, who is very ill, and to Robert Morris's place to see the people at work on the canal.

June 30.—Joseph Wharton informed me of the death of Robert Erwin this afternoon.

July 1.—Went to the burial of Robert Erwin from his house on Sixth Street to Christ Church yard on Second street, where he was laid alongside of his wife. I walked with Mr. Barge and my sons Robert and Thomas.

July 4.—Breakfasted at the Governor's with Mr. Barge and his friend Bernhard, of Easton, Mr. Bird and Mr. Wright. Dined at Mr. Barge's, and drank the following toasts : "The Fourth of July, 1776;" "the President ;" "the Governor." At night, with my daughters and friends, viewed the fireworks on Market Street from the roof of the President's house kitchen.

July 13.—As Mr. Barge and I were going to the meadow we were called in to Charles Jarvis's place by Colonel Williams and Captain Boys to drink punch. Afterward we went to see Mr. Ricketts ride, and saw there the President and his lady.

July 20.—Mr. Barge and I called at C. Jarvis's place and dined under the trees with Colonel Williams, Nathan Boys, J. Commons, Dr. Hutchinson, N. Handlin, Harrison, Dr. B. Duffield, Hill, Brown and others.

July 24.—At ten o'clock set out in the Bethlehem stage with Moses Cox and daughter, Mrs. William Simmons, and my two daughters; Dr. Redman and daughter we took up at Turner's Lane. Dined at Morris's, stopped at Craig's, and at Rothrock's nighted.

July 25.—Left Rothrock's and proceeded to Brown's to breakfast. Arrived at Bethlehem after twelve o'clock and dined at the Sun Inn. F. Beutel, the farmer of the Moravian estates, called to see me and we walked over some of the farms, the care of which he has had since 1788.

July 26.—To-day we visited the Girls' school, Sisters' House and other buildings, and at night went to the place of worship.

July 27.—Rode to Easton to breakfast, visited John Bernet's mill on the Bushkill, built by Evans of the Brandywine Mills, thence to Nazareth to dinner and then returned to Bethlehem.

July 28.—Went to church three times; Mr. Van Vleck preached in English, Mr. Klingsohr in German. Bishop Ettwein called to see me at the Tavern.

July 29.—Left Bethlehem early in the morning and reached my house at 8.30 P. M., without a change of horses.

August 1.—This afternoon Matthew Clarkson and I took a ride in my chair to Robert Morris's place to see Arthur Donaldson at work on the canal. Afterwards called at George Ogden's ferry and had punch.

August 7.—Mr. and Mrs. Barge breakfasted with me, after which I took them with my daughter Hannah, ten miles up the Lancaster road to the Widow Miller's, to see the new turnpike, about a mile of which is laid. It is twenty-four feet wide and covered with small broken stones eighteen inches in depth. Philip Sheapp is superintendent. Tench Francis drove out to meet us and at four o'clock we set out for home.

August 9.—With my daughter Hannah visited the Governor and drank tea with Miss S. Morris. The Governor, Miss Morris, and A. Powell will set out for Black Point to-morrow.

August 12.—Had to breakfast with me, Hon. Albert Gallatin, United States Senator elect. Dined with Mr. Barge.

August 15.—Took Abraham Hunt and his sons Pearson and Wilson to Mr. Morris's, where Arthur Donaldson is working on the canal. The rain of last night carried away the dam which he has been erecting for the past three weeks.

August 22.—While riding to Gravel Hill and just above the one mile stone my mare fell, and although I tried to slip off, she fell on me and I was much hurt. Two wagoners took me to Mr. Wister's, when Jonathan Mifflin driving by in his chair, took me home.

August 25.—This evening I was able to hop down stairs to tea. My friends continue to call on me.

August 27.—Attended at the State House and found a quorum of the members present. William Wister called to see me.

August 29.—Met the Assembly, and at one o'clock the House and Senate met, when the Governor read his address. Then the House adjourned to Monday next, owing to the infectious disorder in the city, and in particular as a young man by the name of Fry is lying dead at the west end of the State House.

August 30.—Dined at Mr. Barge's with Mr. Morton, from Cumberland County. A small cannon was hauled through the streets and constantly discharged, as the flashing of gunpowder is thought will prevent the spreading of the disorder. This is being done by order of Governor Mifflin and Mayor Clarkson.

September 5.—The Assembly adjourned to-day after a short session of ten days, owing to the disorder in the city—the members would not remain any longer.

September 11.—About nine o'clock to-night my daughter Betsey was taken suddenly ill.

September 12.—This forenoon Dr. Rush called to see my sick daughter, and informed me she has the disorder. He ordered eight ounces of blood to be taken from her, and left some powders.

September 14.—My daughter is mending.

September 17.—My daughter Betsy came down stairs, seemingly very well.

September 18.—Called at Matthew Clarkson's on Arch Street, and observed a hearse with a blind horse in the Friends' graveyard. Was informed that it was stationed there daily to receive the corpses of those who belong to the Society; that carriers were not allowed to handle the coffins, owing to the infection. I have also observed a one-horse covered cart with a bed in it, which is used to convey the sick to Bush Hill Hospital. Mr. Clarkson and I called to see Mr. Cox at Gray's Ferry, who moved from his house on Spruce Street, being afraid of the fever.

September 19.—Took my daughter Betsey in my chair for a short ride, the first time since her illness. The disorder is not abating, but appearing in every part of the city, and the Doctors say that there are two sorts of fever—the yellow, which nearly always results fatally, and the other which is not so mortal, since Dr. Rush's mode of treating it—purging and bleeding—is followed. Very few people are seen on the streets, and they keep at a safe distance from each other, and if it is known that you have sickness in your family or among your neighbors you are avoided. One-half of our citizens have gone to the country.

September 20.—The burials in the Potter's Field were upwards of twenty to-day. My daughter Betsey was bled again to-day.

September 22.—After breakfast drove to the meadow. The number of burials in the Potter's Field was greater to-day than yesterday.

September 23.—Took a ride to the Blue Bell and returned by State Island ferry. Drove to Gravel Hill and from thence to see what progress had been made on the canal.

September 25.—Obtained an order from the Committee to move a colored woman from General Daniel Brodhead's to Bush Hill Hospital. When the cart came to the door she refused to go, so I got two colored men who led her away, to their home.

September 29.—Dined with Mr. Barge and young Sergeant, after which we drove to Mr. Cox's near Gray's Ferry.

October 1.—To-day nine bodies were buried from Bush Hill Hospital (the first) in the new ground on the public square between Race and Vine Streets, opposite the new road between Bush Hill and the place lately John Penn's, now the property of Joseph Depart, a French baron.

October 2.—By request of Mayor Clarkson the water engines began sprinkling the streets of the city, as it is said that a moist atmosphere will add to the general health. I have been watering Seventh Street from Market to half way to Chestnut Street, for the past ten days. Mr. Joseph Ogden, who superintends the burial of the poor, told me that 517 bodies have been interred in the Potter's Field between August 19 and October 1.

October 9.—I was very sick last night, but feel better this morning. Received a notice of my election as a member of the House of Representatives—the eighth time.

October 14.—Mr. Barge and I drove to Germantown and found the place filled with Philadelphians, who were very anxious to hear the news from the city. They kept at a distance when informed that we had just left the city. We called at Leonard Stoneburner's, who was not at home, but his daughters brought us some cake and wine to the garden. On our way home dined at the Widow Lesher's, afterward went to see the canal works.

October 15.—Mr. and Mrs. Barge have gone to the Widow Miller's, eleven miles from the city until the disorder abates.

October 16.—Took my two daughters a ride, and found it cold enough for an overcoat. Only three applications were made to the Committee for the removal of sick to Bush Hill.

October 17.—My two daughters took a ride. Mr. Kerr of the Committee told me that there were only two applications to-day for the removal of the sick, the average heretofore being thirty to forty daily. The burials as reported by Joseph Ogden, however, do not lessen much.

October 18.—Drove to the sign of the Buck, and dined with Mr. and Mrs. Barge, Captain Sadder, his wife, and her mother, and young Dr. Glentworth and mother.

October 22.—Cloudy but no rain, though it was never more wished for or wanted. Drove to Gravel Hill and Middle Ferry, and two of my daughters took a ride to Hugh Roberts's on Shippen's Lane.

October 26.—Visited Mr. and Mrs. Barge at the Widow Miller's, who were pleased to see me and to learn of the decrease in the number of deaths in the city. Israel Whelen, Mr. Thomas, an Englishman, and Mr. Downing dined with us.

October 28.—Mr. Barge returned to town with Peter Kuhn and Henry Sheaff. Mr. William Hall, Joseph Rakestraw and William Gray called to see me.

November 3.—Before breakfast went up the Lancaster Road to the nine mile stone, and met the Hon. William Bingham, from the Southward, who is on the way to his family at Black Point. He will not enter the city.

November 9.—Many citizens are returning from the country. Mr. Barge and I dined with the Governor at his house on Market Street, to which he returned last night.

November 15.—Mr. Barge and I became security for £2000, for my son Thomas Hiltzheimer, who was appointed by Governor Mifflin, Vendue officer.

November 24.—My son William, who has been sick, was somewhat easier this morning—his complaint will not permit him to lie down. Dined at Mr. Barge's with Mr. and Mrs. Myer, Mr. Sontag, William Sergeant, and Nicola.

November. 25.—The Asthma troubles my son William, who is very poorly and for some time back has been consumptive. Dr. Wister is attending him.

November 28.—Between one and two o'clock this morning I went into the room of my son William, and sat beside him. After a while he urged me to go to bed, but I said "how can I when I see and hear you in such distress," but after again requesting me to retire I left his room and he directed the nurse to close the door that I might not be disturbed. I could not sleep and about five o'clock hearing everything quiet re-entered his room, and found him just breathing. I took him in my arms, but my children coming in led me away, and he breathed his last before six o'clock. He was thirty-one years old the 30th day of last June.

November 29.—At four o'clock this afternoon I was called to attend the burial of my son, who was buried alongside of his mother in the Friends' ground at Fourth and Arch Streets. I appreciate this favor shown to me by that good and religious society, as neither my late son nor I belong to this Society. A large number of men attended the funeral, considering the late mortality in the city.

December 2.—Matthew Clarkson and Colonel Wadsworth, member of Congress, from Hartford, Connecticut, called to see me and remained to tea.

December 3.—A quorum of the members of the House present at the State House.

December 4.—The House met and elected George Latimer as their Speaker.

December 6.—Attended at the State House. A committee of Friends appeared and handed to the Speaker a memorial against all kinds of gaming and play-houses.

December 10.—Attended at the State House, and after we adjourned dined with the Governor and some friends.

December 17.—Attended at the State House. At twelve o'clock, Dennis Whelen, Thomas Lily, and myself, a committee of the House, with Lindsay Coates, Abraham Smith, and Robert Brown, of the Senate, escorted the Governor from his house to the Senate

Chamber, where the oath was administered to him by Benjamin Chew, Esq., in the presence of the Assembly seated and the joint committee standing.   We then marched to the Court House steps in Market Street, under direction of High Sheriff William Will, where the Governor's election was proclaimed by Timothy Matlack, Clerk of the Senate.   We then marched back to the Senate Chamber, where the Governor was conducted to the chair, from which he expressed his thanks to the public for entrusting him again with the office for another three years.   The committee then escorted him back to his own house, where they remained to dinner.

December 19.—At three o'clock went down to the waterside in Pine Street and dined with our Speaker, Mr. Latimer, and B. R. Morgan, J. Swanwick, Henry Kemmerer, Thomas Britton, Joseph Magoffin, Thomas Paul, Jacob Morgan, Mathias Barton, James Morrow, John Whitehill, Abraham Carpenter, and Isaac Ferree, all of the Assembly.

December 22—Breakfasted at the Point House, and dined with Mr. Barge.   My son Robert had to dine with him at my house, on a saddle of venison, General Brodhead, James Biddle, Esq., Presley Neville, Esq., Peter Baynton, Andrew Tybout, and several other gentlemen.

December 29.—Had to breakfast with me Thomas Bull and Mr. Ross, member from Chester County, and Mr. Old, from Lancaster.

December 30.—In the forenoon attended at the State House.   Dined with Mr. Barge, and afterwards we took a ride to the canal, where Johnson's men are hard at work.

December 31.—Attended in my place at the State House, and remained at home during the afternoon.

1794.

January 3.—Had to breakfast with me Colonel Wadsworth, of Congress, Mr. Kelly and Gardner of the House. Afterward met at the State House the Committee on Claims.

January 11.—John Stewart, member from York County, fell to the floor in a convulsion, which for a time caused considerable excitement in the House.

January 12.—Dined at Mr. Barge's, after which we took a walk. Attended the Lutheran Church on Fourth Street and heard Mr. Helmuth preach.

January 14.—The Senate and House to-day elected Colonel C. Febiger, Treasurer.

January 16.—Had to breakfast with me Messrs. Evans, Tyson, Shoemaker, and Davis, from Montgomery County ; Judge James Biddle, and Mr. Slough,'after which we went to the House.

January 17.—The following gentlemen dined with my son Robert at my house : Colonel Wadsworth, A. Hunt, Mr. Van Borckel, Richard Bache, J. Duffield, Andrew Tybout, J. Lawrence, William Jones, William Gray, and a few others.

January 21.—The members of the House from Lancaster County breakfasted with me. In the afternoon session, when the bill was called up giving the late Proprietors seven thousand pounds, which was lodged with the State Treasurer for pretended arrears of taxes, it occasioned a two hours debate, and was left unfinished.

January 22.—The bill of yesterday was again before the House, and the sum of £7249 2s. 10d. allowed.

February 1.—Attended at the House. Took my three daughters and Molly Ogden sleighing.

February 2.—Dined at Mr. Barge's, and afterward took Mr. Barge, William Jones, Colonel Wadsworth in my sleigh to Point no Point, and then went down to the place where Anthony Morris lives.

February 3.—Had to breakfast with me seven members of the Assembly: Mr. Stokely, Mr. Minor, Mr. Ritchie, and Mr. White, from Washington, Mr. Torrence, and Mr. Cunningham, from Fayette, and Mr. Maclay, from Franklin. Afterwards met the Committee on Claims. Dined at the Governor's with Colonel Henry Miller, Mr. Campbell, Mr. Scott, Dr. Redman, and Mr. Hall.

February 5.—The report was again taken up dividing the State in twelve districts to elect thirteen members for the House of Representatives of the United States. Yesterday Mr. Benjamin R. Morgan handed to the Speaker a motion that the State at large should elect the members on a general ticket; a long debate ensued. The yeas and nays being called, forty-two votes were given for the district system and twenty votes for the general system.

February 8.—Dr. Chapman and Gerardus Wynkoop, from Bucks County, breakfasted with me. In the afternoon took a sleigh ride with William Jones to the Point House.

February 17.—After the House adjourned, many of the members called at Mr. Oellers's Hotel and drank punch. His daughter was married yesterday. This evening the first play was acted at the new theatre at corner of Sixth and Chestnut Streets.

February 26.—At noon the House met with the Senate for the trial of John Nicholson, Comptroller General. Benjamin R. Morgan, chairman of the committee of five appointed by the House, opened the case on behalf of the House. I found that four lawyers are employed by the House at $300 each, and the Comptroller a like number: Messrs. Wilcox, Rawle, Ingersoll, and Dexter for the House; Messrs. Lewis, Tilghman, and Bradford for Nicholson.

February 27.—Mr. Morgan resumed his remarks on the articles of impeachment.

March 1.—The impeachment of the Comptroller continued. Mr. Morgan reported that owing to the sickness of a witness he could not proceed regularly, whereupon the trial was continued.

14

March 2.—The following gentlemen dined at my house on a roast of beef out of my large ox, Commodore Trunnion: James Donaldson, Jr., Peter Baynton, Samuel Clarkson, Colonel Lutz, the son of John Duffield, and my sons.

March 4.—The trial of John Nicholson was resumed and Mr. Morgan concluded his presentation of the charges against him.

March 5.—Edward Tilghman, Esq., opened on behalf of the Comptroller and examined seven witnesses, viz.: W. Montgomery and J. Smilie, members of Congress; William Bingham, A. Smith, and Thomas, of the Senate; Alexander Hamilton, Secretary of the Treasury, and Robert Hare.

March 6.—Albert Gallatin, who a few days ago lost his seat in the Senate of the United States, owing to his not being a citizen long enough, was called by the Comptroller's counsel to give evidence, but I believe it will be to no advantage for their case.

March 7.—Mr. Tilghman continued in behalf of Mr. Nicholson. With Dennis Whelen, Haines, and several more friends went to see the play, "Every One has His Faults," at the new playhouse.

March 8.—The trial of John Nicholson was resumed. A long argument took place as to admitting the testimony of Hans Hamilton, which Nicholson obtained some time ago, when Hamilton was in town, without notice to the counsel for the State to be present. Finally, the counsel on both sides agreed to proceed, and to take up later Hamilton's testimony. When Mr. Tilghman finished, Mr. Gibson and other gentlemen for the defense explained the laws of the United States and this State concerning the debts and certificates of both in a masterly manner. In the afternoon drove down to the Point House and witnessed a quarrel between Mrs. Marshall and a pilot named Crow, concerning her daughter.

March 10.—The trial of the Comptroller resumed. William Rawle spoke on behalf of the State and stated facts that I believe cannot be refuted by the opposing counsel.

March 11.—Mr. Higgins, one of the counsel for Nicholson, spoke nearly three hours, with much force. But argument without facts seldom prevails. In the afternoon Mr. Higgins was too unwell to continue his argument.

March 12.—Mr. Higgins concluded his argument in three-quarters of an hour, when he was followed by Mr. Dexter, for the State. His language was beautiful, his reasoning clear, expressive, and, I think, convincing, that the new loan certificates stated in one of the articles of impeachment were not subscribable to the loan of the United States.

March 13.—William Bradford, of counsel for Nicholson, spoke until two o'clock. His language was smooth and eloquent, and he tried to counteract what was said by Mr. Dexter yesterday.

March 14.—Mr. Bradford concluded his argument in two hours. His ending was beautiful, and he defended his client in a masterly manner. The trial was postponed to Monday.

March 17.—St. Patrick's Day, clear and very pleasant. Mr. Wilcox spoke on behalf of the Commonwealth in the trial of the Comptroller.

March 18.—Mr. Wilcox finished his argument. In the afternoon drank coffee at the Widow Marshall's, at the Point House.

March 19.—William Lewis, Esq., spoke two hours in behalf of Nicholson.

March 20.—Owing to Mr. Lewis, of counsel, being unwell, we adjourned until to-morrow.

March 22.—Mr. Lewis, who was still sick yesterday, concluded his argument in two hours, and was followed by Mr. Ingersoll on behalf of the Commonwealth.

March 24.—Mr. Ingersoll spoke six hours but did not finish his argument. He is a beautiful speaker, an excellent reasoner, and did the case of the Commonwealth great justice.

March 25.—Edward Tilghman, Esq., for the Comptroller, and William Rawle, Esq., for the Commonwealth, concluded the arguments in the case in about one hour each.

March 29.—Before dinner took a walk down Third Street to South, and then up Front Street, and called on Lownes, the silversmith, and paid him for the six silver tankards which I had made for my children, from the sale of my large ox.

March 30.—Mr. Barge and I rode to Robert Morris's place, where Arthur Donaldson's men are digging the canal. Dined at Mr. Barge's with Matthew Clarkson, Maud H. Keppele, her sister, and Miss Hubley and George Lauman.

March 31.—Paid eight dollars for a box at the theatre and took my three daughters, Mr. and Mrs. Barge, Moses Cox and daughters, and Matthew Clarkson. The play was "The Grecian Daughter."

April 1.—The House and Senate elected James Ross, from Washington, to serve as United States Senator.

April 6.—Had to dine with me Mr. and Mrs. Barge and all my children, and gave the latter six silver tankards, costing $30 each.

April 10.—Dined at George Latimer's with five members of the House: John Lardner, Dennis Whelen, T. Britton, T. Lilly, and J. Shoemaker.

April 11.—Was informed that John Nicholson resigned his office of Comptroller General after the Senate had decided in his favor, and that John Donaldson was appointed in his place. In the afternoon the House attended the funeral of Jacob Morgan, one of the members from this county. He was buried in the graveyard at corner of Fifth and Arch Streets.

April 12.—This afternoon the members of the Legislature went to the Lutheran church to hear the new organ.

April 14.—About noon a large body of sailors went to the Governor's house in a riotous manner, complaining of being out of employment owing to the Embargo Act.

April 21.—Attended at the State House twice. Dined with the Governor with General Brodhead, Dr. J. Redman, Colonel Thomas Proctor, and James Ross. At night went to see the play of " Richard III."

April 23.—The Legislature adjourned yesterday. Dined with twenty-five gentlemen at Burns's tavern, on Tenth Street, kept by Richardet. Present, James Ross, of Washington County; Mr. Bingham and Scott, Speaker Latimer, Kemmerer, Erwin, Barton, Ferree, Lilly, Kelly, Haines, Evans, Forrest, Bowman, Carran, Neville, Paul, Stokley, Shoemaker, Lutz, Dennis Whelen, P. Baynton, young Willing, J. Ross, John Woods, and William Lewis.

April 30.—Had to breakfast Mr. J. Trumbull, of Connecticut. In the afternoon met the Commissioners at the President's house, Ninth Street.

May 1.—Went to Isaac Warner's fish house and dined with Richard Peters, Robert Morris, James Wilson, Tench Francis, Andrew Tybout, G. Latimer, Matthew Clarkson, and others—about eighty in number.

May 10.—Forenoon Mr. Barge and I went to Penrose's wharf to see Sontag and Le Roche's ship launched.

May 12.—Took a ride along the banks of the Schuylkill and stopped at Metz's tavern. In the afternoon Mr. Barge and I attended the burial of Joseph Rakestraw.

May 15.—Drove to my Schuylkill lot and meadow and to the Point House. Dined with Mr. Barge, after which we took a ride to Gravel Hill and down to the Swan tavern, where we had a glass of bad punch.

May 21.—Breakfasted with the Governor. Dined with Mr. Barge, after which we drove to Gravel Hill, crossed at Ogden's Upper Ferry, and went to Gray's Ferry, kept by Weed, thence home by my meadows.

June 4.—Matthew Clarkson, Mrs. Simmons, Miss Ogden and Clarkson, and my daughters went to see the play of "Romeo and Juliet," the occasion being Mrs. Marshall's benefit.

June 13.—Matthew Clarkson and Edward Wells took tea with us. At the table my daughter Betsey was taken ill with a hemorrhage. Dr. Kuhn was sent for and ordered her to be bled.

June 18.—Took my daughter Betsey a short ride. Dined with Mr. Barge, after which we attended the funeral of L. Stoneburner, in Germantown, with whom I have been acquainted for thirty-five years.

June 19.—My daughter Betsey has not improved in health and was again bled. I took a ride with my daughter Molly to the canal.

June 23.—Visited Samuel Sansom's country place, and brought home for my daughter Betsey some fine raspberries. In the afternoon attended the funeral of John Cornman, sugar refiner, from his house, Spruce and Tenth Streets.

June 26.—Took Governor Mifflin in my chair and went down to the Stillhouse wharf to examine the stone purchased for Fort Mifflin, a great quantity of which is stored there.

July 29.—At six o'clock set out with my daughter Betsey in my chair for Trenton. Breakfasted at the Red Lion in company with Miss M. Harrison, Francis, Wister, and Eddy.

July 31.—Returned home from Trenton. Dined with Mr. Barge, after which we called on the Governor and drank some wine with Colonel Henry Miller, M. Slough, Nathaniel Falkner, Mr. Britt, and several strangers to me. Met Miers Fisher at the City Tavern, agreeably to his note left at my house, concerning some reports propagated against him in his absence last week. There were present Thomas Willing, Mr. Ingersoll, John Vaughan, George Latimer, H. Kemmerer, Mr. Wynkoop, and myself. As no person appeared to substantiate the charge, Mr. Fisher's explanation had full weight, and the gentlemen present appeared to be satisfied—that he had no conversation with the pilot or pilots, as was reported.

August 4.—My two daughters, Kitty Cox and Molly, took a ride before breakfast. Lewis Farmer's wife was buried to-day. My son Thomas arrived from Trenton and informed me that my daughter Betsey was very ill and desired to see me.

August 5.—At four o'clock A. M. my daughter Molly and I set out for Trenton, and, notwithstanding the day was very hot, reached there at eleven o'clock, and found my daughter very ill.

August 8.—Brought my two daughters home to-day—Betsey better for the ride.

August 9.—My daughter Betsey seems to be better and much more satisfied since she is again at home. Yesterday General Neville, and D. Lennox arrived from Allegheny County, from which they had been driven by the rioters for being officers of excise. They burned the General's house and barn, and would have shot him had he been caught.

August 29.—Drove down to Hoch's, near the Schuylkill, and got some grapes for my daughter Betsey, who is again spitting blood.

September 1.—This afternoon the Legislature assembled by proclamation of Governor Mifflin.

September 3.—Weather very warm. Took my sick daughter with her sisters a short ride, and after our return Betsey became very ill.

September 6.—At nine o'clock, with Mr. Barge in my chair, and in company with Governor Mifflin and the French Minister, set out for Fort Mifflin, where we met Jacob Morgan, John Chapman, Thomas Bull, James Morrison, Jonas Hertzel, and Thomas Hockley, of the Committee appointed by the House, of which I am Chairman. Major Charles L'Enfant, engineer, attended and explained to us the several works under way and to be done. In the evening we returned, some by land and some by water.

September 12.—Took my daughters Betsey, and Molly, a short ride. In the evening went to Dunwoody's and there met the Committee on Fortification of Mud Island.   Major L'Enfant attended.

September 13.—This afternoon took my three daughters out riding— Betsey is rather worse than she has been for several days.

September 15.—After the House adjourned took my daughters riding. During the night I had to send for Dr. Wister, as Betsey, was very ill.

September 18.—Attended the House.   Afternoon took my three daughters to the camp, two miles over Schuylkill, where they rested in the Governor's tent.   The troops are to march to-morrow against the opposers of the Excise Law in the western part of the State.

September 19.—My daughter continues very ill.   This morning about one hundred and twenty horsemen, among them my son Robert and son-in-law Cox, marched through the city, with a company of infantry and the artillerists with fifteen cannon.

September 20.—Attended at the State House, and in the afternoon took my daughters riding.   Colonel Isaac Warner, proprietor of the Fish House, was buried to-day.

September 21.—Breakfasted with the Governor, who returned from Montgomery County last night, where he has been forwarding the troops to quell the insurrection in the West.

September 23.—The House adjourned for half an hour, when Mr. Swanwick invited all the members to Oellers's Hotel to a lunch with punch.

September 30.—That great and good man, General Washington, President of the United States, set out from his house on Market Street, with Secretary Hamilton on his left and Private Secretary on his right, to head the troops called out to quell the insurrection to the westward.

October 1.—Last night in returning from Thomas Fisher's, who gave a permit for the burial of my son Thomas's child in Friends' ground, I sprained my foot so badly that I went to Mr. Cox's and had it bathed, and afterward went home on horseback. At four o'clock my son's child was buried.

October 27.—Colonel F. Johnson's people moved his office into my new house, adjoining the one in which I live, at a rental of $200 per annum.

October 29.—Took my daughters Betsey, and Molly, a ride. Colonel F. Johnson, with nine light-horsemen, brought down four insurgents, among them Herman Husband, from Bedford.

October 31.—Took my daughters riding. Bought two barrels of flour for £6 4s. 4d.

November 3.—This evening Mr. Barge and I went to Elliot's on Fourth Street and met the members of the Amicable Fire Company.

November 19.—Norton Pryor went with me to see President Washington enter Congress, to deliver his address in the lower room, which only took half an hour.

November 28.—This morning Captain McConnell's troop of horse returned from the westward. Dined with Mr. Barge and afterward drove to the Middle Ferry, where we met Captain Singer with his troop of horse. Later we attended the burial of the wife of Mayor Clarkson. Hon. Mr. Kittera and Mr. Barge spent the evening with me.

November 30.—After breakfast with Mr. Barge called on Governor Mifflin, who returned from the westward on Friday evening last. Jacob Cox returned last evening and my son Robert this evening from the westward expedition.

December 3.—Only a bare quorum of members of the House being present, we postponed electing a Speaker until to-morrow.

December 4.—George Latimer was elected Speaker of the House ; Peter Baynton, Clerk ; James Martin, Sergeant-at-Arms and J. Fry, Doorkeeper.

December 7.—In the forenoon took a ride with the Governor, John Nicholson, and Jonathan Mifflin to Governor Mifflin's farm on the west side of the Schuylkill, and after viewing Nicholson's building being erected for a glass house, crossed at the Falls and returned to dinner.

December 10.—Went with the Committee to visit the westernmost part of the market, which is allotted to the country people, and found several butchers using the stalls. After the House adjourned went to see Colonel Macpherson's volunteers enter the city from the western expedition. They were escorted by the troops of light-horse of Captains Dunlap, McConnell, and Singer, who crossed the Schuylkill to meet them.

December 13.—The city troops marched to the Schuylkill to escort the remainder of the troops from the western expedition.

December 18.—At noon the House adjourned and the members, with their Speaker, attended the commencement at the Methodist church on Fourth Street, where several young ladies from Mr. Poor's Academy spoke before a large audience.

December 25.—Colonel White, of the New Jersey light-horse, arrived with the prisoners from the westward, who were lodged in the Gaol on Walnut Street.

December 26.—About eight o'clock this evening, while at Mr. Barge's, heard the cry of fire and found it was in the back part of the Lutheran church at Fourth and Cherry Streets, where the steeple was to be built. This was consumed before nine o'clock, and the church building was thought safe. Later a fire broke out under the roof and the beautiful building was burned to the ground.

December 28.—Remained at home all day, as my daughter Betsey is very low. She suffered so much that I sent for Dr. Kuhn.

December 29.—My daughter Elizabeth died this afternoon at four o'clock. She was born September 1, 1773, in the house where all my children, seven in number, were born. She was an ingenuous and dutiful child, and left us with a sweet smile on her countenance.

December 31.—At three o'clock this afternoon I was called to attend the funeral of my child to the Friends' graveyard at Fourth and Arch Streets.

1795.

January 2.—Mr. Kelly, member from York County, took breakfast with me. In the House he brought up the matter of the election in the four western counties for members of Assembly, thought to be unconstitutional on account of the insurrection.

January 3.—Mr. Kelly again brought up the subject of yesterday's debate, and after he had concluded Albert Gallatin spoke in opposition, and asked in whom does the power lay to set aside an election. At my request Dr. Kuhn called on me concerning the practice of physic, a subject now before the House, and gave me all the information I desired.

January 5.—The matter of the elections in Washington, Westmoreland, Fayette, and Allegheny Counties was again taken up, and Mr. Gallatin spoke three hours in support of the election.

January 7.—Attended the House; Colonel Forrest in the chair. B. R. Morgan and Robert Frazer spoke against and Jacob Nagle, of Bedford, in favor of the western election.

January 8.—Attended the House; Colonel Forrest in the chair. After speeches by Mr. Gallatin against it and Mr. Evans for it, the resolutions setting aside the elections in the western counties was adopted.

January 9.—When the subject, that has been before the Committee of the Whole for some days past, came before the House, it was carried in the affirmative, upon which the eleven members from the four counties withdrew.   The Senate had decided in the same manner on the 3d inst.

January 26.—After leaving the State House, Colonel Jacob Morgan and I called to see Mr. Barge and there met Tench Francis, busy spinning on Mrs. Barge's wheel.

January 27.—After the House was called to order, neither Mr. Baynton nor Mr. Bullock, our Clerks, appearing (owing to the death of Mrs. Markoe, a sister of the former and sister-in-law of the latter), Matthias Barton, member from Lancaster, was good enough to officiate.

February 12.—Mr. John Penn, a former Governor of this Province, was buried from his house in Pine Street at Christ Church on Second Street.

February 19.—Thanksgiving Day, by proclamation of President Washington.   Two days ago I received an invitation from the Hon. William Bingham to dine with him to-day, but finding myself so unwell, I sent a note of regret.

February 26.—To-day Hon. William Bingham was elected United States Senator in the place of Robert Morris, who declined serving again.

February 27.—Mr. Mitchell's resolution for moving the seat of government was debated, and carried by a majority of eleven votes.

March 4.—Attended at the House.   Had to dine with me Colonel Thomas Forrest, of the House of Representatives ; Thomas Boude, Matthias Barton, Isaac Ferree, and Daniel Buckley, of Lancaster County ; John Montgomery, of Cumberland ; Robert Frazer, of Chester ; Presley Neville and Dunning McNair, of Allegheny ; and Peter Baynton, Clerk of the House.   Mr. William B. Hockley was buried this afternoon.

March 9.—At four o'clock, with the Speaker and twenty-two members of the House, dined with President Washington. He was exceedingly affable to all.

March 22.—Dined at Mr. Barge's with M. Keppele and Israel Whelen, who was lately elected State Senator in the place of Hon. William Bingham.

March 25.—With Colonel F. Gurney and several members of the Assembly went to the President's House on Ninth Street, to see what progress is being made by the carpenters. Met a committee of the city and county members, and Mr. Dunlap and Tench Francis, concerning the impropriety of erecting a hospital close to the great road near Schuylkill, on the west side.

March 30.—The bill for moving the seat of government to Carlisle was read a third time, and a long debate ensued, even after the ayes and noes were called for. They were at length taken, thirty-six for moving and thirty-four against.

April 6.—In the evening went to the playhouse with Israel and Dennis Whelen, Thomas Bull, Thomas Boude, R. Frazer, and D. Buckley. Our box was so full that my daughter Molly sent for me to come to hers.

April 9.—Dined with the Governor on Market Street, and so did Mr. Barge, Mr. Hall, Colonel Charles Stewart, and a number of members of the Assembly.

April 20.—At noon the House adjourned after being in session since December 2d last. From the State House about twenty members went to Oellers's, where we had a lunch with punch and wine.

May 5.—By invitation of Lawrence Seckel, went down to his house on the meadows, about four and a half miles from the city, and there dined on excellent beefsteaks prepared by ourselves, and drank the best of wine and punch. The following gentlemen were present: George Latimer, Francis Gurney, B. R. Morgan, Robert

Waln, and Messrs. Hollingsworth, Smith, Twells, Hall, Stocker, Clymer, Jones, Foulke, Baynton, and Guyer. After dinner we went down to the river to see the fishermen draw in the shad seine. In crossing a ditch I fell in and got wet all over, and was obliged to make the best of my way home.

May 11.—Went to the playhouse, it being Mr. Bates's benefit. As he is my tenant, I took a box for my family and invited John Duffield's daughter, Colonel Gurney and wife, Colonel John Patton, and William Gray.

May 26.—With my daughters and Peter Gordon and wife, from Trenton, went to see Eckstein's paintings, on Market Street ; visited the house being built for the President, and also Robert Morris's great house.

May 28.—In the afternoon Matthew Clarkson and I went to the burial of Daniel Rundle from his house on Market Street to Christ Church yard on Second Street.

May 30.—My daughter Hannah accompanied Mr. Gordon and wife to Trenton. In the afternoon Mr. Barge and I drove to the meadow, and on our return I left him at M. Keppele's, who was married last Thursday to Miss Caldwell.

June 12.—Drove along Seventh street between Walnut and Spruce Streets, which the city corporation recently reopened.

June 28.—Went to the meadows and breakfasted at the Point House with Mrs. Anderson and one of her daughters. On my way back met my daughter Molly and Mr. Simmons. Went to church and dined with Mr. Barge. After dinner we drove down to G. Ogden's at Gray's bridge, where the stage-wagon fell into the river. All of the passengers were saved, but two of the horses were drowned. Returned home by the middle bridge.

July 1.—Paid John Dunlap and Richard Wells five dollars toward the trees planted on both sides of Market Street to the Schuylkill this spring ; done by subscription.

July 4.—About midnight I was awakened by a knocking at my door, calling for the light-horse to assemble at Market and Fourth Streets in order to proceed to Kensington, where a crowd of people in a riotous manner burned the effigy of John Jay, of New York, who lately returned from England, where he had been sent by the President to effect a treaty, which he did to the dissatisfaction of a discontented party.

July 5.—Dined with Mr. Barge. George Lauman came in and gave us an account of the affair in Kensington. He is a member of Captain Dunlap's light horse, and their number being so few, they were unable to disperse the mob.

July 11.—Colonel Ephraim Blaine breakfasted with me at the Point House, after which we went to the meadow to see some of my cattle.

July 15.—President Washington about eight o'clock this morning set out for Mount Vernon in a two-horse phaeton for one person, his family in a coach and four horses, and two servants on horseback leading his saddle horse.

July 18.—At five o'clock this morning William Jones in his chair and I in mine set out for the seashore. Breakfasted at Waterman's and dined at Bessonet's in Bristol. Crossed the Delaware a mile above the town and rested several times under the trees, it being exceedingly warm. Made a short stop at Bordentown and proceeded to Crosswix, where I got very sick.

July 20.—Mr. Jones was of the opinion that it was best for me to turn back, and at five o'clock we parted. Stopped at Burlington, then went on to Waterman's, sign of George Washington, where I became very sick again. Reached home at two o'clock and sent for Dr. Kuhn, who ordered me to be bled.

July 21.—Very warm. This morning I feel much easier. In the evening Mr. Barge and I took a ride.

July 24.—Went with Timothy Matlack to Joseph Ogden's house on Market Street near Eighth, to see where the lightning struck, without doing any material damage. It struck the east peak of the roof, ran down to the copper gutter, followed that to the west end of the house, and then down to the pavement.

July 27.—At six o'clock this morning, Mr. Barge and I in my chair, Mrs. Barge, Mr. and Mrs. Pearson Hunt and my two daughters in a light wagon, went down the Chester Road to the Blue Bell, where we breakfasted. We reached home after ten o'clock.

July 28.—Accompanied Israel Whelen in his carriage to Warner's fish house and dined with about thirty gentlemen on the banks of the Schuylkill. The dinner was given by Robert Erwin and William Gray, executors of the estate of the late Robert Erwin. The following are some of the gentlemen present: James Biddle, J. Hewes, D. Brodhead, F. Johnson, T. Forrest, P. Brown, J. Baker, B. Scull, A. Tybout, J. Graff, W. Hall, H. Sheaff, J. Morrell, J. Cox, S. Wheeler, C. Jarvis, J. Wharton, R. Keen, Hugh Roberts, G. Weed, and R. Jones.

July 31.—Received of Colonel Ephraim Blaine £40 for a cow and a calf. Mr. Barge and I went to the Middle Ferry, on Schuylkill, to witness the great freshet. The water was eighteen inches on the floor in the house, and ran across the road to the east to within thirty feet of the pump on the hill in Market Street. After we returned home, my daughters drove out to see it. All the meadows on the west side of the river and the stacks of hay were under water.

August 2.—After dining with Mr. Barge we rode out to the Middle and Upper Ferries to see the destruction caused by the late freshet.

August 5.—Set out for Long Branch with John Brown in two chairs, and William Hall with his wife and two ladies in a four-wheel carriage. Crossed at Dunk's ferry, and near Burlington the road was under water 2½ feet, caused by the late rains. Nighted at

Douglass's in Crosswix. The last fourteen miles took one of the ladies in my chair.

August 6.—Breakfasted at the Widow Britton's. As Mr. Hall and his party did not come up, we drove on to the Burnt House, kept by Jewell, and the mercury being 94°, we rested until four o'clock. We then proceeded to the Court House, to Foreman's, where we met Charles Biddle with his family returning from the seashore. Mr. Hall and party arrived some time in the night, his delay being occasioned by the swingletree of his carriage breaking.

August 7.—Went on to Jacob Hart's at Colt's Neck, and after breakfast set out again. At noon the mercury stood at 98°. One of Mr. Hall's horses gave out and I put my horse in his place and drove. Left the driver to bring up the sick horse in my chair. At Hankinson's, in Edenton, we waited until the sick horse came up, when Mr. Brown and I went to Thomas Chandler's at the shore. Very hot at noon.

August 8.—Early this morning took a bath in the ocean. There dined with us Samuel Morris, governor of the Schuylkill Fishing Company, and his son and brother Israel, John Morrell, and A. Tybout. The following guests are at our house : Leaming and wife, Joshua Bond and wife, Peter Kuhn, wife and daughter, William Jones, Robert Hysham, Mr. Kerr, and Robeson.

August 9.—William Jones went with me in my chair to visit Mr. Morris and Hall, at Green's, and there met Israel Morris, Thomas Morris, and John Wharton. Accompanied them to McKnight's White House, and from thence returned to our lodgings. In the evening Jones and I drove to Hankinson's, at Edenton, to escape the mosquitoes.

August 10.—Mr. Jones and I returned to our lodgings for breakfast. Went with the following gentlemen to the White House : Mr. Jones, Mr. Bond, and Mr. Hysham, and there dined with Samuel Morris, his son Benjamin and two brothers, E. Perot, A. Tybout,

15

John Craig, Jesse Waln, John Morrell, and John Wharton, of Philadelphia; Mr. Sterling, of Burlington, and two gentlemen I did not know. There were five ladies also present.

August 11.—Cool and pleasant, which happens almost daily between ten and four o'clock, owing to the sea breeze; at other hours the mosquitoes are exceedingly troublesome. Arrived to-day, Johnson and sister, from Germantown, Mrs. Howard, and a young lady recently from England.

August 12.—Have been very unwell all day. This evening arrived from Philadelphia Messrs. Franklin Wharton, Merkin, and Allen.

August 13.—On invitation of William Hall dined at Green's, where we had an excellent dinner, besides the pleasure of the company of Mrs. Hall and her niece, Mrs. Cowell, the two Miss Reeds, the three Morris brothers, and John Wharton. After dinner we all drove over to my lodgings.

August 14.—At five o'clock this morning Peter Kuhn, wife, and five children left for Philadelphia, and this afternoon Joshua Bond and wife for New Brunswick. In the afternoon Samuel Morris and Mr. Hall called, and in the evening William Jones and I went to the Widow Brindly's and bought some cake.

August 15.—William Jones and I left for home and breakfasted at Colt's Neck, Here we were overtaken by Benjamin Morris, from the White House, and Messrs. Whitall, Howell, and Blackwood, of Woodbury, New Jersey. After breakfast we went on to Jewell's, fed our horses, and thence to Smith's Burnt House, where we dined. I had a pair of shoes put on my horse. Nighted at Douglass's, making forty-four miles to-day.

August 16.—Benjamin Morris set out from Douglass's at Crosswix for Trenton, and we five went to Davis's tavern at Bordentown to breakfast. Left for Burlington and dined at Hogland's, where we met Colonel F. Nichols. A mile beyond the town we parted with Messrs. Whitall, Blackwood, and Howell, three clever, sociable gentlemen. Jones and I crossed at Dunk's Ferry and proceeded to Waterman's at the sign of General Washington, where we rested until five o'clock, and arrived home at dark.

August 20.—Mrs. Barge, Pearson Hunt and wife, and my daughter Hannah in carriage, Mr. Barge and I in my chair, drove to J. Woodward's, eleven miles up the Bristol Road, and breakfasted. Returning, stopped at Harrowgate and had punch.

August 23.—Went to church and then dined with Mrs. Barge. My old friend is laid up with gout, which I regret, as I shall be lost without his company.

August 26.—Went to the supper of Robert Erwin given to a few friends and his workmen on the raising of his house on Eighth Street.

August 27.—This afternoon drove to the meadow and on the way met William Jones. We went to the French house near the Hospital and drank a bowl of iced punch.

August 31.—I have been reading Brissot de Warville's "Travels" with some interest. My son-in-law, Jacob Cox, returned from the sea-shore.

September 4.—Dined with Mr. Barge, after which we drove over to Mr. Penn's place, but missed Mr. Physic.

September 11.—To-day I finished reading de Warville's "Travels." I can readily understand why he makes so many errors, for his stay was too short to give an accurate account of matters and things.

September 13.—Went to church and afterward dined with Mr. Barge. In the evening went with General Brodhead, William Jones, and A. Tybout to the White Horse, kept by George Weed, and had some good punch.

September 16.—Went to the President's house on Ninth Street, where John Smith has twenty-three men at work on the circular stairs.

September 17.—Visited Mayor Clarkson concerning Governor Mifflin's proclamation in reference to the sickness in New York. Called at Captain Loxley's, on Arch Street, who made a bowl of punch. Mr. Barge and I took a drive in the afternoon along the banks of the Schuylkill.

September 18.—Mr. Barge and I visited the President's house on Ninth Street, and also Robert Morris's, both unfinished.

September 21.—Drove Mr. Barge down to Inglis's rope walk, where he bought some hemp to wrap up his feet when he has an attack of gout.

September 24.—Dined with Governor Mifflin and Miss Susanna Morris, at the Falls.

September 26.—Mr. Barge and I took a ride; stopped at the race ground, near the Lower Ferry Road, and watched them exercise the horses.

October 15.—Received my certificate of election as a member of the House of Representatives, in which I have served since October of 1786.

October 21.—Joseph Wharton with Jacob Craver, Sheriff-elect of Cumberland County, called to see me. Accompanied them to the Governor's and then to the Chief Justice, to ascertain why the Sheriff's commission is withheld. We learned that it was charged Craver was implicated in the late Whisky Insurrection. This he must clear up.

October 22.—Dined at the Governor's with Major Fisher, of the Artillery.

October 26.—Visited Ricketts' circus with Abraham Hunt, of Trenton, and my three daughters. Bought one and a half cords of oak wood at 52 s. 6 d. per cord.

November 4.—Visited William Jones, on Market Street, who was yesterday married to the Widow Elves—his third wife. His first was

Annie Moss, and his second the Widow Gray.   Drank punch with
Governor Mifflin, J. Donaldson, R. Keen, Israel Whelen, A. Tybout,
William Hall, P. DeHaven, William and Henry Sheaff, William
Pollard, B. Scull, Joseph Wharton, Dr. B. Duffield, Robert Erwin,
William and Joseph Gray, Matthew and Robert Jones, Hugh
Roberts, and others.   In the afternoon took Joseph Wharton in
my chair to the Point House.

November 6.—Called again at William Jones's, where a bountiful re-
past, with punch, was served, and where I met Thomas Forest, Hugh
McCullough, Samuel Mills, Jr., Gibson, the lawyer; Mr. Shaw, the
merchant; Wilson Hunt, Mr. Sperry, Edward Wells, Michael Hillegas, Dr. Kuhn, and others.   By request of Mr. Jones I remained
and dined with Mrs. Jones and the family.   Mr. Barge took a ride
with me along the banks of the Schuylkill.

November 7.—At noon called on Mayor Clarkson, when we visited
William Jones to drink punch.   We met Mr. VanBerkel, Joseph
Anthony, Dr. John Duffield, Hugh Lloyd, Nicholas Diehl, Dr. Paschall, George Westcott, Philip Kinsey, Philip Francis, General Bull,
and Moses Cox.   This is the fourth day that Mr. Jones has kept
open house.   I took a ride all the afternoon to wear off the effects
of the punch and clear my head.

November 8.—Went to church and dined with Mr. Barge.   After dinner we took a ride through Kensington, up the Frankford Road,
then over to Germantown Road, and home via Ridge Road.

November 10.—Dined at Governor Mifflin's, on Market Street, with
General D. Brodhead, John Adlum, William West, and Nathaniel
Newlin.

November 17.—At Robert Morris's house, southeast corner Seventh
and Chestnut, the workmen began to erect the steam engine.

November 24.—At ten o'clock set out in my chair for Lancaster, in
company with Israel Whelen, John Perot, John Hall, A. Witmer,
William Sansom, and James Fisher.   Dined with Mr. Curwen, the

overseer of the turnpike. Nighted at Hunt Downing's, where we had exceedingly good accommodations.

November 25.—After breakfast Richard Downing and Mr. Paulding joined us and we proceeded to Humphrey's tavern, where we stopped for punch. At Reynell's we dined, and afterward stopped at Witmer's bridge, and thence to Slough's, in Lancaster. We found the turnpike in a generally good condition, only here and there the stones were not sufficiently covered with gravel. Visited several friends.

November 27.—Mr. Whelen, General Henry Miller, and I left Lancaster and dined at Reynell's. I frequently got out of my chair and measured the bed of the turnpike, which is full twenty-one feet wide, which is according to law. At Hunt Downing's we met United States Senator James Ross and wife, of Pittsburgh.

November 28.—Set out after breakfast and made a short stop at Robinson's tavern. I frequently measured the turnpike down to the 14-mile stone, from which point to the city it has been viewed by the Commissioners. Dined at the Widow Miller's and reached home by sundown.

December 1.—Attended the House of Representatives; a quorum present.

December 2.—Mathias Young, J. Hall, and myself, who were appointed last month by the Governor to view the turnpike from the 14-mile stone to Witmer's bridge and thence to Lancaster, went to the Secretary's office in the State House.

December 5.—The Governor, Mr. Barge, and myself went to Dunwoody's Spread Eagle Tavern on Market Street, and there dined on venison with the following gentlemen: Jacob Barge, born in 1721; William Jones, 1723; Edward Shippen, 1728; Frederick Kuhl, 1728; Michael Hillegas, 1729; Jacob Hiltzheimer, 1729; James Biddle, 1731; Matthew Clarkson, 1733; Joseph Hewes, 1733; Moses Cox, 1734; Daniel Brodhead, 1736; Andrew Tybout, 1736;

Rey. Keen, 1739; Alexander Wilcox, 1742; Thomas Mifflin, 1742; and Charles Jarvis. After dinner we agreed to meet at the same place the last Saturday in the months of March, June, September, and December.

December 8.—At noon the House adjourned and went to the Congress hall, when President Washington delivered his address to the Senate and House.

December 11.—Mr. Barge called for me and we went to Samuel Miles, Jr's., on Arch Street next to the Free Quaker meeting house, who was married last Friday to the daughter of Caleb Foulke, where we drank punch.

December 14.—Colonel F. Gurney and I, with a number of members of the Assembly, examined the work at the President's house on Ninth Street.

December 17.—To-day Mr. Leib's motion for calling the names of the members of the House in alphabetical order was defeated by the vote of the Speaker. It was also resolved that the Speaker in the future shall vote as other members on every question that may come before the House, and only to decide questions when the votes are equally divided.

December 27.—Went to church. Rev. Mr. Helmuth preached. Our congregation has granted the use of the church every other Sunday to the use of the Lutherans until their church is rebuilt. Dined with Mr. Barge, after which we took a walk to the State House yard.

1796.

January 1.—Took luncheon with the Governor at his house on Market Street, the following gentlemen being present : John Shoemaker, Mathias Barton, Abraham Carpenter, Dennis Whelen, and Dr. Kennedy.

January 2.—This evening went to Rickett's circus with my daughters, Mr. and Mrs. Barge, William Standley, Mr. Twells and his daughter.

January 9.—Yesterday went to the House of Representatives of the United States to listen to the trial of Robert Randall and Charles Whitney, who are charged with endeavoring to corrupt some members of the body concerning a large tract of land. Randall was then at the bar of the House and was being defended by James Tilghman and William Lewis.

January 7.—Forenoon attended the House. Dined with Speaker George Latimer and his brother, United States Senator from Delaware ; B. R. Morgan, Francis Gurney, Lawrence Seckel, Robert Waln, Cadwalader Evans, Mr. Tyson, Mr. Davis, Israel Whelen, and Dr. McKinley.

January 12.—The Senate met the House, and Christian Febiger was elected Treasurer of the State.

January 22.—Joseph Erwin's wife was buried. Met with the Committee on Claims on the petition of John Jones. He brought his two daughters before us, who testified that his store was taken by Messrs. Paul Cox, Joseph Marsh, and S. Massey for the use of the State at £100 per annum, and that the same gentlemen gave Mrs. Jones to understand that if the store was destroyed by the British the State would make good the loss.

February 6.—This afternoon General Wayne came to town from the Indian country, where he has been above three years. Our three troops of light-horse met him four miles from the city, and when he crossed the bridge over Schuylkill a salute of fifteen guns was fired from Centre Square. The spectators were very numerous, notwithstanding the muddy roads and streets.

February 7.—On my return from the meadow, I was bled by order of Dr. Kuhn. William Jones called to see me.

February 12.—Met the Committee on Claims, and decided against the claim of John Jones.

February 16.—Met Messrs. Worrell, Boude, Smith, and Cunningham, and decided in favor of the petition of the Trustees of the Academy of Lower Dublin.

February 22.—At noon Speaker Hare, of the Senate, and Speaker Latimer, of the House, with their members, called on President Washington to congratulate him on his birthday. He stood in the centre of the back room, where he bowed to each member as he passed into the front room, where wine and cake were served. At night the ladies and gentlemen had a dance at Rickett's riding place, southwest corner Sixth and Chestnut Streets.

February 25.—The House decided against the resolutions from the State of Virginia for altering the Constitution of the United States, by a majority of fifteen.

March 1.—Attended the House. In the afternoon William Jones and I went to the meadow and ferry house, where we drank coffee. My horse broke loose and ran homeward, but one of the gentlemen of the hunting company secured him and brought him back part way.

March 3.—The bill for moving the Legislature to Lancaster had a second reading and a long debate. Dined at the Governor's with General F. Nichols, John Hall, and David Meade.

March 6.—Dined with Mr. Barge, after which we took a walk. After we parted I met R. B. Morgan and George Roberts on Chestnut Street, and on passing George' Fox's house he invited us in and treated to wine.

March 14.—Spent the evening at Mr. Barge's with the Hon. Mr. Dayton, Speaker of the United States House of Representatives, and his wife, Mr. Kittera and his wife, and Pearson Hunt and wife.

March 17.—Very windy. Attended at the State House. My barn at Gravel Hill, 50 feet long by 22 feet wide was blown down.

March 18.—The Committee on Claims resumed the consideration of the claim of General John Gibson, when we decided against allowing him any compensation for the time he was absent from his family in 1794.

March 20.—Took a walk with Mr. Barge, and went to his house to dinner, which I usually do on Sundays.

March 26.—Attended the House. Dined at Dunwoody's on Market Street, with Governor Mifflin, Benjamin Chew, Judge McKean, Edward Shippen, Richard Peters, General Wayne, Daniel Brodhead, Edward Duffield, Mayor Clarkson, Charles Jarvis, Captain Anthony, William Jones, Rev. Keen, Tench Francis, Judge Biddle, Andrew Tybout, and Joseph Donaldson.

March 28.—At the State House. Dined with Governor Mifflin, Mr. Haldeman, from Lancaster County, Rev. Dr. William Smith, and an English gentleman. Spent the evening at Mr. Barge's with Hon. Mr. Dayton and wife and Hon. Mr. Kittera and wife.

March 30.—Attended in my usual place in the House. At Gravel Hill found the carpenters at work on my new barn.

April 1.—In the morning at the State House. Took a ride up the Ridge Road to John Mifflin's place, and then along the canal and over to Gravel Hill. After a meeting of the Committee on Claims, we went to Dunwoody's tavern, drank two bottles of wine and two bowls of punch.

April 4.—The Legislature adjourned. In the evening between thirty and forty members of both houses met at Oellers's tavern, when Senator Samuel Postlethwaite was called to the chair and Robert Frazer made Secretary. We agreed to the selection of the following gentlemen for Presidential Electors: Israel Whelen, Samuel Miles, Thomas Bull, Henry Wynkoop, Valentine Eckhart, Robert Coleman, John Carson, John Arndt, William Willson, Samuel Postlethwaite, Jacob Hay, Benjamin Elliott, Ephraim Douglass, John Woods, and Thomas Stokely.

April 21.—This afternoon Mr. Barge and I laid the foundation stone of the house I am to build on Market Street adjoining the southwest corner of Seventh, after which we took a ride along the canal.

April 30.—To-day the question was taken in the House on the treaty with Great Britain. The vote stood 49 to 49, when Mr. Muhlenberg gave his vote in favor of the treaty.

May 2.—At noon, with John Wharton, in my chair took a ride along the canal and on our return crossed the Upper Ferry and went to Warner's Fish House, where we dined with Tench Francis, W. Hall, Mr. Cooper, M. C., J Baker, William Gray, Hugh Roberts, Robert and Thomas Hiltzheimer, J. Cox, and about forty more gentlemen. Mr. Daily and Mr. Marshall sang a number of songs.

May 6.—Observed a crowd of people on Fifth Street going toward Chestnut, and on inquiring found that the constables were taking Bernard Shaffer to gaol for stabbing his brother-in-law, F. A. Muhlenberg, two days ago. Shaffer dangerously stabbed Constable West when making the arrest.

May 9.—This evening my daughter, Robert Erwin, and my son Robert went to see the play called "Alexander the Great," it being Mrs. Marshall's benefit.

May 15.—Miss Higby in my chair, and Abraham Hunt, wife and daughter, in their carriage, set out for Trenton.

May 16.—Mr. Hunt and I rode up to Lambertville on horseback. The fishermen, eight in number, caught 60,200 herring just below the town. They sell for $3 per thousand.

May 17.—Set out from Abraham Hunt's at five o'clock, drove twenty miles to the sign of Washington to breakfast, and arrived in Philadelphia at half past ten.

May 20.—John Wharton and I went to the burial of R. Will's wife, on Third Street, to Friends' burial ground.

May 21.—Took Mathias Slough, of Lancaster, in my chair to Governor Mifflin's, at the Falls, where we dined with Matthew McConnell, Daniel Brodhead, Robert Westcott, John Hall, Robert Erwin, Anthony Morris, William Gray, Thomas Forrest, Benjamin Scull, Alexander Scott, Alderman Keen, and others

May 27.—Called at Mr. Barge's and took him out riding, as he has not been well, and spent the evening with him.

June 4.—Mr. Barge and I went to the State House yard, from thence to my house, where we took my chair and rode to the meadows. On our return we met, just below the stone bridge in the meadows, our President, Washington, and lady in a coach and four, two postillions, and only one servant on horseback. In old countries a man of his rank and dignity would not be seen without a retinue of twenty or more persons.

June 12.—Dined with Mr. Barge and in the afternoon walked with William Jones to Robert Morris's house, which attracts the attention of every one who sees it. One of the workmen told me that it could not be finished under five summers.

June 13.—My daughter, with Robert Erwin, went to the play, and Matthew Clarkson and I called to see William Jones and wife.

June 15.—General Walter Stewart was buried to-day, and I was informed of the death of Mr. Higby, of Trenton.

June 16.—Rode to the meadows and Point House. Walked down to Hunt's wharf with the Governor to see the vessel loaded with cheese from New England.

June 21.—Breakfasted at Mr. Barge's at six o'clock, after which we drove down the Chester Road to the Blue Bell and to the meadows, returning by the way of Mr. Bingham's ferry, the last one down the Schuylkill.

June 24.—Before breakfast Mr. Barge and I drove to the ferry house kept by one William Jones, at the mouth of the Schuylkill, and in the evening repeated our visit to obtain a jug of buttermilk.

June 27.—To-day the well-known David Rittenhouse was buried under a small building in the rear of his house, northwest corner Seventh and Arch Streets.

July 4.—In the morning Jonathan Mifflin, Pearson Hunt, and myself, went to the Governor's garden, back of his house on Market Street, where a lunch with punch was served to the officers of the militia and State Government.

July 9.—This afternoon had the raising supper on the second floor of my new building intended for a store. The following gentlemen were present : Judge John J. Henry, of Lancaster; General Henry Miller, of York ; Mr. Barge, Weidman, Robert Erwin, William and Joseph Gray, Pearson Hunt, Jacob Cox, Edward Wells, Mr. Lybrand, Tonking, Emerick, and others. Some of the gentlemen came over to my house and sat under the grape arbor.

July 10.—Miss Higby, Pearson Hunt, and Mr. Milner went down to the Blue Bell to breakfast. Just as they were leaving, my daughter Molly, Julia Duffield, and two young gentlemen drove up to dine there.

July 12.—Drove to Gravel Hill before breakfast and around by Robert Morris's stone quarry on Schuylkill, where I saw five teams loading stone to be taken to the building at Seventh and Market Streets. At the latter a large number of men are employed, as well as building a wall around the lot.

July 19.—At three o'clock this morning Mr. Barge, his wife, and I set out for the seashore, crossed at Dunk's ferry, and thence to Burlington to breakfast, and to Bordentown and dined at Davis's with Dr. Burns and wife, of that town, and Mr. Bartow, of Philadelphia. Nighted at Crosswix.

July 20.—Set out at three o'clock and breakfasted at David Clayton's Burnt House, thence to Jacob Hart's, Colt's Neck, and arrived at Alexander McGregor's, in Edenton, for the night.

July 21.—After breakfast set out for the seashore, four miles distant. Called at Thomas Chandler's and McKnight's and found both inns full. Returned to Edenton to dinner, and found there Mr. Morrell, and wife and daughters, Mr. Clark, Mr. Compton, Mr. Pointell, Mr. Wagner, Mr. Beck, Mr. Newbold, and others. Returned to the shore, where Mr. Barge and I took a bath, after which we returned to McGregor's for the night.

July 22.—Went again to the seashore and met Anthony Shafto at Chandler's, where we dined. Accompanied Shafto to his house and engaged rooms. Drove to Edenton, paid our bill, and returned to our new lodgings, Shafto's, which is within three-quarters of a mile of the seashore.

July 23.—After breakfast Mr. Barge, wife, and I took a ride along the shore in the direction of New York. Passed through Wardell's plantation and on to the river, near which Mr. Bingham's house stands on high ground, which affords a fine view in the direction of Black Point. Returned to our lodgings for dinner. William Hunter, wife, and three children and Miss Mary Luken arrived here from Philadelphia.

July 24.—After breakfast the Hunter family and we in two carriages drove along the shore to Chandler's, and after dining at Shafto's drove to Edenton and back.

July 25.—Bathed with the Hunter family. In the afternoon Mr. Barge and I drove to Edenton.

July 26.—We accompanied the Hunter family to Chandler's, which is the headquarters for all Philadelphians to call to hear the news of the day.

July 27.—The Hunter family, Miss Luken, and we, drove to Shrewsbury, stopped at Thompson's, and drank punch and returned home to dinner. Called at Chandler's as usual.

July 28.—This morning bathed with the Hunters, and so did Mrs. Barge for the first time. Mr. Barge, after bathing in the sea once, and having tried the shower bath three times, has concluded that neither are of benefit to him. Mr. Hunter, with several of his friends and I drove to Deal, stopping at Brindley's mill to see the curious maple tree, the roots of which in the form of an arch span the stream. Visited the farms of Jacob Herbst, Jacob Corlies, and White, which are fine. At Deal there is a body of water inland called the Crab Pond.

July 29.—Bathed with Mr. Hunter and Miss Luken. After breakfast drove along the shore to Chandler's, where we had some port wine. Mr. Bevan, of Philadelphia, who lodges at Chandler's, dined with us.

July 30.—Mr. Barge was quite ill last night; the rain came through the roof on to his bed, and gave him gout in the knee. Mr. and Mrs. Hunter and I rode down to Corlies to see the water let out of Crab Pond, and dined there with Captain Tingly, wife, and daughter, Mr. Bond and wife, Mr. Rea and wife, Mr. Stockton, Henry, Bevan, and others.

July 31.—At five o'clock Mr. and Mrs. Barge and myself set out for home and left the Hunters at Shafto's. Breakfasted at James Craig's in Monmouth, went on to Crosswix, dined at Douglass's, and remained over night. William Jones arrived from Philadelphia and remained over night.

August 1.—Mr. Barge had a very bad night. We waited for breakfast, then, to my great surprise, Mr. Barge desired to go on, so we carried him to his carriage. Crossed the Delaware at Dunk's, fed our horses at Kimball's, and proceeded to the Sign of General

Washington, where we dined and drank tea. Set out again and reached Mr. Barge's house by dark. We carried him in, suffering great pain from his knee down to his foot.

August 5.—Called to see Jacob Cox, who fell from his horse and was much hurt in the left shoulder. My son Thomas's daughter died—she was born the 23d of March, 1795, and has been ill a long time.

August 6.—My granddaughter's corpse was taken to Friends' ground, Arch Street, in General Brodhead's carriage, in which was her father and my daughter Molly; Rebecca Cox, Hannah Hiltzheimer, and R. Erwin in Hall's carriage. William Gray and I walked.

August 7.—Went to the meadow and Point House before breakfast. Dined at Mr. Barge's, who is still very ill with the gout.

August 8.—Driving down to the meadow, met William Gray, Hugh Roberts, my son Thomas, and William Hall, in the latter's carriage. Stopped at the Sign of the Buck and drank punch.

August 18.—Called at the ropewalk and bought a pint of brown tar for my daughter Molly, who has been sick some days. Went up the canal as far as John Mifflin's, near which I met Anthony Benezet and another gentleman in a chair.

August 19.—This forenoon took Mr. Barge out in my chair, the first time since he was brought home with the gout from the seashore.

August 23.—At six o'clock Christian Byerly and I attended the burial of Mrs. Kidd, from her house in Market Street to Pine Street. Titus Matlack was buried from the house of his son-in-law, William Hunter, in Friends' ground, this morning.

August 26.—Took a ride with Mr. Barge by the Schuylkill, to show him where Robert Morris is erecting the large building to manufacture iron by steam. Dined with William Jones, who lately returned from the seashore.

August 27.—To-night called to see Mr. Barge, who complained much of the gout in his head. Dr. Wister ordered him to be cupped at once, and it was done.

August 28.—Went to church, and afterwards dined with Mr. Barge, who is much better than last night.

August 31.—Received of Mr. Trimble the Governor's warrant for $14,054.55, the balance for completing the President's house, which amount I delivered to my brother commissioner, R. Wells. The total cost was $30.000.

September 1.—Took a ride along the banks of the Schuylkill, and afterwards dined at Warner's Fish House with Samuel Morris, J. Hews, William Jones, B. Scull, William Gray, Thomas Forest, John M. Taylor, S. Wheeler, John Graff, and my two sons.

September 6.—Mr. Barge and I took a ride out Ridge Road, across Turner's Lane and home via Germantown Road.

September 7.—In the afternoon Mr. Barge and I took a ride to Point No Point. By invitation of Governor Mifflin dined at Dunwoody's, on turtle, with General Brodhead, F. Johnston, and John Hall, the three Land officers; Judge Yeates; Dr. James Armstrong, of Carlisle; General Henry Miller, of York; Alexander Scott, George Campbell, Edward Fox, Joseph Thomas, John Baker, Matthew McConnell, General Harmar, and Captain Pike.

September 13.—Breakfasted with Mr. and Mrs. Barge at six o'clock, after which we set out in carriage for Bristol, where we dined at McEllroy's. On returning one of the horses nearly gave out, owing to the extreme heat, within two miles of the city.

September 17.—Forenoon Mr. Barge rode with me out Ridge Road, crossed over, returned through Frankford. Dined with Israel Whelen and family, afterward went to the burial of Anthony Morris's, daughter, who is grand-daughter of William Jones.

September 19.—Mr. Wells, F. Gurney and myself had the eagle taken down from the President's house, repaired and then replaced.

16

September 20.—Mr. Barge and I took a ride up the canal to above Mifflin's place. I read in Brown's paper of yesterday the President's address declining a renomination at the approaching election. The advice he gives to the nation I hope will be remembered by all good citizens to the end of time.

September 22.—Attended the burial of Christian Febiger, State Treasurer, from his house on Market Street to the Presbyterian ground on Arch near Fifth Street. Dined with Mr. Barge, and afterwards we took a ride along the banks of the Schuylkill.

September 23.—Delivered the key of my new store to William Harrison, who rents it at $450 per annum.

September 24.—Called to see my daughter Cox, and her son, who was a week old yesterday and is a stout, good-looking boy. Dined with Mr. Barge, after which we took a ride.

September 29.—This evening went to corner of Spruce and Second Streets, to Jacob Cox's, to witness the marriage of his daughter Susanna to Robert Erwin, by Bishop White. About thirty couples were present.

September 30.—Mr. Barge and I took a ride up the canal as far as Mr. Williams's place; afterward we met Mr. Hysham and B. Scull, and went to Robert Erwin's on Eighth Street, to drink punch with him, where we met a large number of gentlemen.

October 1.—At noon went again to Robert Erwin's and there met Moses Cox. I found still a number of persons going in and out, and was told by the young ladies up stairs that they kept an account of the gentlemen callers yesterday, who numbered 170, and that nearly as many had called to-day.

October 11.—Election day; went to the State House and voted for county and State officers.

October 13.—To-day I received the eleventh notice from the Judges of the Election of my being elected a Representative of the city in the Assembly.

October 18.—Mr. Toderhirst and I drove down the Chester Road to Richard Tutton's, and dug up in his field near the house what is called cotton stone. When it is washed and dried it looks white and fuzzy, and if laid in oil will burn like a candle for a long time, and fire will not consume it. When it has been in use for a long time, and becomes dirty, it is thrown into the fire to clean it.

October 23.—Went to church in the forenoon. After dinner Lewis Weiss, Esq., was buried in the Moravian ground, on Vine Street.

October 26.—The stone-cutter set the top stone of the steps at the President's house on Ninth Street.

October 30.—Went to Samuel Newlin's, a mile below Darby, and dined with his family and seven young ladies and gentlemen. After dinner Hugh Lloyd called and was glad to see me. We used to be quite intimate when he was a member of the Assembly.

October 31.—Weather rainy and unpleasant. General Washington and his lady came to town.

November 1.—This morning about five o'clock a fire broke out in William Hunter's stable, in the rear of his house on the north side of Market Street above Eighth, adjoining Surveyor General Brodhead's office, where all the valuable papers are kept belonging to the State. It is reported that some lime, near some boards by the stable, began to slack from a slight rainfall, which caused the fire.

November 3.—A young gentleman by the name of Braham, from Winchester, Virginia, with a letter from Nancy Clayton, took breakfast with me.

November 4.—Went to the State House and voted for fifteen Presidential electors, who with those from other States, are to choose a President and Vice-President of the United States, to serve for four years.

November 12.—Mr. and Mrs. Barge, Dr. Burns and wife from Bordentown, and myself, went to see the elephant, on the south side of

Market between Third and Fourth Streets. It is the first one I have seen.

November 18.—In the forenoon went with the Governor, Colonel Gurney, John Hall, P. Baynton, Major Lenox, B. R. Morgan and others to the house on Ninth Street, intended for the President of the United States.

November 20.—Before breakfast drove to the meadow and Point House. Went to church, and afterwards had to dinner with me, William Gray, Mr. Levis, Robert Westcott, J. M. Taylor, and my two sons, with daughter Hannah.

November 27.—This morning the first sermon was preached in the Lutheran church on Fourth Street, since it was destroyed by fire, December 26, 1794.

November 28.—Mr. Barge and I took a ride, and in returning by Robert Morris's stone quarry, found the Schuylkill frozen over at the upper bridge. This is very uncommon at this season. The old rule that winter never sets in until the ditches and ponds are filled with water, does not hold good this year, for we have had no rain since the 3d of September.

November 29.—Dined with the Governor and his son-in-law. After dinner we went to General Brodhead's, where we met John Hall and Jonathan Jones.

December 6.—The Legislature met this afternoon, but no quorum was present.

December 9.—At noon the Speaker of the House and the members proceeded to the Senate Chamber, where Thomas Mifflin delivered his address, which occupied fifty minutes. The several subjects were well treated and still better delivered.

December 12.—Dined at the Governor's with Thomas Campbell, Abraham Shultz, Joseph Tyson, Jacob Saylor, and Mr. Weirich, of the House; John Hall and the Governor's son-in-law, Hopkinson.

December 15.—Went to the President's house on Ninth Street, which I usually do once daily.

December 17.—At noon the Assembly went to the Presbyterian church on Market Street, where Dr. Rush, a member of the Philosophical Society, pronounced an eulogium in memory of their late president, David Rittenhouse. The church was crowded, President Washington and lady, with members of Congress being present.

December 20.—At noon the Assembly walked to the Court House on Market Street, and proclaimed the election for the third time of Governor Mifflin. Owing to being confined to his house, the Governor was unable to attend.

December 27.—During the evening my daughters told me that they had crossed the river Delaware on the ice, with Robert Erwin and his wife's sister.

1797.

January 6.—Went to our Speaker's, George Latimer, on Pine Street by the waterside, and dined with Senator James Ross; Senator Tazewell, of Virginia; Senator Latimer, of Delaware; (our Speaker's brother); Francis Gurney, R. Waln, Joseph Ball, members of the House; Mr. Miller, Clement Stocker, Mr. Smith, Mr. Swift, and Mr. Pratt.

January 8.—From Race Street wharf I walked on the ice to Cooper's Ferry and back; saw thousands of people, horses and sleighs, and booths on the ice.

January 10.—The Senate and House elected Peter Baynton, late clerk of the House, State Treasurer, in the place of the late Christian Febiger.

January 12.—Joseph Bullock was elected Clerk of the House on the second ballot, in the place of Peter Baynton, resigned.

January 20.—At three o'clock dined with Levi Hollingsworth, Israel Whelen, Dennis Whelen, Francis Gurney, Lawrence Seckel, John Hulme, Theophilus Foulke, R. Stover, Thomas Boude, Thomas Campbell, John Coolbaugh, Thomas Grant, William Henderson, Samuel Marshall, Jonas Preston, at Robert Waln's, on Second Street, member of the House. He is a man of uncommon understanding, a good speaker, and can reply to a member who is opposed to him, with temper and good reasoning. His house is richly furnished, and he has a large lot and garden in the rear. Mr. Waln sat at one end of the table and his wife at the other.

January 22.—My daughters told me that yesterday when they drove to the upper bridge, they saw an ox roast on the ice on the Schuylkill.

January 26.—Met the Committee on Claims and decided against the claim of John Hazelwood for £132.

January 27.—In returning from the meadows, up Front Street, stopped to look at Mr. Brown's, the printer's house, which was on fire this morning, and was told that Mrs. Brown, two daughters, one son and a negro boy perished in the flames.

January 28.—While at Mr. Barge's this evening, the cry of fire was raised, and ascertained it was the brewery of Jacob Morgan, in Moravian Alley. Mrs. Brown and her children, who were burned to death yesterday, were buried in three coffins in the graveyard of St. Paul's church. (Mr. Brown soon followed his wife and children, —he was buried February 5th.)

February 3.—Went down to Chestnut Street wharf to see the ice move —the river has been closed since December 23d last. To-day the report concerning the controversy about lands in the Wyoming Valley, which was made to the House on January 16th, was read for the second time, in Committee of the Whole, John Shoemaker in the chair. William Maclay, member from Dauphin, spoke first, and he was followed by John Franklin, of Luzerne, until two o'clock.

February 4.—John Franklin resumed his argument and spoke for one hour and fifty minutes.

February 7.—The Wyoming controversy again brought up, and Mr. Maclay spoke two hours in favor of the report, he being a member of the Committee.

February 8.—The House again took up the Wyoming controversy, Mr. Shoemaker in the chair. Mr. C. Evans, of Montgomery county, spoke one hour and forty-five minutes, against the report, and Mr. Power, of Cumberland, about fifteen minutes. The Committee reported progress.

February 9.—Wyoming matter again before the house. Mr. Robert Waln spoke thirty minutes against the report, and was replied to by Mr. Maclay. Mr. West, from Delaware county, made a few observations in opposition to Maclay. Committee reported progress.

February 10.—House went into Committee of the Whole, John Shoemaker again in the chair. Mr. John Smilie, from Fayette county, spoke in favor of the report for forty-five minutes; John Franklin spoke one hour and three quarters, refuting the charges made against him and other Connecticut claimants.

February 11.—The Wyoming controversy again called up. Mr. Maclay followed up his argument of former days; then Robert Frazer, of Chester County, spoke half an hour, opposing Maclay in part. The Committee of the Whole agreed to the report brought in by the Special Committee, and of course Mr. Waln's substitute fell. It was argued by the minority that the report was unconstitutional; besides it was thought it made no distinction between those Connecticut claimants who settled on the lands before the decree of the Commissioners at Trenton, December 30, 1782, and those who settled there afterwards. On the Speaker resuming the chair, Mr. Shoemaker reported that the Committee of the Whole had agreed to report, and it was read to the House and agreed to by a vote of forty-six to fourteen.

February 15.—The House agreed to the address which is to be delivered to President Washington, by Messrs. Joseph Ball, Robert Frazer, and Mr. Power, the yeas and nays being called, 45 to 26.

February 16.—At noon the Senate and House re-elected James Ross, of Pittsburgh, United States Senator.

February 17.—At noon the Speaker of the House with a number of members waited on President Washington with the address of the House.

February 18.—At four o'clock I went with the following members of the House and dined with that great and good man, George Washington, President of the United States, who will retire from office on March 4th next, at which time John Adams, the present Vice-President, will take his place: Speaker Latimer, J. Bull, Gurney, Waln, and Seckel, of Philadelphia; Keys, Boude, Carpenter, and Brown, of Lancaster; Hulme, Foulke, -Stover, and Van Horn, of Bucks; Frazer, Bull, and Hannum, of Chester; McPherson, Turner, Miller, and Stewart, of York; and Marshall, of Huntingdon. Our Speaker sat between the President and his lady, and I on the left of the President.

February 22.—The House adjourned at noon and the members generally went and paid their respects to President Washington, this being his birthday. A salute was fired. At two o'clock dined with my son-in-law, Jacob Cox, southeast corner Fourth and Market Streets, with old Mr. Cox, John Dunlap, William Gray, Dennis Whelen, Abraham Carpenter, John Patton, Benjamin Scull, William Hall, Robert Erwin, Peter Brown, John Graff, William Miller, William Forrest, and Thomas Hiltzheimer. Mr. Barge came in after dinner was over.

March 2.—Mr. Hulme and Van Horn, of the House, breakfasted with me. In the afternoon Governor Mifflin and the members of both houses visited the President's house on Ninth Street.

March 4.—At noon our house adjourned to attend in Congress Hall, where the new President, John Adams, was proclaimed. Cannons were fired from the lot at the northwest corner Walnut and Sixth Streets.

March 6.—General Washington, our late worthy President, set out with his family toward his seat in Virginia.

March 7.—Went from the State House with John Shoemaker, of the House, and about a dozen members, to the gaol, to see the prisoners at work at different trades. We saw six men cutting nails, and twelve making heads to them; a number sawing marble, others making shoes, and women spinning. All the criminals are put to work and are allowed a certain sum of money per week; none are hanged except for murder.

March 9.—In Committee of the Whole, the bill was read which was formed on the report debated from February 3d to 11th, concerning the Wyoming disturbances.

March 10.—The Wyoming affairs again before the Committee of the Whole, Mr. Bull in the chair. Went to the State House in the afternoon, to a Committee meeting; Leiper against Ross, Delaware County. Mr. Dallas spoke in behalf of the former.

March 16.—The Wyoming matter was brought up on the 11th 14th, 15th, and to-day, in Committee of the Whole.

March 18.—The Wyoming bill was again before the House and was gotten through with.

March 26.—President John Adams's proclamation calling Congress together May 15th, for important business, has been issued.

April 2.—Mr. Barge and I drove down to see the Federal ship which is to be launched this week.

April 3.—Drove up the canal as far as Judge Williams's place, formerly Macphersons, and returned by the Ridge Road.

April 5.—The House sat until 9.30 before the business was concluded, when we adjourned to August 28th next.

April 11.—With Mr. Standley and Barge drove in a carriage to Standley's place, and in the meadow, where there were some fine cattle, Mr. Barge and I got out. Before Mr. Standley could alight the horses started off; the driver caught hold of the off horse, but fell and the carriage passed over him. On a full run they started around the field, until they were stopped by striking a fence post, when Mr. Standley got out unhurt. No damage was done and the driver complained only a little of being sore.

April 21.—In the evening went to the play; it being W. Bates's benefit, I bought Box No. 3.

April 27.—Daniel Benezet and wife were buried to-day—they died within ten hours of each other.

May 4.—Mr. Barge and I in my chair, John Dunlap, Robert Erwin, William Gray, Hugh Roberts, and George Weed in Dunlap's carriage; Pearson Hunt and Major Armstrong on horseback, went to see Dunlap's meadows, and on our return stopped at Paschall's, Sign of the Blue Bell, where we had several bottles of wine. My son-in-law Jacob Cox met us there.

May 9.—In the evening Mrs. Barge and I went to Lailson's Circus, on Fifth Street south of Chestnut, where we saw some wonderful equestrian acts.

May 10.—Dined with Mr. Barge, after which we went down in my chair to the old fort in Southwark, where was launched the frigate United States, to carry forty-four guns. The launch was conducted by Commodore Barry, in view of possibly 20,000 spectators, who crowded the shore and on the river.

May 16.—In the afternoon a genteel young man by the name of Glenn, a physician, and grandson of Dr. William Jones, of Georgia, who at the time of our Revolution was a member of Congress and lived in my house at Southwest corner Seventh and Market, called to see me. He boards at Joseph Webster's, Jenkintown, where my son Robert boards, by whom he was desired to call on me.

May 19.—Molly Ogden and my daughter Molly drove in my chair to see Mr. Bartram's garden, on the west side of the Schuylkill.

May 20.—In the evening went to Moses Cox's, to witness the marriage of his daughter Peggy to Major Freeman, by Bishop White.

May 24.—Mr. Barge and I went to Gravel Hill and from thence to Seider's, called the upper Ferry, which he recently bought of John Britton, as the corporation and he could not agree about the rent for the Middle Ferry. Seider told us he offered them £1200 a year for it.

May 26.—William Jones and I in my chair, went to George Esterley's, Harrowgate, and found a fine garden, large, and in good order, laid out with serpentine walks and round ponds of water. We had a glass of punch, with fish, ham, beef and coffee as a relish.

May 28.—At noon met Thomas and Norton Pryor; went with them to the late David Rittenhouse's observatory, to set the time piece there, which they have done since the death of that great man.

June 1.—While out riding with Mr. Barge we called on Robert Morris' s gardener, who made us some very good lemon punch, the fruit grown in the garden, and showed us a number of pine-apples growing and likewise two coffee trees in bloom.

June 11.—Heard that Thomas Blount had sent a challenge to George Thatcher to fight a duel. Both are members of the House of Representatives of the United States.

June 15.—This evening went to Moses Cox's, on Spruce Street, and witnessed the marriage of his daughter Betsey to Captain Poole, by Bishop White.

June 16.—At noon called on Captain Poole and his wife. Attended the funeral of Judge James Biddle, from his house on Seventh Street, to the Church yard on Arch Street.

June 20.—Mr. Barge and I drove to the Middle Ferry to see the mast, ninety feet long, which Witmer brought down on his wagon, of three pairs of wheels and nine horses, from Wright's Ferry, on the

Susquehanna. It weighs about nine tons. It was unloaded into the Schuylkill and is to be towed around to the city. Mr. Tench Francis told us it cost about $200, and that it is intended for the Algerine government, under the treaty.

June 22.—After dinner Mr. Barge and I went to William Sheaff's place on Shippen's Lane; saw his fine garden. He invited us in to lunch, with F. A. Muhlenberg, J. Nixon, Mr. Thomas, Ex-Senator, Ross and Mr. Sperry. We had dried beef and tongue of the tenderest kind and some extraordinary fine wine, for which Mr. Sheaff is noted.

July 1.—I went to the Schuylkill lot; met the Hon. George Latimer, and the two Smith's at Colonel Gurney's place on Schuylkill; in the city, where I was kindly received by the Colonel and his wife, we had a lunch with wine.

July 2.—Went to Mrs. Marshall's, at Gloucester Point, and there had breakfast. Just as I was leaving, my daughter Cox with her two children drove up, and we returned together. Dined at Mr. Barge's, then I went to church, and at seven o'clock attended the burial of Henry Keppele, aged eighty-one years, on Market near Third Street, to the graveyard on Fifth Street adjoining the old Lutheran Church. The attendance was unusually large.

July 4.—In the afternoon Christopher Byerley and I in my chair drove to Harrowgate, where we saw many people, and from thence to Bush Hill, where we saw still more, all spending money.

July 5.—Mr. Cunningham's country seat, late the property of Thomas Lawrence, three miles from the city, was burned down.

July 7.—The House of Representatives of the United States appointed Samuel Sitgreaves to appear before the Bar of the Senate and impeach William Blount, one of their members, and also demand that he be sequestered from his seat. He also entered into bonds for $20,000 and his brother Thomas Blount, and Pierce Butler, each of them $15,000 as his sureties. In the evening Mr. Barge and I took a ride to Bush Hill to see William Bates, and from thence to Peter Kuhn's country seat on Turner's Lane, where we drank tea.

July 10.—I learned that on Saturday the Senate of the United States expelled Mr. Blount from his seat.

July 13.—Mr. Barge and I early this morning went to Germantown, to the burial of Sarah Paris, daughter of the late Mr. Stoneburner. On our way home called at Colonel Thomas Forrest's, and there dined at two o'clock with James Ash, Esq., who is again a candidate for sheriff.

July 16.—Forenoon went to Church and dined with Mr. Barge. In the afternoon we drove up Point no Point road to Geisse's place, formerly William Parr's, where I have not visited for many years.

July 18.—Mr. Barge and I took a ride down to the meadows, at the mouth of Hollander's Creek. After dinner we went with Peter Kuhn to his lot, lately a part of Robert Morris's garden, where he showed us his grape vines loaded down with grapes. I have not seen so many in one place since I left Germany.

July 21.—Mr. Barge and I took a ride. Stopped at Casin's tavern and had a drink, and met Joseph Wharton, with a member of Congress from Connecticut, H. Sheaff and several others.

July 26.—Mr. Barge and I went with Governor Mifflin to his place on the west side of the Schuylkill opposite the Falls. We dined at the Falls, where my son-in-law Cox, joined us.

July 28.—Took a ride to the Upper Ferry to see Seider's contrivance for bringing water from a spring in his garden, through pipes into his bar-room on one side and out on the other, and into the Schuylkill.

July 29.—Mr. Barge and I took a ride down along the banks of the Schuylkill, to view the Frenchman's place, which Mr. James Milligan sold.

August 1.—At six o'clock Mr. Barge and I drove to Elliot's, near Darby, to visit my daughter Cox and children, where they are to board two or three weeks. Breakfasted with the family and then returned home by the way of the lower ferry.

August 7.—To-day I handed Hugh Roberts, one of the Street Commissioners, a petition signed by residents along Seventh Street, for a pump.

August 11.—This evening the Rev. Mr. Helmuth married my daughter Molly to W. Rogers.

August 17.—The letter of Dr. John Redman, President of the College of Physicians, addressed to Governor Mifflin, with regard to the malignant fever which has appeared in Penn Street, was printed to-day.

August 18.—Met at the State House, Governor Mifflin, agreeably to a letter received from Secretary A. J. Dallas, concerning the approaching session of the Legislature, and the fever on Penn near Pine Street. There was present Judges McKean and Smith, Doctors S. Duffield and Wister; Robert Hare, Israel Whelen, B. R., Morgan, Newlin and Z. Potts, of the Senate, Francis Gurney, J. Bull and Laurence Seckel, of the House, and Messrs. Leib, Worrell, Linnard, Eyre, Shoemaker, Evans, Tyson Preston and West. It appears that since the arrival of the Ship Hinde, on the 5th instant, twenty-eight persons were taken down with the fever and eleven died.

August 20.—While out riding met Mr. Mays with his wife and children and Miss de Hart of Virginia, in their coach and four, on the way to Elizabethtown. After parting with them at the Bell we drove to near the mouth of the Schuylkill and crossed.

August 22.—The father of my son-in-law W. Rogers, with Dr. Dewees and wife, drank tea at my house.

August 27.—The number of deaths reported by the different churches of this city and suburbs since the 1st instant, is 211, of which 105 were children. I now remember that in the autumn of 1762, a fever which I believe to be like the present one alarmed the citizens very much, but it was insignificant compared to the present one or that of four years ago.

August 29.—At ten o'clock attended the House. The Governor delivered his address to both houses. An appropriation of $10,000 to the Committee of Health, for the relief of the poor sick, was passed. The House then adjourned sine die. Their abrupt adjournment is owing to the contagious fever in the southeastern and lower districts of the city.

August 30.—The deaths during the last twenty-four hours numbered only eight adults and six children. It is surprising that so insignificant a number should create so much excitement in this city as well as in the country.

August 31.—I sold three lots on Eighth Street near Vine, nineteen feet front by ninety feet deep, at $1.50 per foot a year, to Messrs. Edward Hughes, John Alexander and Jacob Ford.

September 1.—I observe that people are still moving from the city, notwithstanding the mortality is abating.

September 3.—Before breakfast drove over Schuylkill to Benjamin Brannan's, to visit Moses Cox and family, who moved on account of the fever in their neighborhood. After breakfast went to Elliot's, where Jacob Cox and his family are boarding. Returned home after dinner.

September 4.—Breakfasted at Mr. Barge's, after which we took a ride to William Standley's, and from thence through Bensell's Lane and down the Germantown road home. We met a number of our citizens anxious to hear of affairs in the city.

September 11.—With Mr. Barge in my chair we drove to Squire Elliot's to breakfast, and from thence Jacob Cox went with us to his father at Brennan's. We all drove to Miller's Sign of the Buck, where we dined, and then each returned home.

September 12.—Mr. Barge and I drove up the Ridge Road to visit William Standley, who is sick in bed, and found Dr. Wister with him.   The doctor invited us in, we shook hands and then left.

September 29.—Breakfasted with Mr. Barge, after which he and Mrs. Barge rode with me to Jonathan Miller's Sign of the Buck, on the Lancaster road, and dined there with Mr. and Mrs. Graff, Mr. Kress, and two gentlemen.   From there we drove to Brannan's to visit my daughter's family.

October 3.—Mr. Barge and I took a drive up the Ridge Road to engage 100 heads of cabbage for sour kraut.   Claypoole's paper contains the account of a man who fell suddenly on Arch Street and was examined by two physicians who pronounced him dead.   A coffin was sent for, into which his body was placed, and as it was being carried off, he began to rap on the lid, upon which he was helped out.   The man is now alive.

October 5.—Dined at Warner's Fish House with William Jones, William Gray, William Hall, Edward Shoemaker, Joseph Cowperthwaite and my son Thomas.

October 8.—Dined at Mr. Barge's, which I have done ever since my family went out of town, the 15th of last month.

October 10.—Mr. Barge and I went to the State House and voted for Sheriff, one Senator, six Assemblymen, and one County Commissioner.   Dined at Mr. Barge's with John Dunlap, Henry Sheaff, a son of William Sheaff, and Levi Hollingsworth.

October 15.—Breakfasted and dined with my family at Brannan's, after which we walked over to neighbor Garritt's and found him sick with gout.   On our return found John Sellers and another neighbor who called to see me.   Returned home in the afternoon.

October 18.—A false report of the death of General Washington reached the city.

October 20.—Went over the Schuylkill to Brannan's, and after dinner brought my family home.   It is just five weeks since they left the city.

November 10.—John Adams, President of the United States, arrived at his house on Market Street, escorted by the three troops of light-horse.

November 13.—To-day Congress met, but no quorum was present.

November 23.—Messrs. Wells and Gurney came to my house, where we examined and signed the accounts for the President's house on Ninth Street, after which we lodged them with Receiver General Samuel Bryan.

November 30.—Matthew Clarkson and I took a ride in my chair to the Schuylkill and found it frozen over.   We returned by the canal and Ridge Road.

December 5.—This afternoon went to the State House, it being the day appointed by the Constitution for the Legislature to meet.

December 6.—Went to the State House and elected George Latimer, Speaker.

December 13.—Attended the Assembly, and after adjourning Joseph Webster of Montgomery county dined with me.

December 16.—Attended at the State House.   A committee was selected to try a contested election in Lycoming county, between Jacob Shoemaker, the sitting member, and Hugh White.   First the names of members present were called (seventy), then their names were written on the same number of pieces of paper, rolled up and placed in three different boxes.   Clerk Bullock then took out one at a time and handed it to the Speaker, who opened them and called out the name.   Two tellers, Mr. Leib and Henderson, wrote them down.   The contestants sat near the table to object to such members as they deemed proper, without giving any reason, until seventeen were selected.   Then the parties withdrew to a Committee

17

room with the Clerk, when eight names were stricken off, reducing the number to nine. On the return of the nine members the Speaker administered the oath, that they will truly try and decide which party shall be admitted to the House. John Lloyd, of Montgomery county, dined at my house.

December 20.—A committee was selected to try the election contest between Boileau, the sitting member, and Pauling, of Montgomery county. After the House adjourned Speaker Latimer with myself and several members went to George Bickham's, on Market street, to drink punch, whose daughter was married to Washington Finney.

December 25.—Dined at Mr. Barge's with young Mr. Bohlen, and his relatives Knoll and Souder, recently arrived from Germany.

December 28.—On my way to the State House, paid twenty-five cents to see a lion.

1798.

January 1.—Forenoon Edward Wells brought his accounts for building a small house adjoining the one I live in; an addition to the one my son Thomas lives in; and a store in Market Street, adjoining the corner house. In the afternoon attended at the State House, as a member of the House of Representatives.

January 4.—Attended at the State House forenoon. Dined with my son-in-law, Jacob Cox, and so did the following gentlemen:— Governor Mifflin, my son-in-law's father, Peter Baynton, William Gray, Robert Erwin, Mr. — Pool, and William Hall. John Hall came in after dinner and sat down with us. From thence I went to the State House to meet the Committee on Claims, of which I am chairman.

January 10.—Had to breakfast with me Thomas Campbell, from York County; Mr. Kirk, from Chester County, and Doctor Preston, from Delaware County, all members of the House of Representatives; afterwards we went to the State House.

January 15.—Went with Philip Gardner, a member from York County, to the House at the southwest corner of Chestnut and Fourth Streets to see the dwarf, Calvin Phillips, born in Massachusetts. He is seven years old, twenty-six inches high, weighs twelve pounds, is very smart, and it was pleasing to see him walk about the room.

January 19.—Attended in my usual place. Afternoon met at the President's house, Ninth Street, a committee, on a memorial from fifty-one subscribers praying to be incorporated to build a bridge across the Delaware at Trenton.

January 22.—At the State House we had before the House four witnesses, and examined them concerning a certain magistrate, Henry Shoemaker, Esq., of Lycoming County, holding out threats to prevent the above witnesses coming to Philadelphia to attend on the committee of nine members elected by the House to try and decide the contested election between Jacob Shoemaker and Hugh White, of said county, which they have done in favor of Hugh White, Esq. Jacob Shoemaker was the sitting member.

January 24.—The resolution before the House to address the Governor, to remove Henry Shoemaker, Esq., from office, was debated three hours and a half, and at three o'clock the House adjourned.

January 25.—To-day the subject was again debated concerning H. Shoemaker. The following gentlemen were re-elected directors of the Bank of Pennsylvania: George Bickham, Jacob Morgan, and Charles Biddle.

January 26.—Forenoon attended in my place. The resolution concerning H. Shoemaker was again taken up, and at last a committee of seven members appointed to make out specifications against him and report to the House. The House went into a Committee of the Whole, Doctor Preston in the chair. On the bill for a turnpike road through Germantown to the twelfth mile stone on the Reading road, Mr. C. Evans spoke one and a half hours, stating the impropriety of a toll road ; that it will be against the will of a large majority of the people.

January 27.—Forenoon attended in my place. The House went into Committee of the Whole, Dr. Preston again in the chair. The turnpike bill was before the House. Mr. Evans again spoke, and followed up his yesterday's speech, and Mr. Waln and Mr. William Maclay replied. The question on the first section was put, and carried. Mr. Evans yesterday expressed himself unbecomingly, I think, saying that the members' noses were made of wax and would draw anywhere. I suppose he meant those who did not vote with him.

January 30.—Attended in my place. The turnpike bill, as yesterday, was again proceeded on, Doctor Preston in the chair.

February 1.—Attended the House. Dr. Preston again in the chair. Dined at my son-in-law Cox's, so did William Hall, and Doctor Preston from Delaware County. After dinner would have gone to the burial of Richard Willing, who was brought from his farm on the west side of the Schuylkill, to his brother's in Third Street, but having to attend the Committee on Claims, at the President's house on Ninth Street, could not attend the burial of my worthy old friend.

February 2.—After the House adjourned the Speaker, Mr. Latimer, and the larger part of the members, went up Market to Twelfth Street, to drink punch with Mr. John Dunlap, who had a daughter married last night to Mr. William Forrest, son to Colonel T. Forrest, of Germantown. The turnpike bill so long in hand got through in the Committee.

February 12.—Colonel Will, late Sheriff, was buried.

February 16.—Reading Claypoole's paper of this day I observed another fracas had happened yesterday in the House of Representatives of the United States, between two members of the same. Mr. Griswold with a walking stick beat Mr. Lyon severely before Lyon could get something to defend himself. This fracas was occasioned by the insult of Lyon spitting in Mr. Griswold's face a few day since, in the same place.

February 21.—At 11 o'clock, the House adjourned to Monday, ten o'clock, on account of the room being wanted to-morrow for the election of a Senator in the place of Israel Israel, whose seat was declared void by a Committee of the Senate recently, on account of some unlawful votes being received at his election in October last.

February 24.—The House of Representatives of the United States finished debating on the disorderly behavior of two of its members, Roger Griswold of Connecticut and Matthew Lyon of Vermont. Afternoon went to look at the river at Market Street wharf, and observed the ice was still going off. A flat with wood came up; hickory wood sold for $18 a few days ago.

February 28.—Attended the House. The report on the Wyoming matter in Luzerne County was taken up in the Committee of the Whole, Colonel Forrest in the chair. Mr. William Maclay spoke first, Mr. Waln answered him, and Mr. Welles from Luzerne County, spoke fifteen minutes exceedingly well, in opposition to Mr. Maclay.

March 5.—Forenoon attended the House. The bill for moving the seat of government to Wright's Ferry on the Susquehanna, debated to two o'clock in Committee of the Whole, Thomas Forrest in the chair.

March 6.—Attended in my place; at five o'clock went with many of the members of both branches of the Legislature to the burial of the late Colonel A. Hubley, of Lancaster, who died at the hospital and was buried from the house of Henry Keppele, Esq., on Chestnut Street.

March 8.—In the evening went to the schoolhouse in Third Street, adjoining the meeting-house at the corner of Arch Street, and there met four members of the Senate, Israel Whelen, Mr. Brown, Mr. Erwin and Mr. Brandon; Mr. Ball, Mr. Seckel and myself from the House of Representatives; where also appeared Mr. Rogers,

Mr. Green and Mr. Ustick of the Clergy ; and three friends of the people called Quakers ; also Mr. Ralston and Magoffin, to hear their proposals concerning the enactment of laws to prevent vice and immorality.

March 17—Forenoon attended the House and half after eleven o'clock the bill for moving the seat of government to Wright's Ferry was debated in Committee of the Whole, Thomas Forrest in the chair. The debate lasted until four o'clock.

March 20.—Attended the House. Mr. Maclay, from Dauphin County, offered and handed to the chair a resolution, that this House instruct our Representatives in Congress to oppose the measures of going to war with any nation or nations of Europe, in particular not with France, without they invade our Territory by land; which was followed by a debate of three hours.

March 23.—The bill for moving the seat of Government had its third reading, 38 votes for, to 36 against it.

March 24.—Forenoon attended in my place. The House went in Committee of the Whole on the report concerning the Wyoming controversy, Colonel Forrest in the chair. This is the fourth time this session this report has been debated.

March 26.—Both branches of the Assembly, with their Speakers, Mr. Hare and Mr. Latimer, attended the burial of Samuel Ainsworth, a member of the House from Dauphin County. His remains were taken from his lodgings on Fourth Street, to the graveyard in Arch Street a little above Fifth Street.

April 13.—Subscribed for two shares, ten dollars each, of stock of bridge across Schuylkill at Market Street, and paid down two dollars. Spent part of the afternoon and evening at Mr. Barge's ; so did Mr. Hasenclever and Mr. Bohlen the younger.

April 28.—Breakfasted at Mr. Barge's, after which he, F. A. Muhlenberg, Jacob Sperry, his son-in-law, and a nephew of Muhlenberg's, from Lancaster, and Mr. Barge's boy, George, and myself went in

Kuhler's wagon to Fort Mifflin, where we dined with Henry Muhlenberg, who commands the soldiers at the Fort. About 200 men were at work, and a French gentleman with one arm is engineer.

May 3.—My daughter Hannah and her sister took a ride with my horse and chair before breakfast. After breakfast Mr. Barge and I rode up to Mr. Standley's at Point, and on our way called at the Widow Sanders's. Called at Easterly's, Harrowgate, and had a drink. In the afternoon, Mr. Barge and I, by an invitation in writing of my neighbor John Stock, went to his new paint shop, and there saw Moses striking the rock, out of which came wine. We held our glasses under and drank. Present Revd. McGaw, R. Keen, Rawle, Gray, Roberts, Emerich, Graff, Geyer, Nicholas, young Hillegas, Little Kuhl, and a number of others, about thirty-five in all.

May 7.—Forenoon Mr. Barge and I took a ride to my meadow. At twelve o'clock the.volunteers, in a body of about one thousand, took their address to the President, John Adams.

May 8.—Forenoon went up to the Falls to see Governor Mifflin; found him in bed very sick. Afternoon went to the State House yard with Mr. Barge.

May 9.—Went to church in Race Street. This day is set aside by the President, John Adams, for Fasting and Prayer. Dined at my son-in-law Cox's, and so did William Hall, William Govet and Robert Erwin.

May 10.—Last evening there was some disturbance in the streets, occasioned by men of the Black Cockade and those of White Cockade, and some arrests were made. The Light-Horse were called and they paraded the streets.

May 20.—Before breakfast took a ride with Nancy Clayton, up the canal, down Ridge Road and by Gravel Hill lot home. Dined at Mr. Barge's, none but Mr. and Mrs. Barge present.

May 24.—In the afternoon Henry Sheaff and I went to Lombard Street, opposite the Hospital, to an exhibition of different animals, conducted by a Frenchman.

May 26.—This afternoon Mr. and Mrs. Franklin, my son-in-law William Rogers, his wife and son, Hannah Hiltzheimer, and Nancy Clayton, went in a two-horse carriage down to Casin's Tavern.

May 31.—This afternoon Molly Rogers and Nancy Clayton took a ride; had my horse and chair. I went on horseback to the Powder house, near the Schuylkill, to see Captain Morrell's troop of horse. The three companies of Light-Horse, Dunlap's, Singer's, and Morrell's, came down Market Street and made a short halt at the President's, John Adams's house. I think there was about 130, and they made a grand appearance.

June 3.—General Morgan, member of Congress from Virginia, came to my house; he and I took a ride in my chair up Ridge Road and down the canal, after which he breakfasted with us. Afterwards I went to church and again in the afternoon.

June 9.—Mr. Barge and I took a ride to Peter Kuhn's wood land in Turner's Lane, where he is digging a well, and marked out the ground for a house in the woods. From thence we went to Mr. William Standley's place, then down the canal, and to Seider's Upper Ferry, and had punch. Dined at Mr. Barge's. At six o'clock a fire broke out in the workshops in the gaol yard.

June 19.—Mr. Barge and I went up Ridge Road and across to Harrowgate, from thence to William Standley's, at Point no Point. Dined with him and returning home met some of our city Light-Horse, who are to meet the Hon. Mr. John Marshall, of Virginia, one of our Commissioners just returned from France via New York and on his way to Congress, which is yet in session here. At sunset he arrived in town escorted by the three troops of horse, Captains Dunlap, Morrell, and Singer. Mr. Marshall, and Pinckney received their passports 14th of April last. Mr. Gerry, the other Commissioner, remains in Paris.

June 22.—I am very much troubled with a cough at night. Afternoon Mr. Barge and I went to the meadow, and afterward to Oellers's Hotel, and drank two bottles champagne wine.

July 4.—Before breakfast Mr. Barge and I took a ride up Point Road to Mr. Geisse's place, to see the shed where Captain Dunlap with his company of dragoons is to dine to-day. At ten o'clock went to Mr. Passmore's house, corner of High and Seventh Street, with my daughter Hannah, Mrs. Franklin, Mrs. Haslet, and three young women, to see the great parade of soldiery coming down High Street and past the President, John Adams's house, which was a pleasing sight, to find that the people of the United States will no longer be duped by the French, but will unite and defend their country. Dined at Mr. Barge's, so did F. A. Muhlenberg, Peter Kuhn, Jonathan Miller, and Israel Whelen. Towards evening Mr. Barge and I took a ride.

July 9.—Afternoon Mr. Barge and I took a ride along the banks of the Schuylkill and distributed several little books in German, telling how the French soldiery used the people in Germany in the summer of 1796.

July 11.—I read in Claypoole's paper of yesterday the death of Mr. Adam Poth, who lived until lately at the southwest corner of Market and Sixth Streets. The paper states he is one hundred and three years, six months, and three days old, which agrees with what he told me at my house eleven months ago.

July 13.—Set out for Mr. Matthew Clarkson's country seat, eleven miles up Bristol Road; there breakfasted and dined with him.

July 16.—Forenoon Mr. Barge and I took a ride ; called at the Muhlenberg's. At six o'clock William Forrest, a member of Captain Dunlap's Troop of Horse, and his son-in-law, died at his father's, in Germantown. The body was brought from there to Dunlap's, corner of Market and Twelfth Streets, and from thence the funeral procession 'came down Market Street; three troops of horse,

Macpherson's Blues, Moore's Grenadiers, and other soldiery. Young Forrest was only married 1st of February last.

July 19.—Yesterday General Washington's letter, dated Mount Vernon, 13th July, of his acceptance of the command of the armies of the United States, appeared in print. This is another token of his great goodness of heart and love of country, to again consent to leave his peaceful retirement to enter upon trouble and responsibility at his late period of life, but who can account for the feelings of a man who sincerely loves his country. I have no doubt but that the contents of this letter will unite the people, and this prudent man at the head of the army, with the assistance of Providence, will preserve our independence.

July 21.—Forenoon Mr. Barge and I took a ride down to the Blue Bell, across to the late Province Island, crossed Schuylkill and thence home. Observed on our way that the people are cutting their oats generally and have uncommon good crops. Afternoon went to Gravel Hill on horseback.

July 23.—Dined at Mr. Barge's, so did F. A. Muhlenberg; afterward Mr. Barge and I went to see Captain Singer's troops exercise, near the Powder house, on Schuylkill.

July 28.—After four o'clock Mr. Barge and I went down to the Powder house, to see Captain Wharton's and Captain McKean's troops of horse exercise.

August 2.—At nine o'clock John Swanwick, late member of Congress, was buried in St. Peter's Church yard. Dined at my son-in-law, J. Cox's, so did Robert Erwin, who is married to his sister.

August 10.—I observe in Mr. Brown's paper of yesterday, an account of the deaths in the several congregations in the City and Liberties; from the 1st instant to the 8th are 53.

August 20.—At four o'clock set out with my daughter Hannah towards Trenton. Breakfasted at the Cross Key Tavern, Bristol, and there met with Mr. Ingersoll, of Philadelphia, and had some conversation about the present·sickness. He said that the Legislature ought, and he hoped it would, grant a sum of money to complete the canal from Norriton, near Schuylkill, to the neighborhood of Philadelphia, to bring the water into the city, for the great benefit of its health, and in case of a fire. Mr. Ingersoll also said, that he is informed that the cost of said canal is already one hundred and eighty thousand dollars, and a like sum will complete it. At twelve o'clock, I arrived with my daughter at Peter Gordon's, at Trenton. I dined with my friend, Mr. A. Hunt.

August 21.—I was weighed at Mr. Hunt's—162℔s. Lodged at Mr. Peter Gordon's, last night. I took a walk before breakfast. Mr. Hunt and I rode in my chair to Lambertville; there met with Mr. William Summers, who took us to Mr. Glenn's, where he and family board, and gave us a glass of wine.

August 22.—Half-past four o'clock left Trenton, came down the road to 11-mile stone, to Matthew Clarkson's, where I breakfasted and dined.

August 23.—Breakfasted at Mr. Barge's, then he and I took a ride. We called at Peter Kuhn's new house, building. in Turner's Lane, and afterward at Mr. Muhlenberg's in the Northern Liberties. Dined with Mr. Barge.

August 31.—At six o'clock, Mr. and Mrs. Barge and I set out in Dunwoody's carriage; went to Spring Mill to see Mr. ——, a French gentleman's vineyard, who told us that he began it twelve years ago, and increased it, and that he has now about 8000 plants. I confess it did not come up to my expectation. Returned to the 10-mile stone, to Mr. Schneider's ; there dined, and then came home.

September 2.—Set out for Trenton ; breakfasted and dined at Mr. Satterthwaite's, at the mouth of the Pennypack Creek, eleven miles; afterward went on and arrived at Trenton near sunset. Found my daughter Hannah well, and all my friends.

September 4.—After breakfasting at Mr. Gordon's and paying my bill, I set out for Philadelphia. Called at Mr. Clarkson's, then at Satterthwaite's, and there dined on fish just taken out of the Delaware, and exceedingly good. At the 8-mile stone Mrs. Oellers begged that I would take her housekeeper and little daughter to town with me, which I did. Deaths to-day, 66.

September 5.—[Here the diary ends. On this day Mr. Hiltzheimer was taken down with the yellow fever, and died on September 14th. His remains were interred in the cemetery of the German Reformed Church, now a part of Franklin Square.]

INDEX.

262   INDEX.

www.ingramcontent.com/pod-product-compliance
Lightning Source LLC
Chambersburg PA
CBHW020348030726
47496CB00007B/2057